The earl caught at her chin, and turned her face toward him, studying it in perplexity. Then suddenly comprehension dawned.

"You…you are teasing me!"

For a moment Helen felt as though her fate hung in the balance. It was the height of impertinence for one of her station to treat a man of his rank with such lack of respect.

But then he smiled.

Really smiled, as though she had just handed him some immensely rare and unexpected gift.

Her stomach swooped and soared, just as it had done when, as a little girl, she had taken a turn on her garden swing.

She had thought him attractive, in a dangerous sort of way, when she had believed he was merely a footman. Had imagined maidservants queuing up to kiss that mouth when it had been hard and cynical. But the intensity of that smile was downright lethal. As she gazed, transfixed, at those happily curved lips, with his hand still cupping her chin gently, she wished that he would pull her closer, slant that mouth across her own…

With a gasp, she pulled away from him.

* * *

A Countess by Christmas
Harlequin® Historical #1021—December 2010

Author's Note

When I was writing this story, set during a Regency Christmas house party, I spent a lot of time considering what is most important to me about the season. If I'm not careful, I have to confess, I can get totally stressed out by all the extra shopping, baking and general organizing the season can entail. But sitting down to really think about the themes of this story reminded me that Christmas, for me, is essentially about family. I want to spend time with them, see them enjoying the day, find them that special gift that will make them happy.

The hero of the story, Lord Bridgemere, has, like me, very strong views about the importance of family. Even though he finds many of his own relatives hard to get along with, he is determined to do the right thing by them, at least at this time of year. Even if he has to do so with gritted teeth.

And a man who is so determined to do the right thing deserves to find a woman who can see past the outer, prickly shell. And love him for who he really is.

And so I wish you and your own family all the joys and blessings of this season.

Merry Christmas!

A Countess by Christmas

ANNIE BURROWS

HARLEQUIN®

TORONTO • NEW YORK • LONDON
AMSTERDAM • PARIS • SYDNEY • HAMBURG
STOCKHOLM • ATHENS • TOKYO • MILAN • MADRID
PRAGUE • WARSAW • BUDAPEST • AUCKLAND

Recycling programs
for this product may
not exist in your area.

ISBN-13: 978-0-373-29621-7

A COUNTESS BY CHRISTMAS

Copyright © 2010 by Annie Burrows

Praise for
Annie Burrows

The Earl's Untouched Bride
"Burrows cleverly creates winning situations and
attractive characters in this amusing romance. A
desperate bride, a hostile husband and an outrageous
proposal will win your attention."
—*RT Book Reviews*

In this, the fiftieth anniversary of the Romantic Novelists' Association, I would like to dedicate this book to all those writers I meet with regularly at local chapters.

Since I have joined the RNA I have found your support, enthusiasm, friendship and advice invaluable.

And if not for you, I might never have found out about PLR!

Chapter One

An Invitation is extended to
Miss Isabella Forrest
To attend the celebration of the Season
at
Alvanley Hall

Helen was tired and cold. The private chaise she had hired for the last stage of the journey across Bodmin Moor was the most uncomfortable and least weather-proof of all the many and varied coaches in which she had been travelling for the past three days.

She shot her Aunt Bella an anxious glance. For the past half-hour she had kept her eyes fixed tightly shut, but she was not asleep. Helen knew this because every time they bounced over a pothole she emitted a faint moan.

She had never thought of her aunt as old until quite recently. Aunt Bella had always looked the same to her, right from the very first moment they had met. A determined-looking but kind lady, with light brown hair shot through with silver. There was perhaps just a little more silver now than there had been twelve years ago, when she had taken Helen home with her. But in the months since their local bank had gone out of business, and all their money had disappeared into some kind of financial abyss neither of them fully understood, she had definitely aged rapidly.

And now, thought Helen with a pang of disquiet, she looked like a lady of advancing years who had been evicted from her home, endured a journey fraught with innumerable difficulties in the depths of winter, and was facing the humiliation of having to beg a man she detested to provide her daily bread.

The transition from independent, respected woman to pauper had been hard enough for Helen to contend with. But it looked as though it was destroying her aunt.

At that very moment a flare of light outside the coach briefly attracted Helen's attention. They were slowing down to negotiate the turn from the main road onto a driveway, the wrought-iron gates of which stood open.

'Almost there, Aunt Bella,' said Helen. 'See?'

She indicated the two stone pillars through which their driver was negotiating the chaise.

Aunt Bella's eyes flicked open, and she attempted a tremulous smile which was so lacking in conviction it made Helen want to weep.

She averted her head. She did not want to upset her aunt any further by making her think she was going to break down. She had to be strong. Aunt Bella had taken her in when she had discovered nobody else wanted a virtually penniless orphan—product of a marriage neither her father's nor her mother's family had approved of. Aunt Bella had been there for her, looking after her, all these years. Now it was Helen's turn.

Through the carriage window she could see, one crouching on top of each pillar, a pair of stone lions, mouths open in silent snarls. Since the wind which howled across the moors was making the lanterns swing, the flickering shadows made it look just as though they were licking their lips and preparing to pounce.

She gave an involuntary shiver, then roused herself to push aside such a fanciful notion. She had only imagined the lions looked menacing because she was tired, and anxious about her aunt's health now, as well as already being convinced neither of them was truly welcome at Alvanley Hall. In spite of the Earl of Bridgemere sending that invitation.

He had sent one every year since Helen could remember. And every other year her aunt had tossed the gilt-edged piece of card straight into the fire with a contemptuous snort.

'Spend Christmas with a pack of relations I cannot abide, in that draughty great barracks of a place, when I can really enjoy myself here, in my snug little cottage, amongst my true friends?'

Yet here they were, whilst the cottage and the friends, along with Aunt Bella's independence, had all gone. Swept away in the aftermath of the collapse of the Middleton and Shropshire County Bank, to which all their capital had been entrusted.

Her feeling of being an unwelcome intruder into the Earl of Bridgemere's domain only increased the further along the carriageway they drove. It had its foundation,

Helen knew, in her aunt's statement that the Earl was as loath to open up his home to his extended family as she was to attend the annual gathering.

'It is about the only thing we have in common,' she had grumbled as she wrote her acceptance letter. 'A disinclination to go anywhere near any other member of this family. In fact, if it were not for his habit of going to Alvanley to preside over the Christmas festivities for the tenants at the family seat, nobody would know where to locate him from one year's end to the next, so assiduously does he avoid us all. Which is why he issues these invitations, I dare say. We would run him to earth there whether he did so or not. And at least this way he knows how many of us to cater for.'

Though torches had been lit and set at frequent intervals along the winding driveway, ostensibly to help strangers find their way more easily through the rapidly falling winter dusk, the only effect upon Helen was to make her wonder what lurked beyond the pools of light they cast. What was waiting in the depths of the menacing shadows, poised to pounce on anyone foolish enough to stray beyond the boundaries the Earl had set for those he so grudgingly permitted thus far?

It seemed to take an inordinately long time before the carriage drew to a halt in the shelter of a generously proportioned *porte-cochère*. A footman in black and silver livery came to open the coach door and let down the steps. Her aunt slumped back into her seat. The light streaming from the porch lamps revealed that her face was grey, her eyes dulled with despair.

'Aunt Bella, we have to get out now. We are here!' Helen whispered in an urgent undertone.

'No…' the old lady moaned. 'I cannot do this. I want to go home!' Her eyes filled with tears. She shut them, and shook her head in a gesture of impatience, as though reminding herself she no longer had anywhere to call home.

Their landlord had visited promptly, as soon as the rumours began to spread that Aunt Bella had lost her entire fortune. To remind her that their lease expired in the New Year, and that if she had not the cash to meet the rent she would have to leave.

Leaving her eventually with no alternative but to apply to the Earl of Bridgemere—the head of the family—for aid.

'That it has come to this,' Aunt Bella had said three days ago, when they had climbed into the mail coach at Bridgenorth. 'To be obliged to go cap in hand to that man of all men! But I have burned my bridges now. I can never go back. Never.'

She had sat ramrod-straight, refusing to look out of the window for miles lest she catch the eye of anyone who knew her. She had faced every challenge such a long journey had entailed with an air of dogged determination.

But it looked as though her redoubtable spirit had finally crumbled to dust.

Helen clambered over her, got out, and leaned back into the coach.

'Come!' she urged gently, putting her arms around her. 'Let me help you out.'

Helen had to practically lift her aunt from the coach. And had to keep her arm about her waist once she had reached solid ground to keep her standing. It was a shock to feel her trembling all over, though whether from exhaustion, fear, or the cold that had pervaded their hired carriage, she could not tell.

A second footman materialised. He was a little older than the first flunkey, and dressed more soberly. Helen assumed he was the head footman, or possibly even the under-butler.

'Welcome to Alvanley Hall, Miss Forrest—' he began, in the bland, bored tone of an upper servant who had spent all day parroting the same words.

'Never mind that now!' Helen interrupted. 'My aunt needs assistance, not meaningless platitudes!'

Both footmen goggled at her as though she had sprouted two heads.

She very nearly stamped her foot in irritation.

'Can't you see she can barely stand?' Helen continued. 'Oh, for heaven's sake!' she snapped, when they just continued to stare at her as though in shock. 'Make yourselves useful, can't you? Get her a chair. Or…no…' She immediately changed her mind as her aunt gave another convulsive shiver. 'We must get her inside first. Into the warm.'

Her aunt blinked owlishly about her. 'I do not think I shall ever feel warm again,' she observed.

And fainted.

To do him justice, the head footman had very quick reflexes. And very deft, sure hands. He managed to disentangle Helen from her aunt before she lost the fight to keep her from slithering to the ground, and scooped her up into his arms with an insouciance that suggested catching fainting guests was a task he performed every day.

Then he strode into the house without a backward glance, leaving Helen to her own devices.

After tamping down a fresh wave of annoyance she trotted behind him, arriving in the hall just in time to hear him addressing a young housemaid, who had been scurrying across the hall with a pile of linen in her arms.

'What room does Miss Forrest have?'

The maid's eyes grew round at the sight of the unconscious woman in his arms.

'Well, I just finished making up the drum room at the foot of the tower,' she began, 'but…'

'Very well. I shall take her up there myself.'

'B…but sir!' stammered the first footman.

The head footman shot him one look, which was so withering it was enough to reduce him to red-faced silence.

'Follow me, Miss…?' He raised one eyebrow, as though expecting her to enlighten him as to her name.

But Helen was in no mood to waste time on introductions.

'Hurry up, do! The sooner we make her comfortable the better!'

He nodded curtly, then demonstrated that he had caught on to the severity of her aunt's condition by striding deeper into the house. He bypassed the rather ostentatious staircase which swept upwards from the main hall, going instead along a corridor to a plainer, more narrow stone staircase, with wooden handrails darkened and glossy with age.

Helen had to trot to keep up with his long-legged stride, and was quite out of breath by the time they came to a heavily studded oak door set into a small gothic arch that led into a perfectly circular room. With its unadorned ceiling, which contrasted starkly with the bright frieze running round the upper portion of the walls, it did indeed feel like being on the inside of a drum.

The footman laid Aunt Bella upon the bed, frowned down at her for a moment or two, then went across and tugged on a bell-pull beside the chimney breast.

'Someone will come and see to Miss Forrest,' he said curtly. 'I really should not be up here.' He stalked to the door, opened it, then turned to her. 'I am sure you know what is best to do for her when she has one of these turns.' He ran his eyes over her dismissively. 'I shall leave her in your…capable hands.'

Helen opened her mouth to protest that this was not a *turn* but the result of exhaustion, brought on by the sufferings her aunt had endured over the preceding weeks, but the footman had already gone.

How *dared* he look at her like that? As though she was a dead pigeon the cat had brought in! And as for saying he should not be up here! She tugged the strings of her muff over her head and flung it at the door through which he had just gone.

Pompous toad! For all his quick reflexes, and the strength it must have taken to carry her aunt's dead weight up all these stairs, he was clearly one of those men who thought that showing an ailing female any sort of compassion was beneath his dignity!

Unless he was just hiding a streak of venality beneath that cool, efficient demeanour? She had heard another carriage approaching just as they had been going into the house. It probably contained one of the Earl's *titled* relatives. He had a score of them, her aunt had warned her as they had lain in bed the night before, neither of them quite able to do more than doze on and off because of the noise the other occupants of the coaching inn were making.

'Each one more pompous than the last,' she had said. 'Lord Bridgemere's two surviving sisters are the worst. Lady Thrapston and Lady Craddock are so starched up it is a wonder either of them can bend enough to sit down.'

Helen had giggled in the darkness, glad her aunt was still able to make a jest in light of all she was going through—and all she still had to face.

But she was beyond the stage of joking about anything now. With agitated fingers Helen untied the strings of her aunt's bonnet, loosened the top buttons of her coat, and pulled off her boots. Aunt Bella's eyes flickered open briefly as she tucked a quilt over her, but she did not really come properly awake.

Helen pulled a ladder-backed chair beside the bed, so that she could hold her hand while she waited for a maid to arrive.

Helen waited. And waited. But the promised help did not come.

She got up, crossed the room, and yanked on the bell-pull again. Then, in spite of the fact that the room was so cold she could see her breath steaming, she untied her own bonnet, shaking out her ebony curls and fluffing them over her ears, and peeled off her gloves before returning to her aunt's bedside to chafe at her hands. Even though a fire was burning in the hearth it was making little impact upon the chill that pervaded this room. Her aunt's hands remained cold, and her face still retained that horribly worrying grey tinge.

After waiting in mounting irritation for what must have been at least twenty minutes, she began to wonder if the bell-pull actually worked. They had not been quartered in the best part of the house. Even trotting behind the footman, with one eye kept firmly on her aunt, she had noticed that the corridors up here were uncarpeted, the wall hangings faded and worn with age.

This was clearly, she decided in mounting annoyance, all that an indigent, untitled lady who was the mere aunt of a cousin of the Earl warranted by way of comfort!

But then her aunt finally opened her eyes.

'Helen?' she croaked.

'Yes, dear, I am here.'

'What happened?'

'You...had a little faint, I think,' she said, smoothing a straggling greying lock from her aunt's forehead.

'How embarrassing.'

Her aunt might feel mortified, but the pink that now stole to her hollow cheeks came as a great relief to Helen.

'You will feel better once you have had some tea,' said Helen. 'I have rung for some, but so far nobody has come.'

Lord, they must have been up here for the better part of an hour now! This really was not good enough.

'Oh, yes,' her aunt sighed. 'A cup of tea is *just* what I need. Though even some water would be welcome,' she finished weakly.

Helen leapt to her feet. Though the room was small,

somebody had at least provided a decanter and glasses upon a little table under a curtained window. Once her aunt had drunk a few sips of the water Helen poured for her and held to her lips, she did seem to revive a little more.

'Will you be all right if I leave you for a short while?' Helen asked. 'I think I had better go and see if I can find out what has happened to the maid who was supposed to be coming up here.'

'Oh, Helen, thank you. I do not want to be any trouble, but…'

'No trouble, Aunt Bella. No trouble at all!' said Helen over her shoulder as she left the room.

But once she was outside in the corridor the reassuring smile faded from her lips. Her dark eyes flashed and her brows drew down in a furious scowl.

Clenching her fists, she stalked back along the tortuous route to the main hall, and then, finding it deserted, looked around for the green baize door that would take her to the servants' quarters.

She did not know who was responsible, but somebody was going to be very sorry they had shoved her poor dear aunt up there, out of the way, and promptly forgotten all about her!

The scene that met her eyes in the servants' hall was one of utter chaos.

Trunks and boxes cluttered the stone-flagged passageway. Coachmen and postilions lounged against the walls, drinking tankards of ale. Maids and footmen in overcoats clustered round the various piles of luggage, stoically awaiting their turn to be allotted their rooms.

Helen could see that there must have been a sudden influx of visitors. She could just, she supposed, understand how the needs of one of the less important ones had been overlooked. But that did not mean she was going to meekly walk away and let the situation continue!

She strode past the loitering servants and into the kitchen.

'I need some tea for Miss Forrest,' she declared.

A perspiring, red-faced kitchen maid looked up from where she was sawing away at a loaf of bread.

'Have to wait your turn,' she said, without pausing in her task. 'I only got one pair of hands, see, and I got to do Lady Thrapston's tray first.'

The problem with having a Frenchman for a father, her aunt had often observed, was that it left Helen with a very un-English tendency to lose her temper.

'Is Lady Thrapston an elderly woman who absolutely *needs* that tea to help her recover from the rigours of her journey?' asked Helen militantly. Even though a very small part of her suspected that, since she was the Earl's oldest surviving sister, Lady Thrapston might well be quite elderly, she felt little sympathy for the unknown woman. She was almost certain that Lady Thrapston was getting preferential treatment because of her rank, not her need. 'I don't suppose *she* dropped down in a dead faint, did she?'

The maid opened her mouth to deny it, but Helen smiled grimly, and said, 'No, I thought not!' She seized the edge of the tray that already contained a pot, the necessary crockery, and what bread the kitchen maid had already buttered. 'Miss Forrest has been lying upstairs, untended, for the best part of an hour. You will just have to start another tray for Lady Thrapston!'

''Ere! You can't do that!' another maid protested.

'I have done it!' replied Helen, swirling round and elbowing her way through the shifting mass of visiting servants milling about in the doorway.

'I'll be telling Mrs Dent what you done!' came a shrill voice from behind her.

Mrs Dent must be the housekeeper. The one who by rights ought to have made sure Aunt Bella was properly looked after. It was past time the woman got involved.

'Good!' she tossed back airily over her shoulder. 'I have a few things I should like to say to her myself!'

It was a far longer trek back up to the little round room with a heavy tray in her hands than it had been going down, fuelled by indignation. She set the tray down on a table just inside the door, feeling the teapot to see if it was still at a drinkable temperature.

'My goodness,' said Aunt Bella, easing herself up against the pillows. 'You did well! Did you find out what was taking so long?'

'It appears that several other guests have arrived today, and the servants' hall is in uproar.'

Her aunt pursed her lips as Helen poured her a cup of tea which, she saw to her relief, was still emitting wisps of steam.

'I should not be a bit surprised to learn that *everybody* has arrived today,' she said, taking the cup from Helen's hand. 'Given the fact that we have only two weeks for all of us to make our petitions known, while Lord Bridgemere is observing Christmas with his tenants. And it is only to be expected,' she added wryly, 'that without a woman to see to the minutiae things are bound to descend into chaos.'

'What do you mean?'

'Only that he will not have either of his sisters acting as hostess,' Aunt Bella explained. 'Absolutely refuses to let them have so much as a toehold in any aspect of his life.'

'He is not married, then?'

Her aunt sipped at her tea and sighed with pleasure. Then cocked an eyebrow at Helen. 'Bridgemere? Marry? Perish the thought! Why would a man of his solitary disposition bother to saddle himself with a wife?'

'I should have thought that was obvious,' said Helen tartly.

Her aunt clicked her tongue disapprovingly.

'Helen, you really ought not to know about such things. Besides, a man does not need a wife for *that*.'

Helen sat down, raised her cup to her lips, took a delicate sip, and widened her eyes.

'I simply cannot imagine where I learned about… men's…um…proclivities,' she said. 'Or why you should suppose *that* was what I was alluding to.'

'Oh, yes, you can! And I do not know why you have suddenly decided to be so mealy-mouthed.'

'Well, now that I am about to be a governess I thought I had better learn to keep a rein on my tongue.' Once Helen had made sure the Earl would house her aunt, and provide some kind of pension for her, Helen was going to take up the post she had managed to secure as governess to the children of a family in Derbyshire.

Her aunt regarded her thoughtfully over the rim of her teacup. 'Don't know as how that will be doing your charges any favours. Girls need to know what kind of behaviour to expect from men. If they have not already learned it from their own menfolk.'

'Oh, I quite agree,' she said, leaning forward to relieve her aunt of her empty cup and depositing it on the tea tray. 'But perhaps my employers would prefer me not to be too outspoken,' she added, handing her a plate of bread and butter.

'Humph,' said her aunt, as she took a bite out of her bread.

'Besides, I might not have been going to say what you *thought* I meant to say at all. Perhaps,' she said mischievously, 'I was only going to remark that a man of his station generally requires…an heir.'

Quick as a flash, her aunt replied, 'He already has an heir. Lady Craddock's oldest boy will inherit when he dies.'

'So that only leaves his proclivities to discuss and disparage.'

'Helen! How could you?'

'What? Be so indelicate?'

'No, make me almost choke on my bread and butter, you wretched girl!'

But her aunt was laughing, her cheeks pink with amusement, her eyes twinkling with mirth. And Helen knew it had been worth ruffling a few feathers in the servants' hall to see her aunt smiling again. She would do anything for her dear Aunt Bella!

But Aunt Bella had still not got out of bed by the time they heard the faint echoes of the dinner gong sounding in the distance.

'I am in no fit state to face them,' she admitted

wearily. 'Just one more evening before I have to humble myself—is that too much to ask?'

Aunt Bella had prided herself on maintaining her independence from her family, in particular her over-bearing brothers, for as long as Helen had known her.

'All these years I have kept on telling everyone that I am quite capable of managing my own affairs,' she had moaned when the invitation to the Christmas house party had arrived, 'without the interference of any pompous, opinionated male, and now I am going to have to crawl to Lord Bridgemere himself and beg him for help!'

It was quite enough for today, Helen could see, that she was actually under Lord Bridgemere's roof. It would be much better to put off laying out her dire situation before the cold and distant Earl until she had recovered from the journey.

'Of course not!' said Helen, stacking the empty cups and plates back on the tray. 'I shall take these back down to the kitchen and arrange for something to be brought up.'

She had already asked the boy who had eventually dumped their luggage in the corridor outside their room if it was possible to have a supper tray brought up. He had shrugged, looking surly, from which she had deduced it would be highly unlikely.

So Helen once more descended to the kitchen, where she was informed by the same kitchen maid she had run up against before that they had enough to do getting a meal on the table without doing extra work for meddling so-and-sos who didn't know their place. This argument was vociferously seconded by a stout cook.

'Very well,' said Helen, her eyes narrowing. 'I can

see you are all far too busy seeing to the guests who are well enough to go to the dining room.' Once again she grabbed a tray, and began loading it with what she could find lying about, already half-prepared. 'I shall save you the bother of having to go up all those stairs with a heavy tray,' she finished acidly.

There were a few murmurs and dirty looks, but nobody actually tried to prevent her.

In the light of this inhospitality, however, she was seriously doubting the wisdom of her aunt's scheme to apply to the Earl for help in her declining years. She had voiced these doubts previously, but her aunt had only sighed, and said, 'He is not so lost to a sense of what is due to his family that he would leave an indigent elderly female to starve, Helen.'

But the fact that his staff cared so little about the weak and helpless must reflect his own attitude, Helen worried. Any help he gave to Aunt Bella would be grudging, at best. And her aunt had implied that had it not been Christmas it would have been a waste of time even writing to him!

Thank heaven she had come here with her. She shook her head as she climbed back up the stairs to the tower room, her generous mouth for once turned down at the corners. If she had not been here to wait on her she could just picture her poor aunt lying there, all alone and growing weaker by the hour, as the staff saw to all the grander, wealthier house guests. Helen was supposed to have taken up her governess duties at the beginning of December, but when she had seen how much her aunt was dreading visiting Alvanley Hall, and humbling herself before the head of the family, she had been on the verge of turning down the job altogether. She had longed to find something else nearby, something that would enable her to care for her aunt in her old age as she had cared for Helen as a child, but Aunt Bella had refused to let her.

'No, Helen, do not be a fool,' Aunt Bella had said firmly. 'You must take this job as governess. Even if you do not stay there very long, your employers will be able to provide references which you can use to get something else. You must preserve your independence, Helen. I could not bear it if you had to resort to marrying some odious male!'

In the end Helen had agreed simply to postpone leaving her aunt until after Bridgemere's Christmas party. After all, she was hardly in a position to turn down the job. It had come as something of a shock to discover just how hard it was for a young lady of good birth to secure paid employment. After all the weeks of scouring the advertisements and writing mostly unanswered applications, the Harcourts had been the only family willing to risk their children to a young woman who had no experience whatsoever.

'I should think,' her aunt had then pointed out astutely, 'that if you were to tell them you mean to spend Christmas in the house of a belted Earl they will be only too glad to give you leave to do so. Think what it will mean to them to be able to boast that their new governess has such connections!'

'There is that,' Helen had mused. The Harcourts were newly wealthy, their fortune stemming from industry, and she had already gained the impression that in their eyes her background far outweighed her lack of experience. Mrs Harcourt's eyes had lit up when Helen had informed her that not only had her mother come from an old and very noble English family, but her father had been a French count.

A virtually penniless French count—which was why her mother's family, one of whom was married to the younger of Aunt Bella's horrible brothers, had shown no interest in raising her themselves. But Helen hadn't felt the need to explain that to Mrs Harcourt, who had indeed proved exceptionally amenable to her new governess attending such an illustrious Christmas party.

That night, though she was more tired than she could ever remember feeling in her whole life, Helen lay in the dark, gnawing on her fingernails, well after her aunt began to snore gently. She did not resent the fact they were having to share a bed yet again. It had been her decision to book only one bed between them on their journey south. It had saved so much money, and given both of them a much needed feeling of security in the strange rooms of the various coaching inns where they had broken their journey. And tonight the room was so cold that it was a blessing to have a body to help her keep warm. Besides, she would not have felt easy leaving Aunt Bella alone for one minute in such an inhospitable place!

If Lord Bridgemere could employ staff who would so casually ignore a guest who was far from well, it did not bode well for her aunt's future. Not at all. What if, in spite of her assurance that he would not permit a female relative to suffer penury, Lord Bridgemere decided he could not be bothered with her? What would she do? Helen wished with all her heart she was in a position to look after her aunt. But the reality was that there were precious few jobs available to young ladies educated at home—especially educated with the rather eccentric methods her aunt had employed.

Aunt Bella had decried all the received wisdom regarding which subjects were appropriate for a girl to learn. Instead, if Helen had shown an interest in any particular topic she had bought her the relevant books or equipment, and hired people who could help her pursue her interest. So she could not teach pupils watercolour painting, or the use of the globe. And the post she *had* been able to obtain was so poorly paid she would not be able to survive herself were her meals and board not included.

Not that she minded for herself. She was young and strong and fit. But her aunt's collapse today had shocked her. She had never thought of Aunt Bella as old and infirm, but the truth was that these last few months had taken their toll. And in a few more years she might well fall foul of some condition which would mean she needed constant care.

If her cousin's nephew proved as cold-hearted as Aunt Bella had led her to believe, and as the treatment she had received since arriving appeared to confirm...

She rolled over and wrapped her arms about her waist.

Her aunt's future did not bear thinking about.

Chapter Two

She woke with a jolt the next morning, feeling as though she had not slept for more than a few minutes.

But she must have done, because the fire had gone out and the insides of the lead paned windows were thick with frost feathers.

She got up, wrapped herself in her warmest shawl, raked out the grate and, discovering a few embers still glowing gently, coaxed them into life with some fresh kindling. Then she looked around for the means to wash the soot and ash from her fingers. There was no dressing room adjoining their tiny room, but there was a screen behind which stood a washstand containing a pitcher of ice-cold water and a basin.

Washing in that water certainly woke her up completely!

She did not want her aunt to suffer the same early-morning shock, though, so, having made sure the coals were beginning to burn nicely, she put the fire guard in place and nipped down to the kitchens to fetch a can of hot water.

By the time she returned she was pleased to find that the little room had reached a temperature at which her aunt might get out of bed.

'You had better make the most of this while the water is still warm,' she told her sleepy aunt. 'And then I shall go and forage for some breakfast.'

'My word, Helen,' her aunt observed sleepily, 'nothing daunts you, does it?'

Helen smiled at her. 'Thank you, Aunt Bella. I try not to let it.'

She had discovered within herself a well of ingenuity over these past months, which she might never have known she possessed had they not been so dramatically plunged from affluence to poverty. Seeing her aunt so upset by their losses, she had vowed to do all she could to shield the older woman from the more beastly aspects of losing their wealth. She had been the one to visit the pawnbrokers, and to haggle with tradespeople for the bread to go on their table. Not that they had been in any immediate danger of starving. So many of the townspeople had banked with the Middleton and Shropshire that a brisk system of bartering had soon come into being, which had done away with the immediate need for cash amongst its former clients. The silver apostle spoons, for instance, had gone to settle an outstanding grocer's bill, and the best table linen had turned out to be worth a dozen eggs and half a pound of sausages.

Once her aunt had finished her toilet, Helen tipped the wastewater into the enamel jug provided for the purpose and set out for the kitchens once more.

At least this morning there was an orderly queue of maids who had come down to fetch a breakfast tray. She took her place at the back of it, completely content to wait her turn. In fact she thoroughly approved of the way they all got attention on the basis of first come, first served. Regardless of whom they were fetching and carrying for. It was much more fair.

What a pity, she thought, her lips pursing, the same egalitarian system had not prevailed the evening before.

The kitchen maid scowled when it came to her turn.

'I don't suppose there are any eggs to be had?' Helen asked politely.

'You don't suppose correct!' her nemesis answered. 'You can have a pot of chocolate and hot rolls for your lady. Eggs is only served in the dining room.'

Really, the hospitality in this place was…*niggardly*, she fumed, bumping open the kitchen door with her hip. But then what had she expected? From the sound of it the Earl of Bridgemere thoroughly disliked having his home invaded by indigent relatives. And his attitude had trickled down to infect his staff, she reflected, setting out once more on the by now familiar route back up to the tower, because their master was a recluse. What kind of man would only open his doors—and that reluctantly—to his family over the Christmas season? An elusive recluse. She smiled to herself, enjoying the play on words and half wondering if there was a rhyme to be made about the crusty old bachelor upon whose whim her aunt's future depended.

Although what would rhyme with Bridgemere? Nothing.

Earl, though... There was curl, and churl, and...

She had just reached the second set of stairs when round the corner came the broad-shouldered footman who had carried her aunt so effortlessly up to her room the night before.

Instead of stepping to one side, to allow her room to pass, he took up position in the very centre of the corridor, his fisted hands on his hips.

'I hear you have been setting the kitchen in a bustle,' he said. 'I hope you have permission to take that tray, and have not snatched it from its rightful recipient as you did last night?'

'What business is it of yours?' she snapped, thoroughly fed up with the attitude of the staff in Alvanley Hall. She knew they were not used to entertaining visitors, but really! 'And how dare you speak to me like that?'

His light coffee-coloured eyes briefly widened, as though her retort had shocked him. But then he said icily, 'Mrs Dent is most put out by your behaviour, miss. And I must say that I can quite see why. I do not appreciate servants from other houses coming here and thinking they know how to run things better...'

'Well, first of all, I am nobody's servant!' she snapped. At least not yet, she corrected herself guiltily. 'And if this place was run better, then I dare say visiting servants would abide by Mrs Dent's regime. As it is, I deplore the way rank was placed above my aunt's very real need last night.'

She had really got the bit between her teeth now. She

advanced on the footman until she was almost prodding him in the stomach with her tray.

'If I had not gone down to the kitchens myself, I dare say she would still be lying there, waiting for somebody to notice her! And as for situating a lady of her age up so many stairs—well, the least said about that the better! Whoever arranged to put her up in that room ought to be—' She could not think of a suitable punishment for anyone who treated her beloved aunt with such lack of consideration. So she had to content herself with taking her temper out on the unfortunate footman, since he was the only member of His Lordship's staff actually in range.

'She is supposed to be a family member, yet Lord Bridgemere has had her stashed away up there as though he is ashamed of her! No wonder she has stayed away all these years! Now, get out of my way—before I…before I…' She barely refrained from stamping her foot.

'Do you mean to tell me you are a *guest*?'

Helen could not tell what it was about him that irritated her the most. The fact that he had ignored all her very real complaints to hone in on the one point she considered least relevant, or the way he was running his eyes insolently over her rather shabby attire, his mouth flattened in derision. If she had been less angry she might have admitted that the gown she was wearing was one she had kept precisely because it *did* make her look more like a servant than a lady of leisure. Her wardrobe would now have to reflect the position she was about to take up. Nobody would take a governess seriously if she went about in fashionable, frivolous clothes. She had ruthlessly culled her wardrobe of such items, knowing, too, that the more fashionable they were, the more money she would get for them from the secondhand clothing dealers. For, although the bartering system had worked up to a point, cash had been absolutely necessary to purchase tickets from their hometown to Alvanley Hall, and to pay for their overnight stops *en route*.

This morning Helen had also wrapped her thickest shawl round her shoulders, to keep her warm as she scuttled along the chilly corridors. She'd knotted it round her waist just before she'd left the kitchen, to leave her hands free to deal with the tray, and now she noticed that it was blotched with ash from when she had made up the fire.

But it was not this man's place to judge or criticise her! Helen drew herself to her full height. Which was not easy to do when weighed down by a tray brimming with food, drink and crockery.

'I mean to tell you nothing! You are an impertinent fellow, and—'

He raised one eyebrow in a way that was so supercilious that if she'd had a hand free she might have been tempted to slap him.

'And my aunt is waiting for her breakfast! So stand aside!'

For a moment she thought he might refuse. But then something like amusement glinted in his eyes. His mouth tilted up at one corner in a smile full of mockery and he stepped to one side of the corridor, sweeping her an elaborate bow as she strode past with a toss of her head.

Well, really! What an abominable rogue he was! So full of himself!

And she could not believe he had goaded her into almost stamping her foot and actually tossing her head. Tossing her head! Like those village girls who loitered around the smithy in the hopes of glimpsing young Jeb Simpkins stripping off his shirt to duck his head under the pump. Who flounced off with a toss of their artfully arranged curls when he shot them a few pithy comments that left them in no doubt as to what he thought of their morals.

Not that she had been thinking about what the footman would look like with his shirt off!

Although he probably would have an impressive set of muscles, given the way he had so effortlessly carried her aunt up all these stairs last night…

She gave herself a mental shake. His physique had nothing to do with anything! He was a…a rogue! Yes, he was probably the type who snatched kisses from the kitchen maids and had stormy affairs with visiting ladies' maids, she reflected darkly. Oh, she could well understand why they would elbow each other aside for the privilege of kissing that hard, arrogant mouth, and ruffling that neat light brown hair with their fingers. For he had that air about him she noticed foolish women often fell for. That air of arrogant disdain which drew silly girls like moths to a candle flame. An air she had observed more than once in men who thought themselves irresistible to women, and who therefore mocked the entire female sex for their gullibility.

Well, she was not silly or gullible! And she had never been the type to find a man exciting merely because he had a reputation as a ladies' man. If she were ever to seriously consider marriage, she would want someone kind and dependable. Not a man who looked down his nose at women! And who was probably planning his next conquest before he had even buttoned up his breeches.

She drew herself up outside the door to her aunt's chamber, out of breath and more than a little shocked at herself. She could not believe the way her mind had been wandering since that encounter with the footman. Picturing him with his shirt off, for heaven's sake! Kissing kitchen maids and…and worse! Why, she could actually *see* the smug expression on his face as he buttoned up his breeches with those long, deft fingers…

It was just as well she was going to be a governess and not a ladies' maid. She did not know how any girl was expected to cope with encounters with handsome, arrogant footmen as they nipped up and down the backstairs.

A rueful smile tugged at her lips as she turned round and bumped open the door with her hip.

She rather thought that any girl who was the least bit susceptible would start to look forward to running into *that* particular footman. It had been quite exhilarating to give him a sharp set-down. To knock him off his arrogant perch and make him look at her twice. And if all she had to look forward to was the dreary grind of service, then…

She shook her head.

She was going to work as a governess, for heaven's sake! Flirting with the footmen on the backstairs was sure to result in instant dismissal.

Besides, the rogue worked *here*. It was unlikely there would be a man of such mettle working for a family like the Harcourts. Footmen of that calibre would not deign to work for anything less than a noble house. It would be very far beneath such a man's dignity to serve a family from *trade*.

Which was a jolly good thing.

She did not set foot outside the drum room for the rest of the day. Her aunt dozed on and off, declaring every time she woke that she felt much better, though to Helen's eye it did not look as though her spirits were reviving all that much.

Whenever Aunt Bella went back to sleep Helen sat by the window, making use of what pale winter sunlight filtered in through the tiny diamond-shaped panes to do some embroidery. There was little money to spare for Christmas gifts this year, and so she had decided to make her aunt a little keepsake, to remind her of their life together in Middleton whenever she used it. Fortunately needlework had been one of the subjects Helen had wanted to pursue. Largely because her mother had begun to teach her to sew, and her sampler had been one of the very few possessions she had managed to salvage from her childhood home.

She tucked her work hastily out of sight every time Aunt Bella began to stir, and occasionally broke off to watch the comings and goings of the other house guests. From up here in the tower she had an excellent view over the rear of the house, and the acres of grounds in which it was set. A party of gentlemen of varying ages went off in the direction of the woods with guns over their arms. A little later a bevy of females sauntered off towards the formal gardens which surrounded the house.

At one point she saw a group of children bundled up

in hats and scarves, loaded up into a cart, and driven off in a different direction entirely from the way their parents had gone, their shouts and laughter inaudible from up here, but made visible by the little puffs of vapour that escaped from their mouths.

It looked as though the house party was now in full swing. She pursed her lips and bent her head over her embroidery. She had to admit that if, as her aunt surmised, all the guests *had* arrived on the same day, the servants might have some excuse for their attitude. They must have been rushed off their feet yesterday. Yet she could not quite rid herself of a simmering sense of injustice. She had only to look out of the window to see that His Lordship had organised entertainment for all the rest of his guests. Only she and Aunt Bella had been completely overlooked. Stuck up in a cold room in the tower and left to their own devices, she fumed, cutting off her thread with a vicious little snip.

Though later, as they prepared to go downstairs and mingle with the other guests for the first time, Helen knew that she must not let her poor opinion of him and his household show.

'Time to face the music,' Aunt Bella sighed, draping a silk shawl round her shoulders. 'I still do not feel at my best, you know, but I cannot hide up here for ever. Besides, I need to collar Lord Bridgemere's current secretary and arrange a private interview with him. The others will have already done so, I shouldn't wonder.'

Because this was the only time of the year he made himself accessible to his relatives, they had to make the most of this brief opportunity to lay their problems before him.

'I do hope it will not be too long before he can see me.'

Helen arranged her aunt's shawl into more becoming folds around her shoulders, and took one last look at herself in the mirror. She had only kept one of her evening gowns. In a deep bronze silk, with very few ribbons or ruffles, she felt that it looked elegant enough to pass muster should her new employers ever invite her to dine with them, without being too eye-catching. Though naturally, since she had bought it in better times, the colour of the silk flattered her creamy complexion. And she had spent hours finding exactly the right shade of chocolate brown for the sash which tied just beneath her bosom to match the deep brown of her eyes.

But it was not vanity alone that had made her keep this dress. Its colouring gave her an excuse to wear the amber beads that had belonged to her mother. She had been quite unable to part with them when disposing of other items of jewellery. They might have fetched quite a tidy sum, but they were worth far more to her as a memento of her mother than any amount of coin.

Both her parents had died when she was only ten years old, of a fever she had barely survived herself. She had recovered to find their chambers full of creditors, stripping the rooms of anything that would settle their outstanding accounts. She had grabbed the beads from her mother's dressing table and hidden them in her sewing case when she had seen what the adults all about her were doing. She ran her forefinger over them now, as she had been doing with increasing frequency over the past few months. They were a tangible reminder that she had been in dire straits before and come through them.

Nothing could be worse than to find yourself an orphan, dependent on the whims of adults who saw you only as a problem they were reluctant to deal with. At least now she was able to provide for herself. And was not, like her aunt, reduced to turning to a wealthy relative for aid.

She whirled away from the mirror, reminding herself that the very least important aspect of tonight's dinner was the way she looked! She must forget about her appearance and concentrate on keeping her tongue between her teeth. Though she still seethed with resentment at the way her aunt had been treated so far, she must do nothing that might jeopardise her aunt's chances of getting into His Lordship's good graces.

They were halfway down the first set of stairs when the dinner gong sounded.

A footman with all the silver lace—the one who had opened the carriage door for them the night before—was waiting at the foot of the second set of stairs to direct them to the blue saloon where, he told them, everyone gathered before processing in to dine.

Her aunt tensed as they crossed the threshold. And Helen could hardly blame her. The amount of jewellery on display was dazzling to the eye, flashing from the throats and wrists of the silken-clad females lounging upon sumptuous velvet sofas. She could not imagine what people who looked so affluent could possibly want from the Earl! Although both she and her aunt had taken care with their appearance, too. They had their pride. To look at them, nobody would know that they had not two brass farthings to rub together. Perhaps she ought not to judge on outward show.

But the boom of male voices definitely struck a

jarring note. Aunt Bella rarely had men in her house. And to be confronted by so many of them at once set Helen's senses reeling. She reached for her aunt's arm and linked her own through it.

A slender young man with an earnest expression hastened to their side.

'You must be Miss Forrest and…er…Miss Forrest,' he said, bowing. 'Permit me to introduce myself. I am His Lordship's personal secretary, Mr Cadwallader.'

'How do you do?' said Helen.

Her aunt drew in a deep breath.

'Young man,' she said, 'I would very much appreciate it if you could arrange for me to have a private word with His Lordship.'

'Of course,' he replied. 'Though that may not be for a day or so,' he added, with a smile Helen thought somewhat supercilious. 'His Lordship has many demands upon his time at present.'

Lord Bridgemere did not participate in many of the festivities laid on for his guests, Aunt Bella had told her, since he was either hearing petitions or deciding what to do about them.

It could not be much fun, Helen thought. But then it served him right for reducing his entire family to such desperation! Besides, he sounded like the kind of person who did not know how to enjoy himself. Even if he were not busy he would still probably not join in with the country pursuits she had seen the others enjoying throughout the course of the day from her window.

Aunt Bella nodded, her air outwardly gracious, but beneath her hand Helen could feel her trembling.

'I have seated you beside General Forrest this

evening,' said Mr Cadwallader to her aunt, 'since I believe he is your brother.' He consulted the sheet of paper he held in his hand at that moment, thus missing the look of utter horror that flitted across Aunt Bella's face.

Helen gave her aunt's arm a comforting squeeze. As if this whole situation was not painful enough, now it appeared that the most odious of her brothers was here to witness her humiliation. And from what she remembered of him, coupled with her aunt's pithy observations over the years, he would be only too delighted to have the opportunity to crow over her downfall.

'And he will be escorting you in to dine.'

'He will?' Aunt Bella gasped. 'Does he know about this?'

For she had not spoken to either of her brothers for years. Twelve years, to be precise. And it was entirely because of this breach with her brothers that Aunt Bella had no recourse but to turn to the head of the extended family now she had lost all her money.

The secretary shot her a baffled look, before turning to Helen and saying hastily, 'And I have placed you opposite your aunt, between Sir Mortimer Hawkshaw and Lord Cleobury. Sir Mortimer will escort you into the dining room…' He trailed off, looking over their shoulders at the next person to arrive, and they felt obliged to move further into the room.

They had not advanced more than a couple of yards before Helen spotted the arrogant footman. One of the groups of gentlemen was breaking up, and he was moving from them towards the dining room doors, which the butler had just flung open. She supposed his duties would include circulating with drinks, and serving at the table.

Suddenly she became aware that the boat-shaped neckline of her gown was particularly flattering to her figure. And felt her cheeks heating at the realisation that he would have an exceptionally good view of her feminine attributes should he reach over her to pour wine.

What on earth had come over her? It had never occurred to her that a footman might *look* at her during the course of performing his duties. She did not think she was a complete snob, but never before had she thought of any servant as…well…as a man! What was more, she had never been the sort of girl who craved male attention. Her aunt was not of the opinion that it was every young lady's duty to marry as soon as possible, so had not encouraged her to mix with the so-called eligible young men of their district. And what she had observed of masculine behaviour, from a decorous distance, had given her no reason to kick against her aunt's prejudice against the entire sex.

Yet every time she saw this footman her thoughts began to wander into most improper territory!

Full of chagrin, she plucked up her shawl and settled it over her shoulders, making sure that it covered her bosom.

'Cold, love?' her aunt asked.

'Um…a little,' she said. Then, because she hated being untruthful, 'Though I think it is mainly nerves that are making me shiver.'

'I know what you mean,' her aunt murmured.

She glanced once more at the footman, warily. He

was standing in the doorway, tugging his wristbands into place as, wooden-faced, he watched the assembled ladies rise to their feet and begin to gravitate towards the dining room.

'So, Bella, you have decided to show your face in society again, have you?'

The booming voice of the ruddy-faced man who stood glaring down at her aunt jerked Helen's attention away from the fascinating footman. General Forrest was, naturally, older than Helen remembered him, though not a whit less intimidating.

He had not stopped shouting, so far as she could recall, from the moment she had arrived on his doorstep until the moment she'd left. 'The girl's mother has plenty of other sisters!' was the first thing she could remember him bellowing at his wife, who had shivered like an aspen leaf under the force of his fury. 'Pack her off to one of them!'

He had then slammed back into his study, where he'd carried on shouting at whoever was inside. When Isabella had eventually emerged, head high, lips pressed tightly together and a suspicious sheen in her eyes, the ten-year-old Helen had immediately felt a strong sense of kinship with her.

She had knelt down in the hall, looked the tearful Helen in the eye, and said, 'Would you like to come home with me? I should love to have a little girl to call my own. Without—' and she had glared darkly up at her glowering brother '—having to go through the horrid experience of having to marry some repulsive man to get one.'

Since the General had already made it perfectly clear

he did not want to be saddled with a half-French brat, she had slipped her hand into that of the older woman.

'If you insist on taking on my wife's niece, on top of all the other outrageous things you have done, then you will have only yourself to blame if I cut you out of my life!' he had bellowed.

They had not looked back. And, just before slamming the door shut on them, the last words he had uttered were, 'That's it! I wash my hands of you, Bella!'

As a child, General Forrest had seemed enormous to her. And, though Helen no longer had to crane her neck to look up at him, the years had added to his bulk, so that he still seemed like a very big man.

But he did not intimidate her aunt, who lifted her chin and glared straight back.

'Needs must when the devil drives.'

'Harrumph!' he replied, holding out his arm for her to take.

He completely ignored Helen. She battened down her sense of affront. Not only was she going to have to inure herself to a lifetime of snubs once she became a governess, but General Forrest had never thought much of her in the first place.

Helen looked beyond the General's bulk and saw, hovering in his shadow, the thin, anxious woman Helen dimly remembered as her real aunt.

A bored-looking man materialised at Helen's side, led her into the dining room, and showed her to a seat about halfway along the table. She assumed he must be Sir Mortimer Hawkshaw, though he did not deign to introduce himself or attempt to make conversation. It was galling to think that even *he* looked down his nose at her, she reflected bitterly. Though they both occupied the lowest social position, so he could only be another of the Earl's poor relations.

They all stood in silence behind their chairs, heads bowed, while an absurdly young clergyman said grace.

Helen could not help glancing down to the foot of the table, where an extremely haughty-looking woman who was dripping in diamonds and sapphires was taking her seat, and then turning to take her first look at her host, the head of her aunt's extended family. The man who held her aunt's entire future in his hands.

And felt her jaw drop.

Because, just being eased into the chair at the head of the table by the stately elderly butler who had earlier thrown open the doors to the dining room and declared dinner was served, was...

The man she had assumed from the first moment she had clapped eyes on him to be nothing more than a footman!

Chapter Three

Ⓢ∽◆∽◆∽Ⓢ

How could he be so *young*?

When her aunt had spoken of her nephew, the head of her family, she had made him sound like a curmudgeonly old misanthrope of at least fifty years. Lord Bridgemere could not be a day over thirty.

And why did he not dress like an earl?

He was one of the wealthiest men in the country! She would have thought he'd be the most finely dressed man in the place. Whereas he was the most plainly, soberly attired of all the men at table. He did not so much as sport a signet ring.

Well, now she knew exactly what foreign visitors to England meant when they complained that it was hard to tell the difference between upper servants and their masters, because of the similarity of dress. Not that she was a foreigner. Just a stranger to the ways of grand houses like this.

And he did not act like an earl, either! What had he been about, carting her aunt upstairs, when there was a perfectly genuine footman on hand to perform that office? And as for loitering about on the backstairs… well, she simply could not account for it!

The Earl turned his head and looked directly at her. And she realised she was the only person still standing. And, what was more, staring at the Earl of Bridgemere with her mouth hanging open.

She sat down swiftly, her cheeks flushing hot. Oh, heavens, what must everyone think?

And what did *he* think? Did he find it amusing to masquerade as a servant and humiliate his guests? What an odious, unkind… If he was laughing at her, she did not care what anyone else thought of her, she would… she would…

She darted him an inimical glare. Only to find that he was talking to the lady on his left-hand side, a completely bland expression on his face, as though nothing untoward had occurred.

She felt deflated. And foolish.

But at least he had not exposed her to ridicule by any look, or word, or…

No, she groaned inwardly. She had managed to make herself look ridiculous all on her own!

Though it had been partly his fault. Why had he not introduced himself properly? Why had he let her rip up at him like that?

She tore her eyes from his and made an effort to calm herself while the real footmen bustled about with plates and tureens and chafing dishes.

Lord Bridgemere struggled to pretend that he was not painfully aware of Miss Forrest's discomfiture. What the devil had come over him this morning that he had bowed and grinned and left her thinking he was merely one of his own servants? She had been so shocked just now, upon realising her error, that she had made a complete spectacle of herself. And no gentleman would willingly expose any lady to such public humiliation.

Though how could he have guessed she would just stand there, gaping at him like that? Or that she would then glare at him, making it obvious to all that he had somehow, at some point, offered her some form of insult? None of the other ladies of his acquaintance would ever be so transparent.

No, they all hid behind their painstakingly constructed masks. The only expression they ever showed in public was mild boredom.

He fixed his gaze on his dinner companion, his sister Lady Craddock, although his mind was very far from her interminable complaining. Instead he was remembering the way thoughts of Miss Forrest imperiously ordering him about had kept on bringing a frisson of amusement to his mind, briefly dispelling the tedium of his day. When he had discovered he had made an error of a similar nature to hers, it had struck him as so funny that he had wanted to prolong the joke. He had even pencilled her name into his diary to remind himself, as if he needed any reminder, to make his way down to his study at precisely the same time he had run into her that morning in the hopes of encountering her again.

Extraordinary.

Most people would say he had no sense of humour whatever.

But they might, with some justification, accuse him of wishing to revel in the novel experience of having a woman react to him as just a man, and not as the Earl of Bridgemere. The wealthy, eligible Earl of Bridgemere. And it *had* been a novel experience. Miss Forrest had not simpered and flattered. No, she had roundly berated him, her dark eyes flashing fire.

He had thought then what an expressive face she had. He had been able to see exactly what she was thinking. Not that he'd needed to guess. She had already been telling him!

Somewhere inside he felt the ghost of a smile trying to break free. Naturally he stifled it, swiftly. It would not do to smile whilst engaged in conversation with either of his sisters. The slightest outward sign that he might be interested in anything either of them had to say would rouse the other to a pitch of jealousy that would make the entire company so uncomfortable they would all be running for cover.

Even now, though, he could tell exactly what emotions Miss Forrest was grappling with. Chief amongst them was chagrin, now that her initial spurt of anger with him had simmered down.

She was quite unlike any of the other guests, all of whom wore the fashionable demeanour of boredom to cloak their dissatisfaction. And they were all of them dissatisfied with their lot, in one way or another. Which irked him beyond measure! They all had so much in comparison with the vast majority of the citizens of this country. Yet they still demanded more.

And Miss Forrest and her older namesake could not be so very different—not deep down, where it mattered. Or they would not be here. It would pay him to remember that.

Only once she felt more in control of herself did Helen raise her head and look about the table. There were at least forty people ranged along its length. For a while conversation was desultory, as the guests helped themselves to generous portions of the vast selection of delicacies on offer. Her aunt looked as uncomfortable as she felt, seated between her brother the General, who was applying himself to his plate with complete concentration, and a man who was conducting a very animated flirtation with the young lady seated on his other side.

It was during the second remove that the General remarked, 'I am surprised at you for bringing that person here, Bella,' motioning at Helen across the table with his fork.

Aunt Bella bristled, while Helen just froze. She had felt uncomfortable enough knowing that she had made such an error of judgement about the station of the man who had turned out to be her host. And in then betraying her consternation by standing there gaping at him like a nodcock. Now, since the General had one of those voices that carried, several other conversations at the table abruptly ceased, and she felt as though once again everyone was staring at her.

'Are you?' replied her aunt repressively. 'I cannot imagine why.'

'I suppose nothing you do ought to shock me any more, Bella,' said the General witheringly. 'You still enjoy courting scandal, do you not?'

'Even if that were true,' Aunt Bella replied with a tight smile, 'which it most emphatically is not, no true gentleman would even touch upon such a topic in company.'

Helen had the satisfaction of seeing the General flush darkly and shift uncomfortably in his seat.

But it was outweighed by the fact that she could also see her aunt's hands were trembling.

There was a moment of tense silence, punctuated only by the genteel clink of sterling silver cutlery on porcelain. Then the lady at the foot of the table drawled, 'The mutton is exceptionally well presented this evening, Bridgemere. You must compliment your cook.'

'I shall certainly do so, Lady Thrapston,' said the Earl dryly, 'since *you* request it.'

For some reason this comment, or perhaps the way it was delivered, made the haughty woman look quite put out.

Lady Thrapston, Helen noted with resentment as she recalled the way Aunt Bella had been neglected upon her arrival, could in no way be described as elderly. She was so stylish that if people did not look too closely, they might take her for a fairly young woman.

There was another uncomfortable pause in the conversation before a few of the younger men, led by a gaudily dressed youth who sat at Lady Thrapston's right hand, began to discuss the day's shooting.

Though the atmosphere had lightened to some extent, Helen was mightily relieved when the meal drew to an end and Lady Thrapston signalled to the other ladies that it was time to withdraw by the simple expedient of getting to her feet.

Helen hurried to the doorway, and waited for her aunt to catch up with her there.

'I am in no condition to go to the drawing room and face any more of that,' said her aunt in an undertone.

'Not after the shock of discovering my odious brother is here!'

Thank heavens for that, thought Helen. But only said, 'I shall help you up to bed, then.'

They left the room arm in arm, and were ascending the first set of stairs when Helen said, 'Would you mind very much if I were to leave you for a little while?'

Aunt Bella's brows rose. 'You surely do not want to face that drawing room without me?'

'No!' She barely repressed a shudder. 'I most certainly do not!'

She chewed on her lower lip, wondering how much to confess to her aunt. She did not want to add to her worries by admitting she had mistaken Lord Bridgemere for one of his footmen and called him an impudent fellow. She cringed as the scene flooded back to her in all its inglorious detail.

'I have decided it would be a good idea if I had a word with that secretary fellow, that is all…' she began. She wanted to see if she could arrange an interview of her own, through his secretary, and get in an apology to Lord Bridgemere before he spoke to Aunt Bella. She would hate to think that her behaviour might prejudice him against her aunt in any way.

'Oh, Helen, what a good idea! I would be so relieved to learn exactly when I shall be able to speak with Lord Bridgemere. I do not think I shall rest easy until I have laid my case before him. And you are such a pretty girl. I am sure you could persuade the young man to arrange for me to see His Lordship before my brother has a chance to turn him against me. I could not believe he would be so unmannerly as to attack me like that over dinner! It shook me, I can tell you.'

Helen had never felt more uncomfortable than to hear the erroneous assumption her aunt had made.

Yet she did nothing to correct it. It would mean making too many explanations, which she was not sure would be helpful to anyone.

Fortunately it took quite some time to run Mr Cadwallader to ground, by which time Helen had managed to regain her composure.

Though he had dined with the guests, he had retreated almost immediately afterwards to a small book-lined room in the servants' hall.

'I am so sorry to bother you,' she said, knocking upon the door and putting her head round without waiting for him to reply, 'but I was wondering if it would be possible for me to have a private interview with His Lordship. As soon as possible. At least…before whatever time you have arranged for him to speak with my aunt.'

Mr Cadwallader looked up from the pile of papers he was working on and frowned.

'Miss Forrest, is it not?' He flipped open a leather-bound ledger and ran his finger down the page at which it opened. His brows shot up.

'Miss *Helen* Forrest?'

'Yes.' She nodded.

'It appears His Lordship has already anticipated your request. He has your name here for seven o clock tomorrow morning.'

'He has?' She swallowed nervously. What did that mean? And was it a coincidence that he had her name down for seven? The approximate time at which she had run into him on the backstairs that very morning?

Forcing a smile, she said, 'Good. Wh…where shall I…?'

'Oh, you had better come in here, if he wishes to speak with you that early,' said the young man, snapping the book shut. 'His Lordship always comes down first thing to see to business before—' He pulled himself up, as though he had been on the point of committing an indiscretion, rose to his feet, and ushered her to the door.

Helen racked her brains as she returned to her room, but could not come up with any reason why he should have decided to arrange a meeting with her that boded anything but ill for her and her aunt. But at least she could see what he might have been doing on the backstairs. Those stairs were probably the most direct route from his secretary's office to his own room. He had probably been on his way down to that office, to see to whatever business he needed to get out of the way before…whatever else it was he did all day when he had a houseful of guests. None of whom, to judge by the set of his face at table, were any more welcome to him than she was. Her aunt had hit the nail on the head when she had described him as a man of solitary disposition. It was not only the plainness of his clothing that set him apart from the rest of the persons gathered about that table. An air of complete insularity cloaked him like a mantle.

And all she had accomplished during the two altercations she'd had with him had been to put herself at the head of the list of people who annoyed him. Oh, bother!

Why was she always letting her temper get the better of her? And why did she have to have lost it with him, of all men? It was her French blood, her aunt would have said. She always blamed her French blood whenever she got into mischief.

She spent another rather restless night, and was pitched even deeper into gloom when she studied her reflection in the mirror the next morning. Somehow she felt that she would have a better chance to make her case without those awful dark smudges beneath her eyes.

But there was nothing she could do about them. She would simply have to appeal to the Earl's sense of fair play and hope that the General had not managed to turn him against her aunt at some time during the preceding evening.

If her own behaviour had not already done so.

She managed to find her way back down to Mr Cadwallader's office without a hitch. As she summoned up all her courage to knock on the door, she reflected that at least her experiences here were good preparation for her new role in life. She was having plenty of practice at taking backstairs, and haunting servants' quarters!

'Come in,' she heard the Earl say from behind the closed door.

She stepped into the room, turning and shutting the door behind her swiftly before anyone saw her. For some reason she did not want anyone to know she had arranged this interview. Not that there was any risk from the rest of the house guests, none of whom were early risers.

But one of the servants might have seen her, and… Oh, bother it all! She spun round, lifted her chin, and faced the Earl, who was sitting behind his desk, idly twirling a pen between his long, supple fingers. What did it matter who saw her come here? She had every right to speak to the man…

Besides, he had been the one to send for her, had he not? Or would have if she had not spoken to his secretary first.

Lord Bridgemere made a motion with his pen towards the chair which was placed in front of his desk, which she interpreted as a signal to sit on it. On rather shaky legs she walked to it, and sank onto it gratefully, placing the candle she had used to light her way down on the floor by her feet.

He could see she was nervous. As well she might be, sneaking down here to meet him unchaperoned. She had taken care to make sure nobody had seen her, though, so at least she was not intending to attempt to compromise him. Still, he was going to take great care that she did not suspect he found her attractive, lest it occur to her to try her luck with him. She would not be the first young female to inveigle her way into one of his house parties with the intention of tempting him to abandon his single state. Though usually it was Lady Thrapston who brought them.

A horrible suspicion struck him then. Might Lady Thrapston have dragged the older Miss Forrest into her matchmaking schemes? Was this lovely young woman the bait by which he was to be hooked? He must observe the interaction between the two ladies closely over the next few days, to see whether they were engaged in some form of conspiracy. His sister might have finally realised that he would strenuously resist *any* female introduced to him by her, no matter how fetching he found her, and switched to a more subtle approach.

Helen was glad she had draped her thickest shawl round her shoulders before setting out from the little tower room, having checked this time that there was no soot on it. She had known the corridors would strike chill at this time of day, and the fire in this room had barely got going. Nobody had been in to light the candles, either. There was just her own nightstick upon the floor, and one very similar on the desk between them. It made the setting somehow very intimate. To think of them sitting alone down here, before anyone else was stirring, just barely able to make out anything in the rest of the room...

She shifted self-consciously in her chair, drawing the shawl more tightly round her shoulders.

Lord Bridgemere made no comment, merely lifted one eyebrow as he regarded her rather tatty shawl in that supercilious way that had so incensed her when she had thought he was a footman.

Mutinously she lifted her chin, and ran her eyes over his own attire. He obviously intended going out riding. There was a whip and a pair of gloves lying on the table. But his jacket was of rough material, and the woollen scarf he had knotted loosely at his throat made him look more like a groom than the lord of the manor!

Their silent duel might have gone on indefinitely had not an odd, plaintive noise emanating from the direction of the fireplace drawn her attention. It appeared to be coming from a heap of mildewed sacking that somebody had carelessly tossed onto the hearthrug.

'Oh,' she said, instantly forgetting her own grievances

as a wave of concern washed through her. 'Has some-body left an injured animal in here?'

Before the Earl could make any reply, something like a huge paw emerged and began energetically scratching at another portion of the tangled mass. A great shaggy head filled with immense teeth rose up, yawned, and then the whole settled back down into an amorphous muddy-coloured mass.

'It's a dog!' she said, then blushed at the absurdity of stating the obvious. Of course it was a dog. Not a heap of sacking. Why on earth would an earl have piles of mildewed sacks about the place?

'Yes,' he said icily. 'Do you wish me to have him removed? Does he offend you?'

'What?' She frowned. 'No, of course he does not offend me. He just took me by surprise, that is all.'

His mouth twisted into the same expression of distaste he had turned on the woman who had presided at the foot of his dinner table the night before.

'You think it beneath my dignity to own an animal of such uncertain pedigree? Is that it?'

It was a complaint he was always hearing from Lady Thrapston. Why could he not live up to his consequence? Why would he not go to town and ride around Hyde Park in a smart equipage? So that she could bask in his reflected glory, naturally. As though she did not occupy an elevated enough sphere in her own right!

And if he must have a dog, why could it not be an animal of prime pedigree, a gundog, the kind every other man would have.

As if he cared about appearances these days.

Helen was determined to hold her temper in check, in

spite of his provoking manner. She managed to return a placating smile to his frown, and say, 'No, not at all.'

The smile and the soft answer did not placate him. Their only effect was to make his scowl deeper.

'I preferred you when you thought I was one of my servants,' he muttered.

At least when she'd thought he was a footman he'd had the truth from her. Now she knew he was the Earl of Bridgemere she was putting on a false face. Smiling when what she really wanted to do was take him down a peg or two.

His comment wiped the smile from her face. She barely managed to prevent herself from informing him that she did not like him in either persona! As a servant she had thought him impertinent, as well as resenting the improper thoughts his proximity had sent frolicking through her mind. As an earl... Well, she had already decided he was a cold, hard, unpleasant sort of man before she had even met him.

Now she *had* met him she could add eccentric and unprincipled to the list of faults she was tallying up against him. Stringing her along like that, when one word would have put her straight!

However, it would not do to tell him what she really thought. Forcing herself to adopt what she hoped was a suitably humble tone, she said instead, 'For which I do most sincerely apologise. It was just that you dress so...' She waved her hand at his attire, which was so ordinary that she defied anyone who did not know to guess that this man held the rank of Earl.

But her speech made no impact on the depth of his scowl.

'And then again, the way you just picked up my aunt and carried her upstairs, as though…'

'You expected me to stand back and watch as she fell to the ground? Is that it?'

He could not tolerate people who were too high in the instep to lend a hand to those less fortunate than themselves. It sickened him when he saw highly bred females hold scented handkerchiefs to their noses as they turned their faces away from beggars. And what kind of man would let a fainting lady drop to the stone flags rather than risk creasing the fabric of his coat?

'You were struggling with her dead weight,' he pointed out. 'And Peters was just standing there gaping. Somebody had to do something.' And from the way she had railed at him on the subject of rank and need he had thought she felt the same. 'As you so forcefully pointed out,' he reminded her.

His eyes had gone so cold and hard it made her want to shiver. She quailed at the reminder of exactly what she had said to him on that occasion. He was clearly still very annoyed with her for being so impertinent.

'Yes, I know I was terribly rude to you, but I thought…'

'That I was merely a servant, and so could be spoken to as though I were of no account. Yes.' He pursed his lips. 'It was a most edifying experience.'

Now she knew he was an earl she would modify her views, no doubt, as well as her manners!

'It was not like that!' Helen objected. 'If you do not wish to be taken for a servant you should tell people who you are! And not loiter around the backstairs the way you do!'

She could have kicked herself. She had sworn she would not antagonise him, and what was she doing? Answering him in a manner that was exceptionally impertinent.

And yet now his scowl had vanished. He leaned back in his chair, eyeing her with frank surprise.

'Do you have no control over your temper, Miss Forrest?'

It was intriguing. She knew who he was. He was certain she had some hidden agenda where he was concerned. And yet she could only play at being obsequious so long before something inside her rebelled.

'Very little,' she admitted guiltily. 'I always *mean* to say what is proper. But usually I just end up telling the truth instead.'

She clapped her hands over her mouth, appalled at having just given him such a clear demonstration of her lack of restraint.

But, far from looking offended, he began to smile. Until now she had only seen a hint of amusement putting a glint into those eyes which were normally so stony, so cold. It was a surprise to see how very different that smile made him look.

Oh, if he were just a footman, and he turned *that* smile on any of the maids, they would swoon at his feet!

'Let me assure you, Miss Forrest, that when the host of a gathering such as this appears on the doorstep to welcome his guests he generally assumes that they know exactly who he is.'

'Oh, well, y…yes,' she conceded. 'I suppose they would…'

'And as for *loitering*, as you put it, on the back-stairs, I do no such thing. I never use the main stair-case because—' He pulled himself up short, astounded by the fact that she had almost made him speak of a matter he never talked about with anyone. Not that most people needed to ask why he avoided setting foot on that staircase.

'I was simply taking the quickest route down to this room when I chanced upon you and ran foul of your temper,' he said irritably.

'Oh!' She sat up straight, feeling as though he had slapped her. All the melting feelings his smile had engendered vanished at once. 'Well, I think I had a right to be angry! My aunt had been treated abominably! And then, to add insult to injury, you accused me of setting the servants' hall in a bustle...'

He held up his hand. 'Unjust of me under the circumstances, I suppose.' Unjust to tease her, too. Had he not realised last night that this kind of behaviour was not that of a gentleman?

It was time to stop this—whatever it was that afflicted him whenever he came into Miss Forrest's orbit— and remember why he had wanted to speak with her privately.

'I had not all the facts at my disposal. I did not know that you were not a servant—'

'You see?' she could not refrain from pointing out triumphantly. 'It is an easy enough mistake to make...'

His lips twitched. Was it so surprising he could not remember who he was when she was around, when she clearly could not either? She was still talking to him as though she had the right to take him to task. As though they were equals.

'*Touché*. Let us cry quits over that issue. Agreed?'

'Oh, absolutely!' She beamed at him. Really, thought Helen, he was being far less difficult to deal with than she had imagined he would be. He could be fair. She only hoped he would be as fair in his eventual treatment of her aunt.

Lord, but that smile packed quite a punch. Miss Forrest was not merely pretty, as he had first thought. She was dazzling.

And women who could dazzle a man, make him forget who he was, the very principles by which he lived his life, were dangerous. As he knew to his cost.

He pulled a sheet of paper across the desk and frowned down at it.

'As for the question of your aunt's accommodations,' he said coldly, 'it appears quite a string of errors have been made. About you both. I wondered at the time I took her up there exactly why my cousin's aunt had been put in a room that should more correctly have been allotted to a visiting upper servant. And upon making enquiries I discovered it had not.'

'Not?' Helen felt puzzled. One moment he had been smiling and approachable. The next it was as though he had pulled up the drawbridge and retreated into his fortress. Shutting her out.

'Ah, no. The room to which I took her is yours, Miss Forrest. And before you remind me yet again that you are not a servant, let me explain that until your arrival it was believed you were accompanying my aunt in the role of paid companion. I have checked the correspondence

by means of which she informed Mrs Dent she was
bringing along a young lady. She referred to you as her
companion and, having read it myself, I am not the least
surprised it created such confusion. We had no idea you
are, in fact, a young relative of hers.'

Helen cast her mind back to the day her aunt had
written that letter. Her nerves had been in shreds. When
she had lost all her money certain people had begun to
cut her in the street. And then their landlord, who had
sometimes come in to take tea with them, had stood on
the doorstep, coldly demanding cash and threatening
her with eviction. She had known she could not apply
to either of her brothers for aid. And then the annual
invitation to Alvanley Hall had arrived, reminding her
that there was still the head of the family, who might—
just might—be able to solve her difficulties. Aunt Bella's
hand had been shaking as she had penned her acceptance
letter. It was hardly surprising that she had not made
Helen's station clear.

When she nodded, he went on, 'I shall have her moved
to the room she should have been occupying today. You
will be relieved to hear,' he said dryly, 'that it is not up
so many flights of stairs.'

She felt her cheeks colouring, but lifted her chin and
said, 'Thank you.'

He regarded her wryly. 'I can see that hurt. And it may
hurt you even more when you are obliged to retract your
accusation that my staff ignored the needs of an ailing
untitled lady to see to a woman of rank. The simple fact
of the matter is that the bell-pull in that room does not
work.'

Helen wanted to curl up somewhere and hide. She had

briefly suspected something of the sort. But then she had lost her temper and gone storming down to the kitchens, flinging accusations in all directions. She could not have made more of a fool of herself if…if… No, that was it. She could *not* have made more of a fool of herself!

'I did wonder about that,' she admitted. 'But then I got so cross that I assumed the worst. I am sorry.'

The Earl cleared his throat, and for a moment he looked as uncomfortable as she felt. 'The only reason nobody came to see to her was that nobody knew she was there. For which oversight I hold myself entirely to blame. I assumed that my staff would take care of her. But immediately after your arrival my older sister Lady Thrapston moved in, and promptly commandeered the services of my housekeeper.' His voice dripped with disdain. 'She seems to think she has the right to order my servants about simply because she once used to live here herself. In retrospect I admit I should have taken a firmer stance over the matter, and personally ensured that at least one maid was not engaged in running round after Lady Thrapston. For which I apologise.'

'That is magnanimous of you,' she said, in some surprise. An apology from a man of his rank was almost unheard of!

She bit back the temptation to point out that during the course of his explanation he had proved that her accusation had, in fact, been correct. Or partially. For his staff *had* been so busy seeing to Lady Thrapston's demands that her aunt had been neglected. Only it had not been done deliberately. But after a brief struggle with herself she decided that it would not be wise to say so. She had more important things to consider than scoring points with this man. To start with she was going to have to go down to the kitchens and apologise in person to all the people she had offended down there. There was nothing worse than mistreating servants—simply because they could not answer back without risk of losing their employment.

And, for another thing, she had still not achieved her ultimate goal.

'I do hope,' she said, clasping her hands together tightly under cover of her shawl, 'that our misunderstanding will not cause you to think any less of my aunt.'

'Ah, yes,' he said, his face suddenly wiped of all expression. 'Cadwallader informs me that she has requested an interview with me to discuss a matter of some urgency.'

In the end, no matter how attractive he found her, it came down to this. Both she and her aunt were here because they felt that he, as head of the family, owed them something.

His face closed up further. Gone was the footman who had teased her and argued with her. In his place sat that cold, hard, remote man who had presided over the dining table the night before. 'Only slightly less urgent than your own request, I believe?' he added sarcastically.

Helen sat forward on her chair. His abrupt changes of mood were unsettling, but she could not waste this opportunity, since the conversation had swung in the direction she'd wished it to go.

'Yes, it was imperative I speak with you before she came to plead her case. I did not want you to be prejudiced against her on my account.'

'You think I am the kind of man who would take some petty revenge on a third party in order to punish someone who has offended me? Is that it?'

Oh, Lord, how had she managed to make it sound so insulting?

'N...no—no, of course not...'

'And yet you insist it was imperative you see me first? What did you think this interview would achieve, Miss Forrest?'

Had she thought to seduce him into a more amenable frame of mind? Dear God, if that was her game...

'I have told you. I wished to apologise for the way I spoke to you and ask that you hear my aunt out on her own account...'

'Which brings us neatly to the matter about which I wanted to see *you*,' he said. 'A remark was made at table last night which gave me cause for concern. That you are not a person who ought to have been brought to Alvanley Hall at all. Would you care to explain what General Forrest meant?'

Chapter Four

'Oh…' She regarded him guiltily. 'Well, I am not strictly speaking a family member. Only Aunt Bella said that it would not matter so long as she notified you. Other people, she said, would be bringing maids and valets and grooms, and heaven knew who else, and you would be making provision for all of *them*…'

It struck her again, that if Aunt Bella had been thinking along those lines when she had written her acceptance note it was no wonder the housekeeper had assumed she actually *was* a servant.

His eyes narrowed. 'That is not the issue. What I wish to uncover is how your association with Isabella Forrest might affect any decision I make regarding the way I deal with her. General Forrest implied that there is some scandal regarding your connection with his sister.'

'That is exactly what Aunt Bella was afraid of! But she has done nothing of which she need be ashamed. The General just cannot stand the fact that she will not bow to his wishes—that is what I think!'

'From what I have so far heard, it is you, Miss Forrest, who has caused the most trouble between the two of them. I believe that her continued association with you—nay, her open acknowledgement of you—has in fact caused a complete breach between them.'

'That is simply not true! Aunt Bella was already at loggerheads with both her brothers before she even knew I existed. You see, much to everyone's surprise, she inherited a substantial fortune when she came of age.' Helen did not think she was betraying a confidence by telling him this much. It was public knowledge. 'She decided to use it to set up house on her own, even though both brothers fiercely opposed her bid for independence. If she no longer wished to live with either of them, they maintained, then she should regard it as a dowry and find herself a suitable husband. They insisted it was scandalous behaviour for an unmarried female to remove herself from their sphere of influence. Taking me in and declaring she would raise me as her own was just the last straw. I admit that neither of them have set foot in her house since the day she formally adopted me, but—'

'She adopted you? You are not, then, her natural daughter?'

'Good heavens, no! Who told you such a dreadful thing?'

He shook his head. 'It was implied…'

General Forrest had sidled up to him in the withdrawing room after dinner the night before and begun to drop a series of vague hints. Which, when added together, had left him with the distinct impression that Isabella Forrest had been a wild, ungovernable girl, who had been forcibly evicted from his life because of the advent of Helen into it.

What kind of man deliberately blackened his own sister's reputation? God knew, he had no great love for either of his, but even as General Forrest had been making those sly innuendoes he had felt revolted by the man's attitude, knowing he would never disparage anyone so closely related to him to a third party even if what he had implied was true. But Miss Forrest was now telling him a completely different version of events.

'If you maintain you are not Isabella Forrest's natural daughter, who exactly are you?'

'My father,' she said, tight-lipped with anger, 'was the Comte de Bois de St Pierre. A penniless French émigré when he met and married my mother, in spite of opposition from her family. They lived a simple but happy life together until their death. At which time I was ten years old. None of my father's family were left alive to take me in. And none of my mother's family wanted me. I was passed from one to another for several months before Aunt Bella came to my rescue. Though strictly speaking she is not really my aunt at all. We are only connected through General Forrest's marriage to one of my mother's sisters,' she explained.

'However, she declared she would be a better guardian to me than any of those more nearly related, since *she* would not resent my presence in her house. As I have already told you, she was already on poor terms with her brothers, on account of her lifestyle. Taking me in and legally adopting me was only the last straw. I admit they did break with her entirely after that…'

The Earl frowned. 'I fail to understand why that should

be. What business was it of anyone else's if she chose to take in and raise a child nobody else wanted?'

'Exactly!'

The Earl was still frowning. 'What do you mean by "her lifestyle"? What was wrong with it?'

'Nothing at all!' Helen flashed. 'Except for the fact that she refused to marry.'

Helen's mouth twisted with wry amusement. When she had asked Aunt Bella, not long after first going to live with her, if she had really never wished to marry, she had given one of her contemptuous snorts and said, 'I had a Season without getting one single proposal. If they did not want me without money, then I certainly was not about to hand it, and myself, over to any of them once I'd got it! Besides,' she had pointed out astutely, 'men always think they know best. If I'd had a husband he would never have permitted me to adopt you. And then where would we both be?'

Helen had gone quite cold inside. If Isabella Forrest had been more conventional, and had meekly married to please her family, Helen shuddered to think where *she* would be. From that moment on she had never questioned the older woman's decision to remain single again. And as she had grown she had found that she too was rather strong-willed, and would likely find it just as difficult as Aunt Bella to have to defer to a man, whether he was right or wrong, simply because convention decreed it.

'Aunt Bella said she saw no reason to hand her fortune over into the hands of some man who would fritter it away.'

Instead she had managed to lose it all on her own. Helen blinked and hung her head. Her poor aunt's humiliation was complete. After a lifetime of striving for independence, she was reduced to begging a man—this man, the head of her extended family—for her daily bread.

'Did she formally adopt you?' Lord Bridgemere asked sharply.

Helen nodded.

'Which is why you go by the name of Forrest now. Although you were born Helen de Bois de St Pierre?'

'Helène, to be precise,' she informed him. 'But, since there is so much prejudice against the French on account of the war, my aunt thought it better to Anglicise me as much as possible.'

He nodded, as though accepting the wisdom of that, and then said casually, 'Did she by any chance make you her sole heir as well?'

She nodded again.

Well, that explained the General's antipathy to this young woman. He would still have had hope, whilst his sister remained unmarried, that some part of her fortune might revert to him upon her demise. Until she had adopted Helen and made *her* the sole beneficiary of her will.

It always came down to money in the end.

A cynical expression swept over his face as he clasped his hands together on the desktop, leaned forward and said, 'Speaking of which, perhaps now you would be good enough to get to the real reason why you requested this private interview with me?'

Helen frowned. 'I do not understand.'

He made a gesture of impatience. 'Do not take me for a fool, Miss Forrest. You all come here each Christmas for one reason and one reason only.' He got to his feet and strode to the window.

'I came with my aunt because I felt she needed my support. That is all.'

'You expect me to believe *you* want nothing from me?' he sneered, whirling round.

'Nothing at all. Except…'

'Yes, now we come down to it,' he said, his face a tight mask of fury. 'Think very carefully before you make your petition known to me. Because once you leave this room you will not get another chance to speak to me in private! I grant each of you one interview and only one.'

It was imperative he put her back with the rest of them. He should never have singled her out for special treatment simply because she had not known who he was when she first came here, and had made the mistake of letting him see her true self.

'My decision,' he warned her, 'whatever it may be, is irrevocable! Do not think you will be able to sway me from it!'

Helen got slowly to her feet. 'I do not know what suspicions you harbour where I am concerned, but I repeat: the only reason I came to you today was to clear the air between us and beg you to put any animosity you may feel for me to one side when you consider Aunt Bella's future. Neither of her brothers is likely to show her any mercy after the stand she took against them in her youth. She has nobody but you to depend on now. And if you will not take pity on her—'

'Do you not want me to take pity on you, too? Is your need not as desperate as hers?'

'No,' she replied calmly. 'My case is not at all desperate. I am young and strong and quite capable of looking after myself.'

'You expect me to believe you want *nothing* from me?'

His implication that she was not only dishonest but also incapable of looking after herself was really beginning to grate. 'Nor any man!' she flashed. No wonder Aunt Bella had taken the almost unheard of decision never to marry. 'I repeat: I am quite capable of looking after myself. And even if I were in need of help, why should I apply to *you*? I have no claim on you. We are not related.'

'That would not stop most women…'

'It would stop any woman with an ounce of pride!' she retorted.

'Of which I observe you have more than your fair share.'

Without her conscious decision, her hands curled into fists at her sides. At this very moment she wished she *were* a man, with the freedom to come to fisticuffs with him! Her only recourse as a female was to tell him exactly what she thought of his horrid opinions of women. But she could not do even that! She had come here to mend fences, to smooth the way for her aunt—not to start a completely new family feud.

He could see her battling with her temper. For one moment he had the impression she was about to fling herself at him bodily. He braced himself for the onslaught, imagining himself capturing her wrists as she tried to strike at him. Subduing her by twisting her arms behind her back. Showing her exactly who was in charge here by stopping that saucy mouth with a hard kiss.

He caught his breath. Took a step towards her.

'Miss Forrest…' His voice, he realised to his surprise, was hoarse.

She put up one hand, as though to ward him off.

'Enough!'

'But—'

'No,' she said through clenched teeth. 'I think I had better leave before one of us says something they will regret.'

It was not what he had been about to *say* she was saving herself from, he reflected grimly as she strode away to the door. But what he had been so sorely tempted to *do.*

'I think for once—' He flinched as she slammed the door shut behind her, sank into his chair, and finished softly, 'I completely agree with you.'

He felt stunned. Yet strangely energised. He wondered if this was what it felt like to be struck by lightning. There had definitely been something elemental about that encounter.

Miss Forrest, he acknowledged with a hollow laugh, could truly be described as a force of nature.

After breakfast Mrs Dent herself came to the drum room, gushing apologies, and a veritable army of staff moved all their possessions to a new suite of rooms, down on the main floor where the other guests were staying.

'Since we have discovered you are a guest, and not a

servant, your things will be moved down here, too,' the housekeeper said to Helen.

Adjoining her aunt's bedchamber was a small but beautifully decorated room, which would afford Helen privacy whilst keeping her close enough to her aunt for peace of mind.

It took most of the rest of the day to organise things to their satisfaction, but as dusk began to fall her aunt remarked, 'I think we had better go down for dinner a little earlier this evening. I do not want anyone to think I am hiding away, as though you or I have anything to be ashamed of.'

An image of the Earl circulating amongst his guests flashed into her mind. The prospect of perhaps speaking to him filled her with mixed feelings. So far their exchanges had been pithy, and strangely stimulating. But tonight, with other people present, they would both be obliged to limit themselves to polite commonplaces. Which would be most unsatisfactory.

Though in all honesty it was unlikely he would deign to speak to her in public. Why should he? He was the head of a large and wealthy family, with immense responsibilities. Whereas she, in another week or so, was to become a governess. What was more, their encounter this morning had hardly ended on…friendly terms.

'Do not look so downcast,' her aunt remarked. 'You will be more than a match for any of them. You are far more clever, as well as having more spirit than any other woman present.'

Helen was loth to admit that it was the prospect of having to interact with one person in particular that had resulted in her looking a little wistful, so she answered,

'Thank you for saying that. But I think I shall have to make an attempt to quench that spirit tonight. I would not wish to say something I ought not, and perhaps give His Lordship cause to think you have not brought me up to know how to behave.'

He had already indicated that his decision regarding Aunt Bella's future hung in the balance. He was half inclined to believe she was Aunt Bella's illegitimate daughter, and that they had both come here to wheedle something from him to which they were not entitled. Unless she could convince him that the General had lied... She shook her head. It was out of her hands now. She had told him the truth, and thank goodness she had, but it was up to him to make up his own mind.

As had become their custom since letting their maid go, they helped each other to get changed. On their way downstairs Helen decided that she would have to make some alterations to her gowns so that she would be able to dress and undress herself unaided in future. Fortunately she was clever with a needle.

The liveried footman was once again on duty at the foot of the stairs, to remind them of the way to the blue saloon. There were already several of the other house guests present, ranged in groups of twos and threes.

Her aunt took a seat on one of the sofas dotted about the room, and Helen sat beside her.

'You have already met Lord Cleobury,' she said in a low voice, cocking her head towards the gentleman who had sat next to Helen at dinner the night before. 'And if I am not mistaken that clerical gentleman, the one who gave thanks for our meal last night, is none other than Barnaby Mullen. Another very distant connection of His

Lordship's. I should not be a bit surprised…' she lowered her voice still further '…if he is not angling for a living. His Lordship has several in his gift.'

Helen took ruthless advantage of the fact that Lord Bridgemere happened to be engaged in an earnest-looking conversation with the young cleric to turn her head and look at him. It almost surprised her to see that he looked the way he always did. What had she expected? That their confrontation this morning, which had left her so shaken, would have made some kind of physical impression on him? He did not even turn his head and look back at her. It was as though he was completely unaware she had entered the room.

He probably was.

At that moment Lady Thrapston walked across her field of vision, severing her tenuous connection to Lord Bridgemere.

There was no need for her aunt to inform her who *this* woman was. She and her aunt watched in silence as Lord Bridgemere's oldest sister sashayed across the room. Tonight she was wearing emeralds to complement the sumptuous outfit of green satin she was wearing.

Helen frowned. Lord Bridgemere had said they all came to Alvanley Hall at Christmas because they wanted something from him. What could a woman as obviously wealthy as this possibly need?

Then Aunt Bella gripped her hand, and said in a voice quivering with suppressed excitement, 'And this boy just coming in now is the one I was telling you about. Bridgemere's heir. The Honourable Nicholas Swaledale.'

Unlike His Lordship, the heir—who was not really a boy at all, although he was certainly not very much past twenty—was dressed in an extravagantly fashionable style. There were fobs and seals hanging from his cherry-striped satin waistcoat, jewels peeping from his cravat, and he wore his hair teased into a fantastic style with liberal use of pomade. Helen tried very hard not to dislike him just because of the way he looked. For he, she recollected, was the youth who had steered the dinner conversation away from her the night before, after General Forrest had been so rude.

'And, *oh*,' Aunt Bella continued wickedly, 'how annoyed Lady Thrapston is that her younger sister produced him, when all *she* managed to have were girls!'

'He does not look to me,' Helen observed, 'like a very happy young man.'

'Money troubles,' Aunt Bella explained darkly. 'His father is not a wealthy man. But because of the title he expects to inherit once Bridgemere dies, he tends to live well beyond his means.'

An idiot, then, as well as a fop, thought Helen as she watched the youth saunter across the room and take a seat in between two damsels who blushed and simpered at him. One of them Helen recognised as the young lady who had been flirting with Aunt Bella's dinner partner the night before.

'I wonder if he is sitting with them on purpose, to annoy his aunt?' mused Aunt Bella aloud. 'Oh—I should perhaps explain that those are the two of Lady Thrapston's daughters not still in the nursery. Octavia and Augustine.'

Even as he acknowledged the adulation of his female cousins, she could still detect a faint sneer hovering about the heir's mouth, which unhappily put her very much in mind of his Aunt Thrapston.

'Which are his parents?' Helen whispered. 'Are they here?'

Aunt Bella made a motion with her fan, to indicate a very ordinary-looking middle-aged couple perched on the edge of a pair of spindly-legged chairs. The lady had been sitting beside Lord Bridgemere at dinner the night before. Talking non-stop and irritating him, she saw on a flash of insight. As much as his other sister had managed to irritate him from the foot of the table, with her condescending remarks about the quality of the food.

What a family!

'You know my brother the General, of course, and his *charming* wife,' her aunt said sarcastically as the couple strolled into the room arm in arm.

When the General saw them, his brows lowered into a scowl.

'I wonder why they have come this year?' her aunt mused. 'He usually goes to spend Christmas with Ambrose.'

It was a great pity he had not gone to spend *this* Christmas with Ambrose, Aunt Bella's oldest brother, sighed Helen. His estate was just outside Chester. Which would have put him at the very other end of the country.

'I can only assume his pockets are to let.'

'Whatever do you mean?'

'Oh, come! You know full well that none of us comes here without a very compelling reason. Had I no need, even *I* would have given my cousin's nephew a wide berth. Indeed, I do not think I have seen him for over fifteen years.'

Helen shifted in her seat. 'It sounds a very odd way of conducting family relations…'

But it helped to explain Lord Bridgemere's conviction that she had come cap in hand, like everyone else. And when she had been so insistent upon speaking to him in private, to put her case, it could only have reinforced that impression.

She wished she had not been so quick to take offence. For suddenly she could see exactly why it had been so hard to convince him that she, personally, wanted nothing from him for herself.

'Perhaps I am being a little harsh in regards to his sisters,' Aunt Bella murmured. 'Not that it is fondness for their brother that brings *them* here, either. It is just that neither of them can bear the thought that the other might somehow steal a march if they are not here to keep an eye on their dealings with Bridgemere.'

How awful! Did nobody ever come to see him merely because they liked him?

Although her aunt had said he actively discouraged visitors by being purposefully elusive. She could not help allowing her eyes to stray in his direction, her heart going out to a man she now saw as an island in the midst of a sea of greedy, grasping relatives. She wondered which had come first. His reclusive habits, or his family's attitude towards him as nothing more than an ever-open purse?

She was startled out of her reverie by the General who, after standing stock still, glaring at them for a few seconds, marched right up to them and demanded, 'I want to know why you have come here, Bella.'

'I do not think that is any of your business,' Aunt Bella retorted.

'Still as argumentative as ever,' he growled. 'And just as prone to stirring up a hornets' nest with your effrontery!'

'I have no idea what you mean,' she replied coldly.

'Don't you? Don't you indeed?' he said. 'You have shunned your entire family for years, and then you march in here, bold as brass, with some devious scheme in your head involving this baggage, I don't doubt…'

'The reason I came here has absolutely nothing to do with Helen—' Aunt Bella began.

'Then why is she here? You have no business bringing that charity case to a family gathering.'

'She is not a charity case. She is family,' Aunt Bella protested. '*My* family.'

Oh, no! Saying such a thing was playing right into the General's hands. Anyone who overheard Aunt Bella's remark would be only too ready to believe she was her natural daughter!

'Well, at least we have that out in the open. You think more of that chit than you do your own family, and that's the truth! Years and years you've frittered your money away on her, and now, when I—'

His wife was tugging urgently on his sleeve.

'Please…not here, not now…' she begged him.

He shook her off as though she were a bothersome fly. 'Well, let me tell you something, madam. *I* know my duty to family. And I have made it my business to keep in His Lordship's good graces over the years. I have let him know what kind of person you are, and if you think you can persuade him otherwise you are very much mistaken.' A nasty smile spread across his face before he turned and stalked across the room, his little wife trailing behind him.

Helen could hardly believe that he bore so much animosity towards both her and his own sister that he would stoop to such tactics. He was a blustering bully! No wonder Aunt Bella had been so determined to make a bid for independence as soon as she'd had the means to do so.

She could not help herself. She just had to see what impression this little scene had made upon Lord Bridgemere. Her eyes flew to his face. To her relief, he was watching the General stalk across the room, his anxious little wife in tow, with barely concealed distaste. As yet she had no way of knowing whether it was dislike for the creation of a scene or a complete rejection of his version of Aunt Bella's past that was bringing that look of cold contempt to Lord Bridgemere's eyes.

But at least he was wise to the kind of man the General was now.

'Do not worry, Aunt Bella,' she murmured, patting her aunt's hand. 'Lord Bridgemere is no fool. I do not think he will accept anything the General says or implies without checking the facts for himself.'

'You seem to have formed a very high opinion of His Lordship, Helen. How on earth did you come by it?'

'I can see it in his face,' she hedged, unwilling to admit she had been to see him in private. Because then she might have to admit to her other encounters with him. 'He did not like the way the General attempted to browbeat you like that in public.'

'You may be right,' Aunt Bella said, though she did not sound all that convinced.

Fortunately for Helen, at that moment another guest caught her aunt's eye.

'My goodness, can that be Sally Stellman? Lady Norton, I should say. I have not seen her since my own come-out. After she married we lost touch, but…'

The lady in question, who was just entering the room, clearly recognised Aunt Bella, too. She tugged upon her husband's arm, steering him straight towards their sofa.

'Bella!' she cried, detaching herself from her husband and plumping herself down beside them. 'It *is* you! I thought it was last night, but you retired so early I never had the chance to renew our acquaintance. How lovely to see you again after all these years!'

The chance for the two ladies to say any more than that was abruptly curtailed when the butler announced in sonorous tones that dinner was served.

Sir Mortimer came to escort Helen in to dine, as he had the night before. This time he did not look bored. No, he looked downright reluctant to associate with her. She had no idea whether it was because he might have heard the rumour the General had started about her being somebody's love-child, or if it was because of the way she had made a fool of herself the night before, or…

Oh, she had never known a Christmas like it. Peace on earth? There was precious little peace here. Let alone goodwill towards men. Why, the whole place was a seething maelstrom of repressed resentments.

She was sorely tempted to remove herself from the field of combat by taking her meals up in her room from now on, if the atmosphere was always going to be as fraught as this in the public rooms. Since she had spent part of the afternoon apologising to the kitchen maid and the cook for her outburst on that first night, she was no longer in *their* black books. In fact, after they had all matched her apology with an explanation of their own errors, which had echoed what Lord Bridgemere had already told her, they had said she was a rare lady to come and make peace with them, when most of the gentry did not give two hoots for the feelings of those below stairs.

Only it did seem a little cowardly to hide away upstairs. And to desert her aunt in her hour of need. She lifted her chin as her reluctant dinner partner escorted her to table. She was as well born as any of them! Better than some. And if Lord Bridgemere did not object to her presence, then nobody else had a right to make her feel like an interloper.

She darted a glance in his direction.

His gaze swept round the assembled guests, his face closed entirely. Until it came to her. She thought for just an instant that he hesitated. That his features softened very slightly.

Her spirits rose. He believed her! Just that slight thaw in her direction, coupled with the utter contempt with which he had regarded the General, was enough to remove the burden of worry that had so weighed her down.

She smiled at him.

His face closed up. He bowed his head.

For the young clergyman was clearing his throat before saying grace.

A stillness gradually descended over them all as they followed the Earl's lead in giving thanks for the food they were about to receive.

Helen clasped her hands at her waist and bowed her own head, truly thankful that it looked as though Lord Bridgemere was not going to believe the General's lies.

She did not notice Lady Thrapston's beady eyes going from her radiant face to her brother's bowed head.

And, since she swiftly bowed her own head, in respect to the convention, absolutely nobody saw the speculative expression that came over Lady Thrapston's face.

Chapter Five

The meal turned out to be every bit as delicious, and the atmosphere quite as poisonous, as it had been the previous night. Only this time when Lady Thrapston got to her feet and the ladies withdrew, Aunt Bella whispered, 'I'm blowed if I'm going to let my brother make me feel as though we have no right to be here. Especially since I have not seen Lady Norton for such a long time. I am looking forward to catching up with her news. Will you come with me?'

'Of course,' Helen replied. She had already decided that nobody was going to make her creep away and hang her head as though she had no right to be here herself. Lifting her chin, she took her aunt's arm and joined the procession of ladies making their way to the winter drawing room. It was the room, her aunt explained, that guests always used in the evenings when they came for Christmas, since it boasted two fireplaces—one at either end of the room.

Lady Thrapston's daughters made straight for the

pianoforte as soon as they entered the drawing room. They played and sang competently, but the way they commandeered the instrument put Helen's back up. Acting as if they owned the place! It reminded her very forcibly of the way their mother had swanned in on the day of their arrival, and been so full of her own importance that poor Aunt Bella had been completely overlooked.

'Be very careful where you choose to sit,' whispered Lady Norton, who had come in just behind them. 'If you are too close to Lady Craddock's camp then Lady Thrapston will take you for her mortal enemy.'

Helen realised that the layout of the room was most unfortunate. People naturally wished to sit as close to one of the fires as they could, but since Lady Craddock had appropriated the sofa nearest the hearth at one end, and Lady Thrapston a matching one at the other, several ladies, apart from her and her aunt, were hanging about in the doorway as though plotting a course between Scylla and Charybdis.

'Is there no neutral ground?' Aunt Bella whispered to her more knowledgeable friend.

'The gaming room. It is just through that door,' she replied with a laugh. 'Only I am not permitted in there until Norton comes.'

Aunt Bella's eyebrow shot up.

'I will explain later,' she said, with a meaningful nod in Helen's direction.

Helen smiled politely, though she took exception to the way the woman was trying to monopolise her aunt and exclude her.

'Look,' she said, indicating a quartet of chairs

grouped around a table towards the centre of the room. 'That looks a safe enough place to sit.'

'We shall have our backs to the piano, though,' said Lady Norton. 'Lady Thrapston might take it as an insult to her daughters…'

'Especially since I intend to sit and gossip with you, rather than listen to their uninspired performance,' agreed Aunt Bella cheerfully. 'But, since I do not care what that woman may think of me, I think we may as well risk it.'

The three of them made their way to the table and sat down, laying their reticules on its highly polished surface before anyone else could steal a march on them.

'You know why they are all here this year, don't you?' Lady Norton said, when the music came to a particularly noisy section that ensured nobody could overhear what she was about to say.

'Augustine is of an age to make her come-out, and I have heard that Lady Thrapston is angling to get her brother to open up Bridgemere House for at least part of the season in her honour.'

'Do you think he might?'

Lady Norton snorted. 'He did not do so for Octavia. Why should he make an exception for Augustine? Besides, their father is still alive. And I am sure Bridgemere will point out that *he* can well afford to launch his girls creditably.'

'Then why on earth is Lady Thrapston making the attempt?' Aunt Bella was leaning forward, her eyes shining with curiosity. Helen had not seen her this animated since well before the collapse of the Middleton and Shropshire Bank.

'Bridgemere House is so much larger than their own London house. And Lady Thrapston, apparently, thinks it is about time Bridgemere spent some time in town again. What better time than to launch his supposedly favourite niece into society?'

'You mean he has not always been such a reclusive person?' Helen asked.

But before Lady Norton could elaborate, they all became aware that the General's wife was approaching their table. With a conciliatory smile, she indicated the one remaining chair and said, 'I do apologise for my husband's outburst earlier. I hope you will not hold it against *me.*'

Before anyone could say anything she sat down and added, 'It is such a pity we have got off on the wrong foot. Especially since the few days we are all going to spend here gives me such a wonderful opportunity to get to know *you* better, Helen.' She turned an anxious smile upon her. 'The breach between my husband and his sister has kept us apart for too long, don't you think?'

'Well, I…' It was such an about-face that Helen did not know what to think.

Mrs Forrest smiled sadly. 'It must have been a terrible blow for you to lose both your parents at such an impressionable age. I would have loved to have raised you myself, but as you know the General is not a man one can cross…'

Helen frowned, trying to recall if her impressions of that time might be faulty. She had not thought her aunt had seemed terribly keen on taking her in, and could certainly not remember her attempting even the smallest argument with the General on her behalf. But then, she had already been through several households where neither adult had wanted the expense of her upkeep, and had begun to feel like a leper.

'Your mother and I were…well, sisters, you know,' she said airily. Then she glanced over her shoulder, as though checking to make sure the gentlemen were not yet joining them, and said, 'I may not stay and chat with you now, but perhaps we could take a walk about the grounds tomorrow? While the men are out shooting?'

Helen hardly had to think about her response. Here was a woman who had known her mother. Though she had no complaints about the way Aunt Bella had raised her, she had never met either of Helen's parents. It would be wonderful to have somebody to talk to who had known them both.

'I should like that very much,' she said.

As soon as they had made arrangements about where to meet, and at what time, Mrs Forrest got to her feet and went to join a group of ladies who were seeking a fourth for a hand of whist.

'She did not invite *me*, I hope you notice, Helen,' said her aunt darkly.

Immediately Helen felt contrite for arranging to meet Mrs Forrest without considering how this might affect Aunt Bella.

'Did you *want* to go out walking tomorrow?' said Lady Norton. 'If you do, then you and I could take a stroll together. Though myself I dislike going out when it is so cold. I would much rather stay within doors and amuse myself with a hand or two of piquet.'

Aunt Bella turned to her with a smile. 'Then that is what we shall do while Helen renews ties with her mother's family. If that is *really* why Mrs Forrest has attempted to detach her from my side.'

'What do you mean?' asked Helen with a frown.

'Well, has it never occurred to you that if she really thought so much of her sister's child she would at the least have written, or sent small gifts for birthdays and Christmas?'

Helen's heart sank. 'Perhaps the General would not permit it.'

'Yes, that *might* be it. But I would not be a bit surprised to learn that she has some other motive than reconciliation on her mind. Take care, Helen. She may smile and say all the right things here, where there are plenty of eyes on her. But I have a strong suspicion she is up to something.'

And so Helen was on her guard when she went to meet her aunt the next morning. And it was just as well, because they had scarcely left the shelter of the house before Mrs Forrest unsheathed her claws.

'We wish to know *exactly* what you are doing here, young woman,' she began coldly. 'And to warn you that whatever your intentions may be we intend to see to it that your days of being a drain upon Isabella's resources come to an end. If my husband had been the head of the family, instead of that ineffectual brother of his, he would never have permitted things to go this far. Indeed, Isabella should never have been permitted to make a home for herself, unprotected, to fall prey to unscrupulous people who only have an eye to her fortune!'

It was so obvious that Mrs Forrest considered Helen to be one of those unscrupulous persons with an eye on

Aunt Bella's fortune that for a brief second she almost blurted out the truth. That there was no longer any fortune for the General to be getting into such a pother about. She found it incredibly sad that this woman had brought her out here simply to squabble over money—non-existent money at that—when they could truly have been spending the season putting aside past misunderstandings and learning to deal better with each other.

Not that she could say as much. For it would feel like a betrayal to talk about Aunt Bella's financial losses behind her back—especially to this woman.

And Aunt Bella had been upset enough about the way the loss of her fortune had affected Helen as it was.

She had gripped Helen's arm so hard it had almost been painful. 'Helen,' she had said, with tears in her eyes, 'I cannot believe I have let you down so badly. I thought I had provided for you. Everything I had would have been yours when I died and now it is all gone. You have nothing. Now or in the future.'

'Aunt, please, do not talk this way,' she had remonstrated. 'You *have* provided for me. You gave me a home. You took me in and raised me as though I was your own child when nobody else wanted me. And do not forget how very poor my parents were. Had they lived, I would *never* have had any expectations for my future.'

Her aunt had seemed much struck by that point. Then Helen had said, 'Besides, you gave me such a broad education that I will surely be able to find work eventually.'

'There is that,' Aunt Bella had said. 'It will be some comfort to know that I have at least ensured you may keep your independence. I have not raised you to think you have to rely on some man, have I?'

No, she had not. To begin with she had loved Aunt Bella so much it had never entered her head to form any opinion that ran counter to her own strongly held beliefs. But as she had grown, and observed the fate of other women of her class, she had begun to regard women who relied entirely on their menfolk with a tinge of contempt. They were like the ivy that had to cling parasitically to some sturdy tree for its support, having no strength in themselves.

Helen eyed her real aunt with a heavy heart. If this woman had kept her, what would she be like now? Cowed and insecure? Afraid to lift her head, never mind her voice, should the General or any other man express his disapproval of something she had done?

Thank heaven she had met Bella Forrest, who had always encouraged her to think for herself. To trust in her own instincts and follow her own heart.

She forced her lips into the semblance of a polite smile.

'I am quite sure you do not include *me* amongst the ranks of people attempting to part Aunt Bella from her fortune? Because you *know* that I was merely a child when she first showed an interest in me….'

'But you are not a child now, are you?' Mrs Forrest put in swiftly. They came to the end of the gravelled path along which they were walking, and passed through an arch in a closely clipped yew hedge into an enclosed garden. 'Though you have got your claws into her now, I am warning you that we intend to take steps to protect her. Steps that should have been taken years ago!'

'This is ridiculous! I—'

But before she could finish her observation she noticed that another party was already strolling across the lawn within the sheltered enclosure. The Countess of Thrapston and her two daughters came to an abrupt halt, and turned round to stare at the sound of raised voices. Helen suspected—although they were all wearing different bonnets and coats—that these were the same females she had observed from the drum room, walking through the formal gardens on her first day here. Oh, how she wished she had observed them more closely. If she had realised this was a favourite walk of theirs she would not have allowed her aunt to strike out in this direction! It was upsetting enough to be having this altercation. It was made ten times worse to have this haughty woman and her proud daughters witness it!

Mrs Forrest recovered first. 'Oh, Lady Thrapston,' she gushed, dropping into a deferential curtsey. 'I am so sorry if we have intruded upon your walk. But really, this girl is such an aggravating creature that she quite made me lose my temper.' She shot Helen a malicious glance. 'I dare say you overheard how she has latched onto my husband's poor sister, and for years has taken shameless advantage of her generous nature?'

'Poppycock!' snapped Helen, finally losing her battle to keep a civil tongue in her head.

'You deny that you have wheedled your way into a defenceless woman's affections? To the extent that she has made a will in your favour? And that you now stand to inherit a fortune that should by rights return to her real family upon her death?'

So *that* was what this was all about. General Forrest

cared nothing for his sister's welfare. He was just desperate to claw back some of the money he believed she had.

At least there was one slur upon her character she could refute without betraying her aunt's confidence, though.

'I do not expect,' said Helen through gritted teeth, 'to receive anything more from Aunt Isabella in future.'

'No?' said Mrs Forrest, with a sarcastic little laugh. 'You do not, surely, expect me to believe that?'

'I do not care what you believe—though what I have just told you is the truth. I intend to work for my living.'

'Oh, really!' scoffed Mrs Forrest. 'As if *any* woman would choose to work for her living if she had an alternative!'

Helen was not about to tell this woman she *had* no alternative. Particularly since the Thrapston ladies were all listening avidly.

Instead, drawing herself up to her full height, she said, 'On the contrary. I am pleased to tell anyone who may be interested that a few days hence I shall be a completely independent woman. I have already secured a post as governess to the children of a family in Derbyshire.'

The girls looked horrified.

'I do not scruple to tell you, young lady,' said Lady Thrapston, shaking her head, 'that it is not at all the thing to boast about taking employment. No true lady would stoop to such measures. I have heard that Isabella Forrest is something of an eccentric, and if this is an example of the kind of thing she has taught you—'

'Though, if it *is* true,' Mrs Forrest interrupted, 'my

husband will be most relieved. Perhaps he need no longer be at outs with Bella, and then she might—'

Helen was by now beside herself with anger. She clenched her fists. What right had Lady Thrapston to make any sort of observation about her conduct? None whatever! And how dared Mrs Forrest assume Aunt Bella would meekly make a will in her brother's favour after the way he had treated her?

Her eyes narrowing, she took a pace towards the three Thrapstons.

She had just taken a breath to make a pithy rejoinder when the hedge to the south of where they were standing suddenly erupted. A dog that was very nearly the size of a pony got its shoulders through and then, barking joyously, bounded straight towards them. From the long, matted hair Helen recognised the hound which had been sprawled on the hearthrug in His Lordship's study the morning before.

Helen had never been so glad to see such a disreputable-looking animal, or so impressed by the effect it had on her erstwhile tormentors. Emitting shrill shrieks, Lady Thrapston and her daughters darted round behind Helen before the dog managed to reach them. Mrs Forrest, even less stalwart in the face of danger, simply took to her heels and fled. Helen could hardly wait to inform Aunt Bella just how athletic her sister-in-law was. How it would make her laugh to hear of that sudden turn of speed!

The hearthrug dog, meanwhile, had reached its target and leapt up, setting its paws on Helen's chest and licking her face. Only the press of females cowering behind her stopped her from falling flat on her back.

'Eeurgh!' Helen could not help exclaiming, screwing her eyes tight shut, wishing that she could somehow stop her nostrils, too. She was not used to dogs, and found the exuberance of his slobbery greeting somewhat too pungent for her liking. Though she did not feel the least bit frightened. She had no doubt it was a doggy sort of friendship the great beast was demonstrating, and felt rather scornful of the two girls who were now squealing with fright, cowering behind her and Lady Thrapston.

'Esau!' the Earl's voice boomed across the lawn. 'Devil take it, what *do* you think you are doing?'

The dog looked in the direction of his master's voice, drool dripping slowly from his lolling tongue.

The Earl forced his way through the hedge just where the dog had broken through. He took the situation in and snapped his fingers. 'Heel, I say! *Heel!*'

To Helen, it looked as though the dog sighed and shrugged its shoulders before obediently dropping to the ground and loping across to his master's side, where he flopped to the ground and rolled on his back, paws waving in the air.

'I am *not* going to rub your stomach, you hell hound!' the Earl snapped.

The dog merely looked up at him adoringly and wriggled encouragingly.

Helen, already struck by the humour of the situation, could barely stifle her giggles. She reached into her pocket for a handkerchief, covering her grin under the pretext of vigorously wiping away the slobber that coated her cheeks.

'Really, Bridgemere,' said Lady Thrapston, emerging from behind Helen. 'Have you no control over that animal?'

'Better than *you* have over your own manners,' he replied coldly. 'You have a very carrying sort of voice, My Lady, and I beg leave to inform you that you have no business berating Miss Forrest upon her future plans. Plans which, in any case, *I* regard as admirable!'

'Excuse me…' Helen put in, suddenly cross all over again. Though it was quite pleasant to hear the Earl say that he found her admirable, she was not in the least bit pleased that he was saying what she would have said herself, had the dog not put a halt to proceedings.

The Earl made an impatient gesture with his hand.

'Not now, Miss Forrest!' he snapped, his eyes fixed upon his sister. 'I find it remarkably refreshing to hear that there is at least one woman in England who does not have marriage to a wealthy man as her goal after having been launched expensively into society!'

At that point Helen's temper came to the boil. It was beyond rude for these two aristocrats to stand there arguing about her as though she was not present. Besides, it was perfectly clear they were not arguing about *her* at all, but about what Lady Thrapston expected Bridgemere to do for her daughters.

Who were both close to tears.

'Don't you assume you know anything about me or my goals, My Lord!' she said. 'It is only women with a dowry and a family behind them who have the luxury of taking the route of which you speak! And, since I have not a penny to my name, I should have thought it would be obvious even to you that route is not open to me!'

'You see?' said the Countess. 'Even this creature

would rather marry than work for a living! You have heard it from her own lips!'

The Earl swung to her, his eyes blazing, as though he felt she had betrayed him.

Not a penny to her name? What nonsense was this? From the preliminary enquiries he had made, it was generally known that she stood to inherit a substantial fortune from Isabella Forrest. Who was already keeping her in some style.

'N…no, I did not mean that, exactly…' Helen stammered, her eyes flicking from brother to sister and back again.

'Come, girls,' said Lady Thrapston imperiously. 'We shall return to the house, since His Lordship chooses to exercise that beast where his guests *should* feel safe to walk!'

Her nose in the air, she swished across the lawns, her two subdued daughters scurrying along behind her.

The dog rolled itself upright and woofed once after them, as though in triumph.

Helen stood frozen to the spot by Lord Bridgemere's glacial stare. He waited until the other ladies were out of earshot before speaking again, while Helen braced herself for yet another battle royal.

'I trust you are unharmed?' he said, completely taking the wind out of her sails. 'For some reason,' he drawled, as though there was no accounting for the working of a dog's mind, 'Esau regards you as a friend. The moment he heard your voice he made straight for you to make his presence known.'

'Straight, yes,' she agreed. 'Straight through the hedge,' she amended, a bubble of mirth welling up inside her as she recalled the consternation he had caused. Then with a perfectly straight face she reached up and plucked a yew twig from the front of Lord Bridgemere's waist-coat. 'And you came *straight* after him,' she observed, tossing the twig to the ground.

'He frightens some females,' he countered. 'He is so large and…'

'So sadly out of control.' She shook her head in mock reproof.

His brows drew down into a scowl. 'No, that is not the case at all. He is very well trained…'

Abruptly she averted her face, as though glancing towards the dog, who was now sniffing away at the foot of the hedge. But not quite quickly enough to hide the laughter brimming.

He caught at her chin and turned her face towards him, studying it in perplexity. Then suddenly compre-hension dawned.

'You…you are teasing me!'

For a moment she felt as though her fate hung in the balance. It was the height of impertinence for one of her station to treat a man of his rank with such lack of respect.

But then he smiled.

Really smiled—as though she had just handed him some immensely rare and unexpected gift.

Her stomach swooped and soared—just as it had done when, as a little girl, she had taken a turn on her garden swing.

She had thought him attractive, in a dangerous sort of way, when she had believed he was merely a foot-man. Had imagined maidservants queuing up to kiss that mouth when it had been hard and cynical. But the intensity of that smile was downright lethal. As she gazed, transfixed, at those happily curved lips, with his hand still cupping her chin gently, she wished that he would pull her closer, slant that mouth across her own…

With a gasp, she pulled away from him.

His smile faded. He looked down at the hand that had been cupping her chin as though its behaviour confused him.

'E…Esau?' she stammered, determined to break the intensity of the mood. 'You called him that because he is so hairy, I take it?'

'And he has a somewhat reddish tinge to his coat,' he agreed mechanically. Then, as though searching for something to say to prolong their odd little conversation, 'Under the mud which unfortunately he chose to roll in this morning.' He looked down at her attire ruefully. 'And which is now liberally smeared all over your coat.'

For the first time Helen took stock of the damage the encounter with his dog had wrought upon her clothing. Helen had wrapped a shawl over her bonnet before setting out. It had slithered to the ground when Esau had jumped up, and the other ladies had trodden it into the ground. Her gloves and cuffs were shiny with the aftermath of Esau's affectionate greeting, and her shoulders bore the imprints of his enormous muddy paws. And, worst of all, when he had dropped to the ground his claws had torn a rent in her skirt.

'You must allow me to replace it.'

'Must?' Taking exception to his high-handed attitude

towards her, she took a step back. 'I *must* do no such thing!'

'Do not be ridiculous,' he snapped, his own brief foray into good humour coming to an abrupt end. 'I saw the way my sister used you as a human shield to protect her own clothing from Esau's unfortunate tendency to jump up on people he likes. And she can easily afford to replace any gowns his paws might ruin. I suspect that you cannot. I have just heard you declare you have not a penny to your name! And I doubt if you have more than two changes of clothing in that meagre amount of luggage my staff carried up to your room.'

Helen stiffened further. 'Mud brushes off when it dries. And I am quite capable of darning this little tear,' she said, indicating her skirts. 'Any competent needle-woman could do it! And, contrary to your opinion, I *do* have a clean gown into which I may change. I am not a *complete* pauper.'

'Nevertheless, you are not the heiress that General Forrest has assumed, are you? What has happened between you and your aunt? Why do you have to go out and work for your living? Will you not tell me?'

'It is not your affair—at least not my part of it.'

She was not going to confide in him. It shook him. Most people were only too ready to pour out a litany of woes in the hope that they might persuade him to bail them out.

He had already told Lady Thrapston that he admired her, but if he were to say it again now it would be with far more conviction. For he realised that he really did.

'That damned pride of yours,' he said, shaking his head. 'Nevertheless, Miss Forrest, you have to admit that it is entirely my fault that your clothing has been ruined. As Lady Thrapston pointed out, I should not have returned to the house by this route when I knew that visiting ladies like to take their exercise in the shelter of the shrubbery. Please,' he said, stepping forward and grasping her by the elbows, 'allow me to make amends.'

For once he would like to be able to do a small thing for someone he suspected had suffered some kind of financial reversal. And what was the cost of a coat to him?

Esau, as though sensing the tension between them, bounded over and sat at Helen's feet, gazing up at her with his head on one side.

'It would be quite inappropriate for you to do so,' she pointed out.

It felt as though the sun went behind a cloud when he let go of her arms and stepped back.

'But thank you for your kind offer,' she said, in a desperate attempt to undo the offence she could see he had taken at her refusal.

It was no use. His face had closed up.

Which was ironic, considering the last time they had spoken he had complained that people only came to him because they wanted something!

'No very great harm has been done by your dog. In fact,' she said, reaching out one hand and tentatively patting the great shaggy head, 'I am rather grateful to him for putting such an abrupt end to my walk.'

'You do not like the gardens?'

'The *gardens* seem very pleasant, My Lord, from what little I have seen so far.'

'Perhaps you would enjoy seeing more of them,' he said, as though he had just been struck by a brilliant idea, 'if you had a more congenial escort? I confess, though I generally only permit Esau to accompany me on my morning ride, I—'

He pulled himself up short, frowned, and made her a stiff bow. 'Miss Forrest, since you will not permit me to replace the clothing Esau has ruined, perhaps you will allow me to make amends in another way. Let me show you these gardens tomorrow, early. Before anyone else has risen. Before the sun has burned the frost away.'

'Oh.' Helen blinked up at him. 'I thought you said you preferred to be alone…'

'To *ride* alone,' he corrected her, with some signs of irritation. 'But I have not asked you to ride with me. Just to walk. Will you?' He clutched his riding crop between his hands, his whole body tensing as he added, 'Please?'

For one wild, glorious moment Helen had the feeling that her assent would really mean something to him. She wondered, given all that she had learned about him, how long it had been since he had asked anyone for anything.

Her heart went out to him. How sad to think that he might be so lonely that he was more or less begging her for an hour or so of her time. She suddenly saw that it was a rare thing for him to come across a person with whom he might spend time safe in the knowledge she would not be pestering him for some kind of favour. Lord, he must be one of the loneliest men on earth.

Especially if he had to resort to asking *her* to go for a

walk with him. She was a virtual stranger to him. And whenever they had met they had ended up arguing.

She chewed on her lower lip. Going for a walk with him, unchaperoned, would be a rather shocking thing for her to do. Especially considering the vast difference between their stations. And yet…and yet…

She was quite certain she would never meet a man like him again.

In the dreary years of servitude that lay ahead of her, would it not be a comfort to look back to this time and recall that once, at least, a handsome, eligible man—a man who made her heart flutter—had urged her to cast convention aside and spend time alone with him? Oh, not that anything would come of it. He could not possibly have any romantic feelings towards her. It was just a walk.

Sometimes, she decided, the conventions were ridiculous. As if he would stoop to attempting to seduce *her*, of all people. A guest under his roof!

She brightened up, knowing that she would be quite safe.

'If the weather is fine, I think I should like that very much,' she said.

While Bridgemere had been awaiting her answer he had felt as though he was teetering on the brink of a precipice. And now he wondered if he had tumbled headlong into it. For the sense of relief and gratitude he felt when she said yes was out of all proportion.

He was more than a little irritated with himself for letting her affect him so much.

'I will wait for you in the mud room at first light, then,' he said brusquely. 'Cadwallader will give you the direction.' He glanced down at her feet. 'Wear sturdy footwear.'

And then he whistled for his dog and strode away, leaving Helen to trail back to the house in a state that was becoming all too familiar after an encounter with Lord Bridgemere. A turbulent mix of exhilaration, irritation, yearning and trepidation—and now, as if that were not quite enough to contend with, more than a dash of compassion for the man who was expected to bear everyone else's burdens but had nobody to help him bear his.

Chapter Six

The next morning Helen woke early. She had escaped up to bed as soon as she could, uncomfortable about lingering in the winter drawing room amongst so many antagonists, leaving Aunt Bella to enjoy some hands of cards with Lady Norton. Helen was not sure what the time had been when her aunt had tiptoed back into their room. She looked down at her now, where she lay sprawled on her back, snoring gently, with a fond smile. It must have been well past midnight. Not even the sounds of Helen rising and having her wash had managed to rouse her this morning!

She rubbed a small patch of frost from the inside of the windowpane with the corner of her towel to see a still star-spangled sky. Not a cloud was in sight. It would be bitterly cold outside. Not that even a blizzard would have doused the excitement that was welling up inside her. Lord Bridgemere had asked her to go for a walk with him. Her! When he so famously shunned others. She simply added several flannel petticoats beneath her gown, as well as a knitted jacket under her coat, and a woollen shawl over her bonnet.

And left the room with a smile on her face and a spring in her step.

Lord Bridgemere was waiting for her in the mud room, similarly bundled up against the cold.

'I would prefer not to take a lantern,' he informed her. 'The sun is only just rising, but I believe we can make our way where we are going quite safely without one.'

'Oh. Very well.' She smiled at him, quite content to go along with whatever he suggested.

He opened the door for her, and with a slight dip of the head extended his arm to indicate she should precede him.

She wanted to laugh out loud. She had expected nothing but slights and insults in her new life as a humble, hardworking governess, but here was a belted earl opening a door for her! Sharing his morning walk with her simply for the pleasure of her company. Well, wouldn't this be something to look back upon when she eventually moved to the Harcourts' home?

She smiled happily up at him as she passed him in the doorway. And breathed in the sharply fresh air with a sense of relish. She had always loved this time of day. It was like having a blank sheet of paper upon which she could write anything.

She darted a surreptitious glance at him as he closed the door behind them. Then averted her gaze demurely when he took her arm to steady her as they set off across the slippery cobbles of the kitchen court. He did not look at her. He kept his eyes fixed ahead, on where they were going. Once they left the cluster of buildings at the back of the main house he led her away from the formal gardens, where she had walked before, and up a sloping lawn towards a belt of trees.

After a while she took the risk of studying his face through a series of glances as they walked along. Most particularly her eyes were drawn to the mouth that had been haunting her imagination from the very first moment she had seen him. When she had thought he was a footman. Now she knew he was an earl, he was no longer beneath her socially, and so...

Guiltily, she tore her eyes from his mouth and cast them to the ground. He was as far from her socially as ever! She ought not to be thinking about kisses—especially not where he was concerned. For it could only end badly for her. Aunt Bella had already told her the man was not the marrying kind. And she had too much pride to become *any* man's plaything.

No matter how tempting he was, she thought, darting another longing glance at his handsome profile.

No, far better to have some innocent, pleasurable memories from this outing to keep her warm in the bleak years ahead.

And she did feel warm, just being with him arm in arm like this. Her heart was racing, and her blood was zinging through her veins in a most remarkable way. She heaved a sigh of contentment, making her breath puff out in a great cloud on the still winter air.

'Am I setting too fast a pace for you, Miss Forrest?' Lord Bridgemere enquired politely.

'Oh, no,' she replied. 'Not at all.'

'But you are becoming breathless,' he said with a

frown. 'Forgive me. I am not used to measuring my pace to suit that of another.'

'I suppose Esau has no problem keeping up with you, though?' she observed.

He frowned, as though turning her remark over in his mind, before replying rather seriously, 'No, he does not. He is an ideal companion when I ride, since he eats up the miles with those great long legs of his. It is, in fact, when he has not had sufficient exercise that he becomes…exuberant.'

Some of her pleasure dimmed. He was having to deliberately slow the pace he would have preferred to set because she was with him. And the way he was smiling now, after talking about his dog, made her feel as if he would be enjoying himself far more if it was the dog out here with him!

It was some minutes before either of them spoke again. Lord Bridgemere seemed preoccupied, and Helen, even though he had slowed down considerably, had little breath left to spare for speech.

It had been getting steadily lighter, and just as they reached the trees the sun's rays struck at an angle that made the entire copse glisten diamond-bright. Since the frosted branches almost met overhead, they looked like the arches of some great outdoor cathedral.

'Oh!' she gasped, stopping completely just to gaze in awe at the magical sight. 'I feel as if, I am in some… church,' she whispered. 'Or a temple. Not made by human hands, but by…'

'Yes,' he said in a low, almost reverent tone. 'That is exactly how I feel sometimes out here, at sunrise.'

She twirled round, her head arched back, to admire

the spectacle from every angle. It made it all the more wonderful that through various gaps in the branches she could make out the moon against the pearly dawn sky, and just one or two of the last and brightest of the stars.

'Oh, thank you,' she breathed. 'Thank you for bringing me here to see this.'

'I *knew* you would appreciate it,' he said, his eyes gleaming with what she thought looked like approval. 'You are the one person I know who would not grumble about the necessity of rising early to witness this,' he said. 'Most of my other visitors prefer staying up all night drinking and gaming, then sleeping half the day away. It does not last long, this rare moment of utter perfection. But just now, as the sun strikes the frosted branches, it makes everything so…' He frowned, shaking his head as though the right words eluded him. 'One can almost embrace winter. For only in this season can one experience this.' He turned around, just as she had done, only far more slowly, as though drinking in the frozen splendour of their surroundings.

Then, without warning, his face turned hard and cynical. 'Nature has a remarkable way of compensating for absence of life. None of this would be possible without bitter cold. And long, dark nights. You can only see this when the branches are stark and dead.'

He turned to her with a twisted sort of smile on his lips. 'Of course before long the very sunshine that creates this glorious spectacle will melt it all away. You can already see the mist beginning to rise. In another hour all that will be left of your mystical temple to nature will be dripping wet branches, blackened with mould, and pools of mire underfoot. Come,' he said brusquely, 'there is something else I wish you to see.'

Puzzled by his abrupt change of mood, Helen plunged through the copse after him. He did not seem to care if she could keep up or not now, and she was soon quite out of breath.

'There,' he said, as he emerged from the trees into a small clearing.

She saw an ancient ruin with a tower at one end, half overgrown with ivy, and at its foot, a sheet of ice almost the size of the front garden of their cottage in Middleton.

'We nearly always get some ice forming up here over winter,' he said. 'The position of the trees keeps the sun from melting it away each morning. This year I have had the staff deliberately extend it. The lake here is too deep to freeze, except a little around the edges, so proper skating is out of the question, but I thought the children would enjoy sliding about on this. What do you think?'

'Me?'

'Yes. You are going to be a governess. You know children. They always seem to love to skate. Don't they? I know I did as a boy.'

Helen's heart plummeted. She had been having fantasies of stolen kisses. He had been thinking of asking her professional opinion, as a woman experienced with children, about his plans for amusing the children of his guests.

Oh, well. She shrugged. It had been only a wild flight of fancy on her part. What would a wealthy, handsome man like him see in an ordinary, penniless woman like her? At least now she did not have to be quite so concerned about what he thought of her.

The notion was quite liberating.

'Only as a boy?' she repeated, grinning up at him. 'Don't you still enjoy skating?'

And, before he had the chance to say a word, she gathered her skirts and made a run at the ice. When her boots hit the slippery surface she began to glide. It had been a while since she had last been skating, and then she had worn proper skating boots. Staying upright whilst sliding rapidly forward in ordinary footwear was a completely different sensation. To keep her balance she had to let go of her skirts and windmill her arms, and lean forward…no, back…no…

'Aaahh!' she squealed as she shot across the ice like a missile fired from a gun. She had totally misjudged how far her run-up would propel her.

She screamed again as she reached the perimeter of the ice, and realised she had no means of slowing down without the blades she was used to wearing for skating. She hit the slightly sloping bank running. Momentum kept her going, forcing her to stumble rapidly forward a few paces, before she managed to stop, with her gloved hands braced against an enormous bramble patch.

'That was amazing!' she panted, straightening up with a huge sense of achievement. She had not fallen flat on her face! Only her skirts had snagged amongst the thorns. Head bowed, she carefully began to disentangle the fabric, to minimise the damage.

'You might want to do something about these, though,' she remarked. 'Somebody might hurt themselves.'

'Only,' he bit out, striding round the ice patch with

a face like thunder, 'if they have no adult to supervise them, and to prevent them from going wild. What the devil were you thinking?' He grabbed her by the shoulders and gave her a shake. 'You little idiot! You could have gone headlong into those brambles and cut yourself to ribbons!'

He had scarce been able to believe it when she had flung herself out onto the ice like that. And when he had heard her scream... For one sickening moment he had pictured her lying injured, her face distorted with pain, frozen for all eternity in agonised death throes...

And then, when he had realised that scream was bordering on a cry of exhilaration, that she was relishing the danger, totally oblivious to the effect her reckless escapade might have upon him...

She gazed up at him in shock, all her pleasure from the little adventure dashed to pieces.

'If you think me an idiot,' she retorted, stung by his harsh words, 'you should not have asked for my opinion!' She swatted his hands away from her shoulders, taking such a hasty step backwards that her skirt ripped. 'And *now* look what you have made me do! Whenever I come anywhere near you it ends in disaster!'

Disaster? he echoed in his mind. This girl had no notion of what disaster truly was. She had come nowhere near disaster.

He tamped down on his surge of fury, acknowledging that it was not her with whom he was angry. Not really. God, Lucinda! Would her ghost never leave him be?

Nobody deserved to die so young. No matter what she'd done. For a moment he was right back in the day he had heard of Lucinda's death, ruing the decision he had taken to wash his hands of her. He should have stayed with her, curbed her. She had been so wild he ought to have known she could be a danger to herself. He had lived with the guilt of her death, and that of the innocent baby she'd been carrying, ever since. Guilt that was exacerbated by the knowledge that a part of him had been relieved he was no longer married to her. Yes, she had set him free. But death was too great a price for any woman to pay.

It was with some difficulty that he wrenched himself back to the present, and the woman who was examining the damage to her gown with clear irritation. It was only a gown. Just a piece of cloth that had been torn. Had she no sense of perspective?

'I have already told you I am willing to replace your gown…'

'That was another gown!' she snapped, made even angrier because he had not noticed she was wearing an entirely different colour today. 'And I have already told you that giving me such things is out of the question!'

That was correct. He had forgotten for a moment that she was merely a guest in his house. That he had no right to buy her clothing. To question her conduct. To be angry with her.

To care what happened to her.

Helen saw his face change. He no longer looked angry. It was as though he had wiped all expression from it.

'I asked for your opinion,' he said in a flat, expressionless tone, 'because you are never afraid to give it. You tell me the truth. Because you care nothing for what I may think of you.'

'Oh, well,' she huffed, feeling somewhat mollified.

It was true that, from what she had observed, most of the people who had come here for Christmas had some kind of hidden agenda. 'Then I apologise for my angry words.' She had lashed out in a fit of pique because he very clearly had no problem keeping his mind off *her* lips. No, he could not possibly have entertained one single romantic thought towards her, or he could not have chastised her in that overbearing manner. Speaking of having some responsible adult to watch over the children, implying he thought *she* was most definitely not!

'Though,' she said ruefully, 'I do not know as much about children as you seem to imagine. The post I am about to take is my first. However, I do think this will be a lovely surprise for them.' Her eyes narrowed as she looked back at the glassy smooth surface he had created. Then she looked straight at him. 'Or for any adult who does not have too inflated an opinion of their own dignity.'

'So you think I have an over-inflated view of my importance?' he replied coldly. 'You think me a very dull fellow, in fact? As well as being hard and unfeeling when it comes to the plight of elderly relatives? I see.'

He gave her a curt bow. 'Perhaps it is time we returned to the house.' He eyed her nose, which had a fatal tendency to go bright red in cold weather. His lips twisted with contempt. 'I can see that you are getting cold.'

She knew it looked most unattractive, but did he really have to be so ungentlemanly as to draw attention to it? Anyone would think he was *trying* to hurt her.

As if he wanted to get back at her for hurting him.

Oh. No…surely not?

But if that were the case…

'I never said I thought you hard and unfeeling. Well, not exactly! Don't go pokering up at me like that!' she protested.

To his back.

He was already striding out in the direction of the house. She would have to trot to keep up with him, never mind catch up with him. She stopped, hands on her hips, and gave a huff of exasperation.

If only it had snowed recently. There was nothing she wanted so much as to fling a large wet snowball at him and knock his hat off!

Except, perhaps, put her arms round him in a consoling hug and tell him she had never meant to insult him. Though she would have to catch up with him to accomplish that. And he had no intention of being caught.

'Ooh…' she breathed, shaking her head in exasperation with herself. What on earth had made her fancy there had been a glimmer of attraction burning in his eyes when he had invited her to come walking with him? Well, if it had ever been there it was gone now. He had just looked at her as though she were something slimy that had crawled out from underneath a rock.

It was not the kind of look she was used to getting from men. Aunt Bella had reminded her only recently that she was a pretty girl. Had urged her to win Mr Cadwallader over with one of her smiles. Had she become vain in recent years? She lowered her head in chagrin as she began to trudge back to the house in Lord Bridgemere's wake. Though she had never actively sought it, she *had* come to regard flattering male attention as her due.

There were some who would say she was getting a

taste of her own medicine, no doubt. Because whenever one of the men of Middleton had sidled up to her in the market, or some such place, under some spurious pretext, to tell her how pretty she was, she had felt nothing for them but contempt. And now the first man she had met who had actually awoken some interest was completely impervious to her charms. He had not paid her a single compliment, nor tried to hold her hand, or snatch a kiss. And yet whenever she was in Lord Bridgemere's vicinity kissing seemed to be all she could think about.

Whereas he, to judge by the stiff set of his shoulders as he drew steadily further and further away, found her annoying.

She flinched, wondering why that knowledge should hurt so much. These days he was out of her reach socially, anyway. Perhaps, she decided glumly, it was just that he represented *everything* that was now out of her reach. The social standing and the affluence that she had taken for granted when she and Aunt Bella had been so comfortably off.

There was nothing so appealing as something that you knew you could never have.

That afternoon Helen took the opportunity to slip away to the library, since the light in there was so much better than it was in their room, with her sewing basket tucked under her arm. She had told her aunt that she intended to make a start on the alterations she had already decided her gowns needed, and the minor repairs her encounters with Lord Bridgemere had made necessary. But really she wanted to get on with the little gift she had been sewing for Aunt Bella. Besides which, the floor-to-ceiling windows contained some heraldic designs which she wanted to sketch. She had decided to use them as a basis for another project which, it had occurred to her, she must complete very swiftly, since it lacked only three days until Christmas.

She made herself comfortable upon one of the window seats with which the room was blessed, and bent her mind to the task in hand. She was not sure how long she had been sitting there when she became aware she was no longer alone.

She looked up from the tangle of silks on her lap to find Lord Bridgemere standing in the doorway. His face was, as usual, hard to read.

Helen felt her cheeks grow hot, and knew she was blushing. It was the first time she had seen him since that early-morning walk of which she'd had such high expectations. And which had resulted in her making such a fool of herself and caused her a morning of quite painful soul-searching as she'd faced up to several unpleasant truths about her character. She had come to the conclusion that whenever Lord Bridgemere looked at her what he saw was a very vain and silly woman.

'I was just passing,' he said, moving his arm towards the corridor outside. 'And I saw you sitting here alone.'

And had been transfixed by the way the sunlight gilded her hair, the pout of her lips as she concentrated on whatever it was that she was doing.

He cleared his throat. 'Why are you on your own, Miss Forrest? Is your aunt unwell?'

Even as he said it he knew that she would not be down here if that were the case. She would be upstairs, nursing her adopted relative. Or down in the kitchens, making some remedy for her. She would not have bothered to ring the bell. A smile kicked up one corner of his mouth as he pictured her marching into the kitchens and elbowing his servants aside to concoct some remedy which only she knew how to make to her own satisfaction.

'Far from it,' replied Helen, wondering what could have put that strange smile on his face. Did she have a smut on her nose? Or was he just recalling one of the many ways she had made a fool of herself since she had come here?

'Aunt Bella is in the card room with Lady Norton. They plan to spend the afternoon drinking tea and gossiping about the fate of mutual acquaintances.'

Her face was so expressive he could not miss a little trace of pique at the way the older woman was treating her. There was something going on between these two ladies that he needed to uncover. The general belief was that Helen was the older Miss Forrest's sole heir. But she had told him she needed to go out to work because she was penniless.

Yet she was still fiercely loyal to her adopted aunt. Whatever had happened between them, it had not soured her.

He found himself walking towards her.

'And what is it you are doing?'

'Oh, nothing much!' Helen quickly stuffed her rough sketches of the Bridgemere coat of arms into her workbasket, and held up the bodice of one of the gowns she was altering. 'Tedious stuff. Making buttonholes and such,' she said.

His brows lowered slightly. 'Is there nothing more amusing you could be doing?'

Helen grappled with a sense of exasperation. She had accused him of neglecting her and her aunt, had felt resentful of the amusements he had provided for the other guests. Yet now he was here, playing the gracious host, she felt uncomfortable. She was not an invited guest. She had done nothing but cause trouble since she had entered his house. And he must have a thousand and one more important things to do with his time. He ought not to be wasting it on her.

'Please do not trouble yourself with me. I am quite content. I…I would actually prefer to be doing something useful than frittering the time away with cards or gossip.'

'Is that so?'

Sometimes Miss Forrest said things that were so exactly what he felt about life himself that it was as though…

He sat down on the window seat beside her and took hold of the piece of material draped across her lap.

'Oh, be careful of the pins!'

He let it go. He had only focussed on it because he had not wanted to look into her face. Lest she see…what? A quickening of interest that she very obviously did not return? She thought him hard and unfeeling, full of his own importance. And worst of all dull. There was no worse character flaw a man could have in the eyes of a girl as lively as this. Had not Lucinda told him so often enough?

It took Helen a great effort to sit completely still. The material which he had dropped back onto her lap was warm from his hand. The fleeting sense that it might have been the touch of his hand on her leg had created an echoing warmth in the pit of her stomach. Which was even now sinking lower, to bloom between her thighs.

Oh, Lord, she hoped he had no idea how his proximity was affecting her! Why did it have to be *this* man, the one man she knew she could never have, who was making her respond in such a shocking way?

'If you really would enjoy being useful, it occurs to me that there is a way in which we could help each other,' he said, laying his arm casually along the edge of the windowsill.

Did he know that extending his arm like that made her feel enclosed by his arms? Was he doing it on purpose, to make her even more conscious of him?

And in what way could she possibly be of any help to him?

Unless she had betrayed her interest in him?

He had no need to marry, but if a woman was silly enough to let him know how physically attractive she found him, might he think he could cajole her into a brief affair?

'I don't think there can possibly be any way I could be of help to you,' she said primly, averting her head. If he was going to insult her by suggesting what she thought he was, then she had no intention of letting him see how much it would hurt!

'You said this morning that you do not have much experience with children, Miss Forrest. And it just so happens that there is a whole batch of them here. They have come with their parents, who have consigned them away upstairs with their nurses. If you wanted to gain some experience with working with children before you take up your first post, then here is an ideal opportunity.'

Experience with children. Of course. She let out the breath she had been holding, chiding herself for once again rating her charms far more highly than Lord Bridgemere obviously did. Here was she, thinking he was about to make her an improper suggestion, while nothing could have been further from his mind. Would she never learn?

'The children of your guests?' she echoed faintly. 'You wish me to go and help…?'

'I have already enlisted the services of Reverend Mullen. He has written the script, which he tells me he has based mostly on the gospel of Luke…'

'Wait a minute. Script?' She raised her head to look at him, quite puzzled. 'What script? What are you talking about?'

'I forgot. This is your first visit to Alvanley Hall, and you are not aware of the traditions that prevail.' He leaned back, his eyes fixed intently on her face. 'Each year I throw a ball for my tenants on Boxing Day, as part of my gift to them to reward them for all their hard work and loyalty to me throughout the year. Out at one of the barns on the home farm. The children who are brought by their parents to stay at the Hall always put on a little entertainment for them to start the evening's festivities. The villagers always perform their mummer's plays for me on Christmas Day, and so I return the favour by getting up this party for them. And, of course, it helps to keep the children occupied during their stay here.'

'Of course,' she echoed faintly, still feeling somewhat

resentful that it had not occurred to him to make her a proposition. Which she would naturally have refused! But still…

'So would you, then? Like to become involved in putting on the production for my tenants?' Or did she consider it was beneath her to spend her time coaching the children to perform for rustics?

She was not quite sure how she could be of *any* help, since he had already told her that Reverend Mullen was writing the script and coaching the children through their parts. She had no experience whatever of amateur theatricals. And the children had their own nurses to see to whatever else it was they needed.

Yet it would be a good opportunity to see how the children of the very upper echelons of society were organised, even if she could contribute very little.

The experience would be of more benefit to her, she suspected, than to Lord Bridgemere.

'Thank you, My Lord,' she said through gritted teeth, wondering why his eyes had turned so cold. 'I should find the experience most beneficial.'

It was ridiculous to let the Earl's treatment of her hurt so much. It was not as if she had seriously believed there could ever be anything between them. And as for those brief flashes of feeling as though she was totally in tune with him…well, they had clearly existed only in her own mind. Lord Bridgemere might have paid her a little attention, but she could see now that it had only been to assess how he could make the best use of her.

'Thank you,' he said, getting to his feet. 'I must leave you now. Cadwallader has arranged a full afternoon for me, and would be most put out if I ruined his timetable. Can you find your own way up to the nursery?'

'If not, I can always ask for directions,' she replied acidly.

She got to her feet and began tidying her work away as soon as he'd left the room. Though she disliked being on the receiving end of Lord Bridgemere's demonstration of his organisational skills, she *would* appreciate the experience of working with some children before she took up her new post. Even though she had decided, when all the money had disappeared, that she would find consolation in moulding young minds in the way Aunt Bella had moulded hers, she was a little nervous about how exactly she would go about the task. Lord Bridgemere could not have hit upon a better way of helping her become accustomed to her new station in life.

Drat him.

Helen enjoyed the rest of the afternoon much more than she had expected. To begin with, the Reverend Mullen welcomed her with an enthusiasm that was a balm to her wounded pride.

'Ah, good, good— His Lordship has managed to persuade you to lend your talents to our little endeavours,' he beamed, when she entered the huge attic space which had been converted into a rehearsal area. 'I have cast the children as best as I can,' he said, 'and rehearsed them once or twice, but they are in dire need of costumes. His Lordship told me you consider yourself a most competent needlewoman, and would be able to help on that front.'

Helen's lips compressed as she recalled flinging those

very words at Lord Bridgemere on the day she had rejected his offer of a new gown to replace the one Esau had spoiled.

But it was hard to stay cross for very long in the atmosphere of jollity over which the Reverend Mullen presided. He was scarcely any older than Nicholas Swaledale, she reflected, yet two youths could not have been more different. The Reverend was earnest, diligent and…well, *worthy* was the word that kept on springing to mind in his regard.

And the children, unlike their parents, all seemed to regard their visit to Alvanley Hall as the highlight of their year.

'Christmas last year was horrid,' said the tubby lad who was to play the part of Joseph, while she was measuring him for his costume. 'Mama and Papa wanted us to keep out of the way while they had their parties. And they forgot all about us. We never got a big feast, like we had the year before at Alvanley. Will we be having a children's feast, this year, Miss Forrest?' he asked excitedly. 'We had cake and jelly and ices last time, I remember.'

'I do not know. This is the very first time I have been here.'

Immediately 'Joseph's' expression turned pitying. 'Never mind, you're here now. Perhaps you will be able to come to our feast with us, and then you'll see!'

'I think I should like that.' She laughed. Far more than the deadly formal banquet she guessed would be provided for the adults.

It would be wonderful to stay up here with the children and servants…

She sucked in a sharp breath. Why had she not seen it before? He had not invited her. She was here as the companion of Aunt Bella, nothing more. He had placed her in a room he'd told her was allotted to upper servants, and when he'd seen her making use of his library, as though she was a guest with the right to make free with the public rooms, he had sent her up here, where the Reverend Mullen could find fitting work for her to do!

She flushed angrily. He thought of her as a servant! It was not his wish to help her gain some experience with children that had prompted him to send her up here. No, he was just putting her in her place! Keeping her out of sight of his relatives, several of whom clearly objected to her presence.

'Did you prick your finger?' asked the pretty little girl who was to play the part of Mary.

When Helen had first come up here the child had run her eyes over her rather plain gown and looked as though she had immediately relegated her to the status of servant. But in spite of that she stopped sifting through the pile of materials that had been provided to make up the costumes the moment Helen gasped.

'I am always pricking my finger when I sew my sampler. You should use a thimble,' she said, nodding sagely.

'Thank you,' said Helen amending her impression of her as a haughty little madam. 'I shall remember that.'

'We get nice presents here, too,' she said absently, resuming her search for something she deemed fit to appear on stage in. 'All of us. *Nobody* is forgotten,' she said, with such a wistful air that Helen suspected she must have suffered such a fate herself. 'And we get to stay up really late to put on our play. And all the grown-ups watch us and clap their hands. Even Mama and Papa.'

Helen could barely refrain from putting her arms round the child and giving her a hug. Her words spoke volumes about the way she was usually treated in her own home.

'I would rather they didn't,' said the slender boy cast in the role of the angel Gabriel, who was sitting on a nearby stool, glumly studying his copy of the play. He was clearly nervous about performing in front of an audience. 'I would rather just stay up here with a book.' He coughed in a most theatrical manner. 'I don't think I will be able to say my lines. I think I'm catching cold.'

'You had better not, Swaledale,' observed 'Joseph'. 'Or you will miss the skating.'

Helen looked sharply at 'Gabriel'. If his name was Swaledale then he must be the younger brother of Lord Bridgemere's heir. Now that she knew he was related, she thought she could see a resemblance. He did have a rather sulky mouth.

'Miss Forrest,' said 'Joseph', turning to her, 'His Lordship has made a skating pond, especially for us children. We are all going to go down tomorrow if the rain holds off. Will you be coming with us?'

'I am not sure,' she replied, tight-lipped. The Earl had specified that he wanted *responsible* adults to watch over his precious young relations, implying that she did not qualify.

'Mary' pouted. 'I expect it is only for boys. The girls will have to stay indoors and…learn lines, or something equally tedious!'

'No, no, Junia, dear,' said Reverend Mullen, who had been passing with a sheaf of scripts in his hands. '*All* the children are to gather in the stableyard, first thing in the morning, where a cart is to be ready to carry them to the pond. Those who do not wish to skate do not have to. They may watch. There will be a warm shelter where hot chocolate and cakes will be served.'

'Joseph's' eyes lit up.

'And did I not tell you, Miss Forrest? His Lordship particularly wants you to accompany the nursery party, since you are such an enthusiastic skater.'

'Are you?' said Junia, dropping a length of purple velvet and looking up at her wide-eyed. 'Would you teach me to skate?'

'Of course I will,' replied Helen, suddenly understanding why her parents sometimes overlooked her. Junia, she recalled hearing, was the name of another of Lady Thrapston's daughters. Her mother must have been furious she had produced yet another girl, when there, in the form of 'Gabriel', was the proof that her sister, Lady Craddock, had produced not only an heir for Lord Bridgemere, but also a potential spare.

As Reverend Mullen hurried away, bent on his next task, Helen's mouth formed into a determined line. No child over whom *she* ever had any influence would be made to feel inferior because of their sex! She would make sure their accomplishments were applauded, their talents encouraged, and—she glanced at the slender, pale young 'Gabriel'—their fears soothed.

Junia sat back and beamed at her. And Helen's opinion of her mellowed still further. She probably could not help being a little haughty, considering who her mother was. The poor girl had clearly been taught that certain behaviour was expected of a young lady. But Helen was going to see to it that tomorrow, at least, she had the chance to break out in the direction her natural inclination carried her!

Then she turned to 'Gabriel'.

'You know, you do not have to say very much,' she said, eyeing his script. 'From what I have seen of the way Reverend Mullen has written it, you mostly have to stand there, looking imposing, while Junia recites the Magnificat.'

'And keep the little angels in order,' said Junia.

Many of the younger children, who could not be expected to learn lines, would be dressed as angels and simply moved about to represent the heavenly host watching over the events taking place in Bethlehem.

He sighed despondently. 'They won't mind *me*,' he prophesied gloomily. 'Nobody ever takes any notice of me.'

'They might,' said Helen on a burst of inspiration, 'if you arm yourself with some treats as a reward for good behaviour.'

'I say, Miss Forrest,' he said, brightening up immediately, 'that's a capital notion. I might ask Cook for some jam tarts, or something!'

Helen had visions of half a dozen little angels, their faces smeared with jam. 'Something like ginger snaps?' she suggested. 'Easier to stow in your pockets for distribution at the proper time. I shall go and have a word with Cook about it later on.'

How fortunate she had already mended fences below stairs, she reflected as Gabriel grinned at her.

Goodness! Helen was beginning to think she might have some natural talent when it came to dealing with children after all.

Chapter Seven

Alas, she had not so much success with adults!

The very moment she walked into the blue saloon that evening she felt out of place. And self-conscious because she had so badly misinterpreted Lord Bridgemere's motives in singling her out for attention. Right now he was moving from one group of guests to another, playing the part of dutiful host. Something inside her squeezed painfully as she saw afresh that it was the duty of a good host to pay a little attention to each of his guests. And she had mistaken his willingness to spend a little of his time ensuring she enjoyed some of the beauty of his estate at dawn's first light as personal interest in *her*. His subsequent attitude had shown her how he really viewed her.

And yet, even knowing this, she was still painfully aware of exactly where he was at any given moment. It was as though she was attuned to the low, melodious timbre of his voice. And, her attention having been caught, she could not prevent her eyes from seeking him out. And then she would feel deflated whenever she caught sight of the back of his head, his light brown hair gleaming in the candlelight. For he would always be intent upon somebody else. So far as he was concerned she might as well not exist.

It was even worse once they sat down to dine and she had an unimpeded view of him at the head of the table. For he talked quietly to those seated on his right hand, or his left.

And ignored her completely.

By the time the ladies withdrew, all Helen wished to do was escape to her bedchamber, where she might have some chance to wrestle her tumultuous feelings into submission.

But Lady Thrapston beckoned to her the moment she crossed the threshold, and she did not see how she could refuse her imperious summons to take a place on the sofa beside her.

Under cover of the noise her two daughters were making at the piano, Lady Thrapston fired her opening salvo.

'I have been observing you,' she said, with a grim smile. 'And I feel obliged to warn you that your tactics will not work with Bridgemere.'

'Tactics?' Helen was so surprised that she hardly knew how to answer Lady Thrapston. They had a knack, she reflected wryly, Lord Bridgemere and his sister, of reducing her to parroting one or two words of their speech.

'Do not play the innocent with me. You fool nobody with all that nonsensical talk about not wishing to marry! It is quite obvious that you have set your cap at Lord Bridgemere.'

Helen's first instinct was to deny the allegation indignantly. She had just opened her mouth to make a pithy rejoinder when she heard her aunt laughing at something Lady Norton had said. And she closed her mouth abruptly. She must not let her temper get the better of her. Aunt Bella was still awaiting Lord Bridgemere's verdict, and until then it would not do to create an even worse impression upon him than she had already done.

She contented herself by lifting her chin and glaring at Lady Thrapston.

'Nothing to say for yourself?' the haughty matron said. 'But then what *can* you say in your defence?'

Helen wondered if she had just made a tactical error. For it looked as though Lady Thrapston thought her dart had gone home. Her next words confirmed it.

'With my own eyes I have watched you making a spectacle of yourself. And let me tell you this. Fluttering your eyelashes at him over the soup plates is one thing, but it has come to my attention that you have now gone to the lengths of luring him to some out-of-the way spot in an attempt to compromise him.'

'That is not true!' Helen gasped. She had not done any luring! Lord Bridgemere had *invited* her to go out walking with him.

How dreadful that somebody had seen them and run to Lady Thrapston with such a tale. She felt quite sick that somebody disliked her enough to do such a thing, without a shred of evidence.

Especially since she would never dream of setting

her cap at any man, or luring him into a compromising position.

But she *had* felt acutely disappointed that his attitude towards her had been so completely impersonal, she admitted to herself. And, her conscience whispered, she'd also had to chastise herself several times for entertaining inappropriate thoughts regarding Lord Bridgemere. Lady Thrapston had obviously noticed that she could not help finding him most attractive. Even when he had made it perfectly clear he was immune to her, she reflected with chagrin.

Her cheeks flushing guiltily, she said, 'I am aware that His Lordship would never consider marrying someone like me.'

Lady Thrapston nodded grimly. 'I trust you will remember that, my girl. If you know what is good for you, you will take care to keep well away from him for the remainder of your visit. It would not do for rumours of indecorous behaviour to accompany you to your new post, would it?'

Was this a threat? Helen reeled at the thought of the damage Lady Thrapston could do to her future if it was. A judicious word in her employer's ear, from a woman of her rank, and her job could well disappear. Nor, if gossip spread about her supposed conduct, would it be easy for her to find another.

Helen wished she might make some clever, cutting rejoinder, but for once she knew it was imperative she keep her tongue between her teeth.

'No,' she whispered. She dared not risk antagonising Lady Thrapston, and have her spread unfounded gossip about her. What General Forrest had begun was bad enough.

'You may return to your aunt,' said Lady Thrapston, a small, but self-satisfied smile playing about her mouth.

She had the look of a woman who had just successfully put a designing trollop in her place, fumed Helen as she walked, stiff-legged and straight-backed, to her aunt, and sat down, her fists clenched in her lap.

It was so unfair!

She caught her lower lip between her teeth, unable to deny that, had she behaved with greater propriety, the woman would not have had cause to think what she had. Her eyes did keep straying towards Lord Bridgemere whenever he was present. Something about him drew her like a magnet. And, from what Lady Thrapston had just said, her attraction towards him must be written all over her face.

She sighed. A proper young lady should never reveal what she was thinking. Her aunt had informed her of that fact many times, without ever managing to teach her how such a feat might become possible. With the result that everyone must be able to tell exactly what she was thinking just by looking at her. She glanced round the room, wondering what everyone had just made of her encounter with Lady Thrapston. And noted several ladies staring at her in a disapproving manner. Lord, did *everyone* think she was fast?

She supposed she could hardly blame them. For she *had* snatched at the chance to spend a few moments with him alone. Even though she had known full well it was most improper behaviour. Oh, she might not have actually set her cap at Lord Bridgemere, but her conduct towards him had definitely been questionable. And had laid her wide open to Lady Thrapston's charges.

Not that his sister need worry. Lord Bridgemere had already taken steps to ensure she kept her distance. He had made sure that she would be busy all day long. Well away from him!

She went cold inside as it occurred to her that *he* might have thought, as Lady Thrapston had, that she was deliberately attempting to entrap him.

How humiliating.

And she had nobody but herself to blame.

'I think I should like to retire early tonight,' said Aunt Bella. 'I have been tired all day after last night's dissipation.'

'I shall come up with you,' said Helen with heartfelt relief. 'Do you wish to go now?' She desperately wanted to get out of the room before the gentlemen joined them. She did not think she could bear to have Lord Bridgemere look at her with the kind of censure Lady Thrapston had just turned on her.

'If you would not mind,' said Aunt Bella gratefully. 'Lady Norton makes me feel old. I simply cannot keep up with her.'

'We are used to living much more quietly,' said Helen, taking her aunt's arm as she rose to her feet. 'That is the problem. Though I, for one,' she muttered under her breath, 'have no wish to fit in with these kind of people.'

Going to bed early solved nothing. Helen lay wide awake, going over and over Lady Thrapston's acid comments, castigating herself for the way she had behaved since coming to Alvanley Hall, and bitterly regretting that second helping of pickled cabbage. She had the worst case of indigestion she could ever remember. Eventually her discomfort became so acute that she knew she would have to find some remedy. In the past she had found that taking a hot drink and walking about provided some relief.

She had no intention of ringing for a servant in the middle of the night. Besides, she knew the way to the kitchens. She could quite easily make herself a cup of tea without disturbing anyone. She got out of bed, thrust her feet into slippers, pulled on her wrapper, and tip-toed across the room so as not to wake her aunt. Then, remembering how cold the corridors could be at any time of the day, she darted back to get her thickest shawl for good measure.

She was halfway down the backstairs when the door at the foot of the staircase opened and somebody with a candle and booted feet began to mount. Assuming it must be a footman, she kept descending until she got to the bend in the stairs, where she gathered the skirts of her nightgown tightly and pressed herself against the wall of the half-landing, to give the man room to get past her.

'Well, well, what have we here?'

Helen grimaced as she recognised in the flickering candlelight not a footman, but the flushed features of Nicholas Swaledale. His neckcloth was awry, his waistcoat buttons undone, and he was swaying ever so slightly with each breath he took.

In other words, he was thoroughly foxed.

And he was standing right in the centre of the narrow

staircase, blocking her path. Running his bloodshot eyes insolently over her.

Her nightgown was not in the least bit revealing. On the contrary, it covered her in voluminous folds of flannel from neck to toe. And yet it was a garment designed for wearing in bed. And the smirk on his face told her he was well aware of the fact.

Helen had never felt so vulnerable.

She had never come across a drunken young man on her own in her entire life, and was not quite sure how to deal with him. If he had been sober she would have curtsied, greeted him formally, and then gone on her way. Perhaps that would be the best thing to do. Remind him of his manners.

'Good evening sir,' she said, dipping her knees in a curtsey as though they were in a drawing room.

Swaledale sniggered as she straightened from her curtsey.

'You don't need to p'tend to be all prim and proper with me, Helen,' he said, climbing up another step so that his face was level with hers. 'Or sh'll I call you Nell?'

He stepped onto the landing and swayed towards her.

Now was not the time to argue about the over familiarity of using her given name. It was the fact that he was standing far too close that was bothering her the most.

She already had her back to the wall. All she could do was turn her head aside as stale brandy fumes assailed her nostrils.

'Please stand back and let me pass,' she said.

'Why? Where you goin'? Or c'n I guess?' His expression turned nasty. 'Off for a little midnight trysht with

Bridgemere, are you? Shneaking down backstairs so nobody will see wass goin' on...'

'There's nothing going on!'

He made a derisive snorting sound. 'The way he goes on about you fair makes me sick. "Paragon!"' He lurched and hiccupped, dripping candle wax onto her shawl. 'Never askin' nobody for nothin', but just goin' out and findin' work. Praising your frugalishity to make the rest of us feel guilty...'

'Fru...frugalishity?' She couldn't help herself. She giggled.

It was just so wonderful to learn that, however he treated her to her face, and whatever suspicions he might harbour in regard to her obvious attraction to him, Lord Bridgemere was still holding certain aspects of her behaviour up to others as an example. And the sudden lift this knowledge brought to her spirits burst forth in a wild surge of hilarity at this drunken youth's muddling of the English language.

With a newfound boldness she reached up and pushed him in the chest, intending to step round him and carry on her way.

But his reflexes were amazingly quick, considering he was slurring his words so badly. He grabbed her wrist and, after a brief struggle, managed to twist her arm behind her back and pin her to the wall.

'Don' laugh at me!' Swaledale's expression had turned ugly. He was leaning against her heavily, his eyes glazed. She could feel the heat of his candle scorching her cheek. She jerked her head away from the naked flame, afraid now that he was so drunk he could easily burn her, entirely by accident.

'Thass wiped that smirk off your face,' he said with a satisfied grin. 'Slut.'

She went still. This kind of behaviour from a man was totally outside her experience. She knew she had no hope of breaking free. And she feared that if she antagonised him further he might really hurt her.

'I am not laughing at you,' she said, in as calm a tone as she could muster, considering her heart was lurching about in her chest. 'Please, won't you let me go now?'

He chuckled.

'No. Don't think I will. Not yet.'

To her utter disgust, he pushed his mouth against hers and licked all the way round her lips.

With the candle held so close to her cheek, she dared not move. All she could do was keep her mouth pressed tightly closed as the revolting assault went on and on. It was just like being slobbered on by Esau! Though at least she had known the dog was trying to be friendly. There was nothing friendly about what Swaledale was doing. It was a deliberate insult!

She whimpered in distress.

He growled. And ran a line of wet kisses down her jaw to her neck.

'What the *devil* do you think you're doing?'

From the staircase below Lord Bridgemere's voice boomed, echoing from the bare woodwork.

'Oh, thank heavens!' Helen cried as Swaledale spun round, letting her go. She wiped her face and neck with the sleeve of her nightgown. Her arm was shaking, she noted. As were her legs.

And she felt sick.

'Having a little bit of sport,' said Swaledale defiantly, 'with a game pullet. Where's the harm in that?'

'The harm,' said Lord Bridgemere coldly, continuing to mount the stairs, 'is that the lady does not appear to me to be willing.'

'She's no lady,' Swaledale sneered. 'Just some jumped-up servant…'

'All the more reason for you to keep your hands off her!'

Helen could not believe how much that hurt. He had not denied Swaledale's assumption that she was a menial. No, his retort only went to confirm that he really did think of her as a sort of servant.

'I will not have my house made unsafe for females whatever their station in life!' Bridgemere continued. 'And if this is an example of what my staff may expect if you take over the reins…'

'Whadya mean, *if*? I'm your heir! When you're gone it will all be mine…'

'*When* I'm gone, and not before!'

He had reached the landing, which now seemed very crowded. Helen was already flat against the wall, and the two men were standing toe to toe.

'I thought I made that quite clear this afternoon,' said Lord Bridgemere in anger. 'You cannot keep running through your allowance, assuming I will mop up all your debts! If this is the way you repay my generosity, then I shall have to think very carefully about doing so again.'

'This is all *your* doing,' Swaledale muttered, giving Helen a dirty look.

'It is nothing to do with Miss Forrest! Oh, for heaven's

sake, go to your room and sleep it off!' he said, running the flat of his hand over the crown of his head. 'We will talk again when you've sobered up.'

To Helen's relief, Swaledale turned and lurched off up the stairs.

But then Lord Bridgemere rounded on her.

'As for you, Miss Forrest, what the devil do you think you are doing, loitering about the backstairs in your nightgown? Have you no sense at all?'

'Loitering?' she retorted, unbelievably hurt by his accusation of deliberate immodesty.

Tears sprang to her eyes as she recalled the way Lady Thrapston had made her feel earlier, when she had accused her of setting her cap at Lord Bridgemere. It was so unfair. She might have been a little reckless, but she had never deliberately set out to lure anyone.

'I assumed that as a guest in your house I would be perfectly safe. I never dreamt I would be accosted and mauled about like that!'

'Well, now you know better.' He laughed bitterly. 'That was just a sample of what you can expect in a devil of a lot of households.' He grabbed her by the shoulders. 'You stay in your room at night, with the door locked,' he grated, shaking her.

He was furious to discover *any* female being subjected to this kind of treatment under his roof. But to think of her going off to some household where there was nobody about to check her natural exuberance, to watch over her, to keep her safe, was ten times worse. He had to make her see that she must modify her behaviour.

'You can never assume anything about men when they have been drinking,' he warned her, 'except that you need to steer clear of them. If you will go prowling around in a state of undress you will have only yourself to blame when some drunken buck helps himself to what is on offer.'

'On offer?' She batted his hands away, her candle guttering as wax splashed down the front of her nightgown. 'How dare you? You make it sound as though what happened was my fault!'

He stepped back and sighed. 'Just get back to your room,' he said wearily. 'And take this as a salutary lesson.'

He was doing it again. Talking down to her as though she was an imbecile…or a child.

'I will not go back to my room,' she said defiantly. 'I have not got what I came down for.'

'If you do not stop acting like this, even I might be tempted to give it to you.'

It was an insult too far. Oh, he might well have commended her frugality to his heir. But only, as the obnoxious toad had said, as a rebuke to a spendthrift youth who seemed to think the world owed him a living.

He really did think she was a…a designing hussy. That she was here on the backstairs in her nightgown for some nefarious reason. And if he could believe that, then he did not know her at all! With a wild sob, she slapped him as hard as she could across the face.

He went very still. Though the breath hissed through his teeth, he said nothing. Merely stared coldly down at her as the marks of her fingers began to bloom across his cheek.

That glacial self-control told her all she needed to

know. Her slap had not hurt him anywhere near as badly as his words had wounded her.

Her breath hitched in her throat as tears streamed down her face.

She felt her self-esteem shrivel to nothing. It was pointless to argue that she had done nothing wrong. In the eyes of the world, a woman who wandered around a house at night in a state of undress, as he had put it, was inviting the wrong sort of attention.

'I d…didn't mean to…'

'I know,' he said, and suddenly he pulled her into his arms and held her. Just held her close while she wept all over his dinner jacket.

It was just what she needed. Someone to hold her and comfort her after the horrible way Swaledale had treated her. Even after the horrible way Lord Bridgemere had spoken to her.

But after only a short while she became aware of the danger of drawing such comfort from Bridgemere, of all men. She knew he would bring Swaledale to book for this night's work. But he would not always be around to fight her battles for her. She was going to have to stand alone. This feeling of security that being in his arms produced was deceptive.

Besides, clinging to him like this when he already thought so poorly of her could only be confirming all his worst assumptions.

Shakily, she pulled herself away, and wiped her face with the back of her hand.

'*Now* will you go back to your room, Miss Forrest?'

He looked completely exasperated. To him, she

must seem like a tiresome child, always blundering into scrapes that he was tired of rescuing her from. Or a servant who did not quite know her place and constantly needed reminding of it.

Not as an equal.

And not, by the way his face had shuttered, as a woman—a desirable woman who might stand a chance of success if ever she *were* brazen enough to attempt a spot of luring!

It felt as though a door had just slammed shut in her face, locking her out, leaving her forever in the cold. Alone.

With a sob, she whirled round and pounded back up the stairs.

The next morning, gritty-eyed from lack of sleep, Helen stumbled outside to the stableyard. She had promised Junia she would help her learn to skate or, to be more accurate, slide about on the ice, and nothing was going to make her break her word to a child.

'Good morning, good morning!' chirped Reverend Mullen, rubbing his hands together for warmth. 'A fine, frosty morning. Perfect for the children's outing,' he beamed.

Helen managed to muster a polite smile as she clambered up into the back of the cart that was already half filled with excited children, all bundled up warmly, with hats and scarves concealing most of their faces.

She had seen them going off in this cart on her first morning here, she remembered, with a pang of nostalgia.

Back then she had felt like an unwelcome intruder. Now, although she was caught up in Lord Bridgemere's plans for his guests, she still felt painfully aware that she did not belong. He would be glad, no doubt, when she left, considering all the trouble she had caused.

She sighed as a groom slammed the tail of the cart closed. Reverend Mullen leapt up in front, next to the driver, and they lurched off, out of the cobbled yard and round a winding drive towards the copse.

The ride through the estate was like rubbing salt into a raw wound. Alvanley Park was just so beautiful this time in the morning. Every bush, tree and lacy spider's web was gilded with frost, which sparkled as the sun caught it. As they swept round the lake she saw tendrils of mist rising from its surface, as well as from the grassy slopes upon which the sun's rays beat down. And she could not help recalling the walk through the woods they were approaching now by the lane. The fleeting feeling of intimacy she had known with the owner of all this magnificence.

Which had melted away like the frost in the sunlight. Leaving behind, as he had predicted, a black mire of misery.

The cart could not get right into the grove in which Lord Bridgemere had created the ice slide. They all had to clamber down from the cart and walk the last few yards.

When they emerged from the last stand of trees Helen was astounded by the transformation that had been wrought on the place overnight. There were coloured lanterns hanging from the overhanging branches, so that what had been a dank, dark place now looked festive and inviting. The door to the tower stood open today, and inside she could see a fire burning in a massive great hearth, so that anyone who got too cold could go and take shelter there.

And, she noted with tears in her eyes, what looked like horse blankets had been draped over the offending brambles, so that if anyone else was careless enough to overshoot the slide they would not get scratched.

Lord Bridgemere had thought of everything, she sniffed. He had taken as much care over this treat for the children as would be given to an entertainment arranged for adults on such estates. He cared equally for all his guests, be they high-born or low, be they young or old.

Why did more people not see this? Why had her aunt described him in such terms that she had thought he was a total misanthrope? He was nothing of the kind!

'Miss? Miss?'

Junia was frowning up at her. 'You said you would teach me...'

Blinking away her tears, Helen saw that some of the boys had dashed straight out onto the ice and were already sliding around, whooping and hollering at the tops of their voices.

Reverend Mullen strode out after them, waving his arms like a shepherd with an unruly flock of sheep, shooing them all to one end so that the smaller ones, and those who were more timid, would have a space where they need not fear getting knocked down.

'I did,' she said, taking Junia's hand. 'Let's show these boys how it's done!'

It was impossible to stay feeling sorry for herself for very long. Soon she was having as much fun as the children. Even Junia forgot her starchy manners and laughed happily as she mastered the art of staying upright whilst sliding about.

Some while later Helen heard the unmistakable sound of Esau's deep throaty bark, carrying to her from the pathway where they had abandoned the cart.

Her heart began to pound heavily. If Esau was there, Lord Bridgemere would not be far behind. Indeed, the moment she lifted her head to gaze in the dog's direction she spotted him, astride a glossy bay stallion, his brows knit in a ferocious scowl as he called his hound to heel.

Esau stood for a second or two, his tail waving in the air, his nose well up, as he watched all the activity on the ice. He would have loved to join the children. But he was so boisterous, and so big, he would be bound to frighten the little ones. Lord Bridgemere called him again, and the dog bounded back to his master's side.

He looked up then and saw her, standing stock still, staring at him.

Her cheeks flushed, remembering the last time she had seen him. How little she had been wearing. And how wonderful it had felt when he had put his arms round her.

And how exasperated he had looked at her clinging to him and weeping all over him.

He had not repulsed her, though. He was too kind for that.

She began to raise her hand, to wave a greeting, but quickly perceived how such a gesture would be interpreted. People already thought she was setting her cap at him. Even such an innocent gesture as waving to him would give them more fodder for gossip. Besides, he had not come down here today to see her. He would want to check for himself, considering all the trouble he had gone to, whether the children were enjoying themselves.

Sucking in a sharp, painful breath, she deliberately turned her back on him, gripped Junia's hand a little more tightly, and pushed herself and her charge in the opposite direction.

Lord Bridgemere felt as though she had slapped him all over again. Last night he had assumed it had been Swaledale she had wanted to strike, that *he* had been the one who had made her so angry.

But now he was not so sure.

The reproachful look on her face before she had deliberately turned her back on him had made him wonder if she could possibly have discerned the effect she'd had on him last night. But, hell, what man could hold a woman like her in his arms and *not* become aroused? She was so warm, so soft, and so very much alive! And as he had held her it had been as though her life force had flowed into him, making him feel, making him want...

If she had not run upstairs like a frightened little girl she would have discovered he could behave every bit as badly as Swaledale. And there would have been nobody to stop him.

Who would dare? They courted him, fawned over him, said *yes, My Lord*, and *no, My Lord* until he could barely stomach the sight of them. All except this proud, vibrant girl, who had barely stopped challenging him from the moment she had set foot in his house. Effortlessly breaching the walls he had built up so painstakingly. Dull but safe bulwarks comprised of duty, cemented together by plentiful application of steady routine. She made him act upon impulse. Brought him back to life…

But with life came pain. He felt it now, in the wake of her reproachful rejection. Almost as badly as he had felt it last night when she had slapped him.

His face twisting in self-disdain, he turned his horse away from the clearing and cantered away into the woods.

Chapter Eight

Upon her return to the house, Helen went straight upstairs to change out of her outdoor clothes.

She was still feeling somewhat disturbed after that fleeting glimpse of Lord Bridgemere. As soon as he had ridden away her pleasure in the morning's activity had dimmed. She had so wished he might have come and joined them. If not for her sake, then for his own. He ought to have been able to take part in the fun everyone else was having. Instead, he had kept his distance.

Dispensing largesse to others whilst staying aloof from them was what he did best. She sighed sadly. Each night, for instance, he provided wonderful food and plenty of drink. Yet he ate but sparingly, and remained sober when the other gentlemen drank to excess. She shuddered as she remembered Swaledale's beastly behaviour. And perceived that Lord Bridgemere would detest being as out of control as that youth.

She wished he were not always quite so serious, though. For a man so young, he carried a great weight of responsibility on his shoulders. She wondered how often he was truly free from care. She wished she might see him smiling more often. Laughing at life's simple pleasures.

But his life was not simple. A great many people depended upon him. And, particularly at this time of year, he had to make a great many decisions about their welfare.

She found herself yawning as she went along the corridor that led to the rooms she shared with Aunt Bella. Heavens, but she was tired! She had barely slept since coming here. And each day had been filled with such emotional turmoil she was quite wrung out with it all. She would be glad when it was time to leave and take up her new post. Being around the insular Lord Bridgemere was too emotionally exhausting.

Yet another shock awaited her when she opened her door. For Aunt Bella was sitting on the chair before the fire, sobbing helplessly into her handkerchief.

A shaft of cold dread struck her in the midriff. For it had been her aunt's turn, this morning, to visit Lord Bridgemere in his study and plead her case.

'Oh, Aunt Bella, whatever is the matter?' she cried, darting across the room and falling to her knees at her aunt's feet. 'What did he say to you to make you weep like this? What is to become of you? Oh, I cannot believe he could be so cruel!'

She could not help thinking of how coldly he had looked at her after she had slapped his face last night. But, surely…? He had vowed he was not the kind of man to take a petty revenge on a third party! Yet her aunt was weeping as though her heart had broken, when she never cried. She had not even cried when their landlord had threatened to evict them from the home that was so dear to her. No, she had just metaphorically rolled up her sleeves and sought a solution for them both.

'C…cruel?' her aunt sniffed, dabbing at her eyes. 'Oh, he has not been cruel at all. So kind. So very kind…' She attempted a wavering smile, but then burst into tears again.

'But you are crying…'

Aunt Bella balled her soggy handkerchief and took a deep breath.

'I have maligned that boy,' she sobbed. 'He was not a b…bit censorious of the way I chose to live all those years, nor did he make me feel inc…competent when I told him what had happened to the b…bank. No snide comments about females not being fit to manage m…money matters and how it would have been better to have been guided by my b…brothers even if I did choose not to marry.'

She drew in a shuddering breath. 'He…he said that this k…kind of thing happens all the time, which is why more experienced men of business n…never put all their eggs in one basket. He laid the blame squarely on my man of business, Ritson, for not spreading my capital amongst a diverse range of enterprises. I told him about the time I wanted to invest in the canal company,' she said, her tears ceasing to flow as the light of indignation came to her eyes, 'and that little manufactory that wanted capital to make modernisations, and how Ritson talked me out of it as being too risky. Risky!' She squeezed her handkerchief so hard Helen knew she was imagining fastening those fingers round Mr Ritson's neck. 'Lord Bridgemere told me that had I had my way on just those two ventures I would now be as well off as I had ever been!'

Helen settled back on her heels, drawing off her gloves with profound relief. Her aunt was drying her eyes, though she had known that she was much more her old self when she had mimed wringing Mr Ritson's neck. Helen could not help admitting to herself that a great deal of her relief stemmed from knowing her faith in Lord Bridgemere had not been misplaced. For a moment, when she had feared he might have refused to help her aunt in her hour of need, it had felt as though her whole world had turned upside down.

'I had been so afraid, Helen, that he would insist my brother resume his responsibilities towards me, even though we have been at daggers drawn all these years. After all, he must be in some kind of trouble himself, or he would not be here, would he? And I thought the price Lord Bridgemere would make him pay for bailing him out would be taking me under his wing again.' She shuddered eloquently.

'Thank heaven it was no such thing. To begin with, His Lordship has offered to look into my finances for me, and see if anything may be salvaged,' she said, dabbing at her nose. 'And if I am really as poor as I fear, he will make arrangements for me to find a new home in which I may be happy. What do you think of that?'

'That,' said Helen, untying the strings of her bonnet, 'it is most thoughtful of him…'

A wave of tenderness towards him swept over her. How tactfully he had dealt with what could have been a most painful interview for her aunt. Aunt Bella was a proud, independent woman. It had not been the poverty so much as the prospect of having to beg for help that had been making her ill.

'He *is* thoughtful, Helen.' Aunt Bella frowned. 'You know, I had gained the impression that he had grown hard and unapproachable in recent years. But perhaps it was just my reluctance to have to approach anyone for help after I had fought so hard to maintain my independence from my overbearing brothers which coloured the way I regarded him.'

In short, she had resented having to humble herself. And therefore resented *him*.

And she, Helen, had absorbed those same views. Her aunt's bitterness had made her suspicious when she need not have been, and angry with him without cause. He had never been intentionally unkind. It had not been his fault that her aunt had worked herself up into a state about casting herself on his mercy. It had not been his fault that she had ended up in that little tower room untended, either. She recalled his chagrin upon discovering the mistake which had resulted in his elderly relative lying up there unattended for hours.

She really had behaved dreadfully, Helen reflected, yet another wave of self-disgust churning through her. She remembered the coldness of his eyes after she had slapped him, now piercing her deeply in such rebuke that it was all she could do to keep her chin up.

The only fault she could find with him now was that he tended to be rather aloof.

She groaned inwardly. But if she had a family like his would not she, too, take care to steer clear of them from one year's end to the next?

'Oh,' said Aunt Bella, leaning back and shutting her eyes. 'It feels as though an enormous weight has rolled off my shoulders.'

'I am so pleased for you, Aunt Bella,' she said. But a wave of sorrow swept through her. Everyone was here because they wanted something from him. But where did he turn when *he* needed help? She shook her head at the ridiculous notion. A man like him would never need help from anyone. Least of all her.

'Before I forget,' said Aunt Bella, sitting up and opening her eyes, 'I should tell you that a letter has arrived for you.' She pointed to the console table just inside the door. 'I put it over there.'

Getting to her feet, Helen went and picked up the single sheet of paper, and broke open the wafer.

'It is from the Harcourts,' she said, quickly checking the signature. 'They want me to go to them straight away. Some domestic crisis.' She frowned at the few lines scrawled upon the page, which explained very little.

'Oh, Helen, I shall be so sorry to see you go.'

'I shall be sorry to have to leave,' Helen admitted. It was ironic that only a few minutes since she had been wishing she could leave Alvanley Hall, and the agonising pain of becoming increasingly infatuated with a man so very far out of her league. Yet now the Harcourts had summoned her the prospect that this was it, she must bid him farewell and never see him again, felt perfectly dreadful. As though a huge dark cloud was hovering above her.

Helen smiled bravely. 'At least I shall not be worrying

about your future, now that Lord Bridgemere has turned out to be so very kind.'

She crumpled the letter in her hand.

'I am just going to take off my coat, Aunt Bella,' she said, darting into her own room to conceal the fact that there were tears in her eyes. 'And then I will see about getting you some luncheon.' She removed her bonnet, hastily dabbing at her eyes with the ribbons. 'This afternoon,' she called, 'I have promised to help Reverend Mullen again, with the theatricals for the children.'

'That is fine by me, dear,' she heard her aunt reply from the other room. 'I shall have forty winks and then go down and join Lady Norton in a hand or two of piquet.'

Helen scrabbled in her coat pocket for a handkerchief and blew her nose. There. She was fine again. Fixing a smile on her face, she returned to the main room.

'I should not be a bit surprised,' her aunt said, 'if His Lordship does not try to see if he can somehow kill two birds with one stone by housing me with her.'

'Do you really think so?'

'Lady Norton,' her aunt said, lowering her voice and leaning towards her niece, 'has such a passion for gambling that even here her husband watches her like a hawk. We play for ivory counters, from some old gaming boxes we found, because he has forbidden her ever to play for money again. And she seems quite scared of disobeying him. His Lordship may well agree to pay off her debts, if that is what they are asking for, in return for taking me in. Though of course that is only conjecture.'

'Would you like to go and live in such a household?'

'Do *you* really want to go and work as a governess for strangers?' Aunt Bella fired straight back at her. 'What we both want,' she said, her lower lip quivering, 'is to be able to go back to the way things were in Middleton. Living simply and quietly, dependent upon nobody, and able to please ourselves. But if you can go out to work for a living,' she said, lifting her chin, 'without uttering one word of reproach to me or anyone else, I can certainly go and act as companion to a woman who is in need of a steadying influence in her life. Not only against her addiction to gambling, but also as a shield against that overbearing husband of hers. And if that *is* the solution His Lordship finds for me, I shall certainly consider it quite seriously. I always liked Sally. After all these years, it is amazing to find that I still do.

'But in any case, I have no need to rush into a decision. Although His Lordship will not be remaining here long after Twelfth Night he has said I may as well stay on, since there are umpteen empty rooms and a small kernel of servants who keep the place up.' A determined look came over her. 'Though you may be sure that if I do stay on here I shall find some way to make myself useful. I dislike the thought of being a charity case.'

Helen was quite sure that Lord Bridgemere would make sure Aunt Bella never felt that way. She sighed. There was really no need for her to stay at Alvanley Hall any longer now that her aunt's future was assured. There was no excuse she could give to put off answering her employer's summons.

'I had better write to the Harcourts straight away and tell them I shall make my way there as soon as is practicable.'

'I wish you need not go,' said Aunt Bella, twisting her handkerchief between her fingers. 'I am quite sure that His Lordship would make some provision for you, too, if you were not too proud to ask him.' She held up her hand as Helen opened her mouth to make her objections known. 'No, you do not need to say it. You have no claim upon him. I know how hard it would be for you to accept his help, since I have found it so difficult to come here myself, and it is his *duty* to look after me. But this one thing I will say. It would be foolish of you not to ask his help with the travel arrangements. You have already partaken of his hospitality, and this would only be an extension of that.'

Helen thought he would probably be so relieved to know she was leaving he would be tempted to load her into the coach himself. He would think it well worth a little inconvenience if it meant ridding himself of a woman he regarded as a conniving hussy who prowled round the house in her nightwear, hoping to lure him into her clutches.

'Do you know?' Aunt Bella continued. 'He said that if we had written to confide the difficulties we were experiencing he would have sent his own coach to fetch us here. He said he was mortified to think of the struggles we had endured, the deleterious effect the rigours of our journey had on my health. Imagine that.'

Helen sighed. She could imagine it all too well. Lord Bridgemere was, beneath that forbidding exterior, a good man. A decent man.

'Then I will ask him if he would be so kind as to make the travel arrangements for me.'

It would probably be best if she went to Mr

Cadwallader and asked him to arrange an appointment. She did not want to have to suffer the indignity of approaching Lord Bridgemere in the blue saloon before dinner tonight, with all those beady eyes on her. All those ears straining to overhear what was her business alone. Besides, she knew only too well that it was completely beyond her capabilities to conceal the effect he had on her. And there was nothing more pathetic than females who made fools of themselves over men who were just not interested.

He would probably not have time to schedule such an appointment before tomorrow. Christmas Eve. She frowned. The day would be packed with so many activities, he might well be too busy to fit her in at all. And had he not said that he only granted each of his guests just one appointment, anyway? And then it would be Christmas Day, and of course he would not make his coachman set out on such a long journey—not on a day which ought to be a holiday for all.

It would be Boxing Day at the earliest before she could leave. And she would probably have to ask Cadwallader to arrange everything without speaking to Lord Bridgemere himself.

But she rather thought that seeing their new governess draw up outside their house in a coach with a crest on the door might compensate the Harcourts for her not arriving sooner.

Two more days. That was all she had left.

And then the rest of her life to recover from the impact the handsome, self-contained Earl had had upon her heart.

* * *

It was a relief to return to the noisy chaos of the schoolroom. Since the children's costumes had all been agreed upon, and suitable materials found, her task that afternoon was to make them up. Lord Bridgemere, she discovered when she went to sit at the large table by the window, had also hired a couple of girls from the village to help out with the sewing.

They were inclined to be on their best behaviour, until Helen explained, 'I have only come here as companion to my aunt. She is the one who really has the right to be here. Once Christmas is over I will be going off to work as a governess.'

After that they began to chat more freely with her as they sat tacking together swathes of velvet, calico and silk for angels, shepherds and kings.

From them, she learned that all the villagers were really looking forward to the ball Lord Bridgemere always arranged for them on Boxing Day.

'Puts on a right good do,' said the plumper of the two, whose name was Maisie. 'And not just for the gentry staying at the house. But for all of us ordinary folk, too.'

'Speak of the devil,' said her thinner companion, jabbing her in the side with her elbow.

Helen looked up to see that the door to the attic room was open and Lord Bridgemere was leaning against the frame, his arms folded, watching over the activity with what looked to her like satisfaction.

Reverend Mullen suddenly noticed him, too. He clapped his hands and said, 'Children, children! Make your bows to His Lordship, who has most generously spared us a few minutes out of his busy day to come and visit us!'

Was it her imagination, or did some of Lord Bridgemere's satisfaction dim?

If it did, it was only for a second, because as the children all stopped what they were doing and turned towards him he produced a smile and said, 'Well, I happen to know that Cook is sending up a tray of her ginger snaps, so how could I stay away?'

At that very moment two maids came into the room, bearing trays of drinks and biscuits which they carried to a table at one end of the room. The children, to Helen's amusement, promptly forgot their company manners to swarm round the refreshments table.

Far from looking offended, Lord Bridgemere was smiling again.

His smile dimmed as he turned towards the table where Helen was working. By the time he reached them his face showed no emotion whatsoever.

'I did not intend the refreshments for the children alone,' he said. 'I do hope you ladies will take a break from your work to sample some of Cook's baking.'

'Why thank you, Your Lordship,' said Maisie, getting up and dropping a clumsy curtsey, her face pink with pleasure. Her friend, too, looked similarly flustered at having Lord Bridgemere address them directly.

It seemed Helen was not the only female upon whom he had such a disturbing effect. Her heart sank as she saw that he had been as impervious to her blushes and sighs as he was to those of these village girls. In his mind he probably consigned her along with them as foolish females who were well beneath his notice! Head lowered, she followed her two companions to the refreshments table.

'Did you enjoy the ice this morning, children?' he asked, when they were all seated with their beakers of milk.

There was a rousing chorus of yeses and thank-yous through milk-moustached smiles.

'Do not forget,' he said solemnly, 'that tomorrow, Christmas Eve, I am relying on you to gather enough greenery to decorate the Great Hall. I need holly and ivy, and mistletoe if you can find it. I think there may be one or two boughs in the apple orchard...'

He frowned, as though uncertain, when Helen was sure he knew exactly where it was to be found. He was deliberately turning the ritual of bringing greenery in for Christmas Eve into a kind of treasure hunt for the children.

The boy who was playing the part of Gabriel, the younger Swaledale, was wriggling where he sat. 'We'll find some for you, sir!' he said earnestly.

'Why, thank you, Charles,' Lord Bridgemere replied, bringing a flush of pleasure to the lad's thin cheeks.

'I know that some of your older brothers and sisters may stir themselves, and there will be a few servants free, but without your help...' He shook his head in mock solemnity.

'We'll do it!' several of them shouted.

Helen couldn't help smiling. It would be servants and perhaps some of the ladies who fashioned the gathered greenery into garlands and wreaths. But after the way he had just spoken the children would feel a real sense of achievement. When Christmas morning came, and they saw the house festooned with the greenery they had helped gather, they would really feel a part of the Christmas celebrations.

No wonder those who had visited before had such fond memories of Christmas at Alvanley Hall.

'Thank you,' he said solemnly. Then, 'Now, make sure you wear suitable clothing. Holly is very prickly. I do not want anyone to forget their gloves. Reverend Mullen, could you perhaps find a few spare pairs of gloves, in case anyone forgets to bring their own?'

Helen could have kissed him. None of the children would want to be left out of the adventure from lack of proper clothing. Yet a few of them, as she had discovered during that morning's outing, simply did not have any. Peter, the little boy who was to play the part of Joseph, for instance, had come back from the skating party with the joints of his fingers horribly distended by angry looking chilblains. If she was being charitable, she would hazard a guess that his parents, Lord and Lady Norton, had so many worries of their own that outfitting their only son for winter had slipped their minds. Except that every time she saw Lady Norton she acted as though she had not a care in the world. It was her husband who went about looking burdened with woes.

She shook her head, her lips pursed. Peter's mother, she feared, did not care about her son, and even if his father did he was such a bellicose kind of man that in all likelihood nobody would dare approach him and remind him of any oversight he might have committed.

Still, once his son left Alvanley Hall Helen had no doubt that he would have been discreetly supplied with enough warm clothes to see him through the rest of the winter. She was convinced that nobody would demand any child return their 'borrowed' gloves.

Lord Bridgemere had such a tactful way of providing for those in need without making them feel like paupers.

She sighed.

It was at that moment, while she was sighing adoringly at his back, that he turned round abruptly and looked straight at her.

Her cheeks flamed guiltily. She swiftly lowered her head and stared fixedly into her half-empty beaker, but she was all too aware of him stalking towards her.

Oh, heavens. After all the lectures she had already given herself about the inappropriate nature of the way she looked at him, he had caught her doing it again!

'Miss Forrest? May I have a private word with you?'

He motioned with his arm to indicate his wish that they step outside.

Her heart sank. She could feel another stinging rebuke coming her way. Yet she placed her beaker on the tray and followed Lord Bridgemere across the room to the doorway. He held the door open as she passed him, then stepped out into the passage, leaving it open behind them. Nobody would be able to hear what they were saying, but since they were in full view of Reverend Mullen, the children, their nurses and various household staff, there would be no possibility of anyone accusing either of them of the least hint of impropriety.

'I spoke with your aunt this morning,' he began, surprising her into raising her head and looking at him properly for the first time since he had caught her making sheep's eyes at him.

He did not look annoyed. More…troubled.

'Her case was far more desperate than I had been led to believe.' He frowned. 'She ought to have written to me straight away,' he said, running the flat of one hand over the crown of his head.

'Oh. Well, perhaps… Only we did not know where you might be found…'

'Nonsense!' He turned and paced away from her, and then back, as though he was seriously agitated. 'A letter addressed to me and sent here would have made its way to me easily enough. I always keep my steward apprised of my movements in case he needs to contact me urgently.'

He was pacing back and forth now, a frown pleating his brow.

'He always forwards any mail. It is unthinkable that she has lost her home because she left approaching me this late. Had she applied to me at once I might have been able to do something to prevent her losing her independence. That she thought me so lacking in proper feeling that she regarded me as a last resort…'

Helen laid a hand upon his sleeve as he passed, arresting his movement. 'Please, do not upset yourself. It is not your fault that she resisted applying for charity.'

'I cannot help blaming myself, though,' he said irritably. 'I have gained something of a reputation over the past few years for being unapproachable. Particularly to my own family. I have sent several of them away with a flea in their ear when I thought they were trying to sponge off me. More than once. But you must believe me, Miss Forrest,' he said earnestly, laying his hand over her own, 'I would never permit anyone for whom I am responsible to suffer unnecessary hardship. Not real hardship.'

'I know that.' She turned her hand over and squeezed his, reassuringly. 'I know.'

She was not sure why he was so determined to convince her that he was not an ogre. When, from what he had just told her, he appeared to have deliberately fostered that image. But it made her feel so happy to think he did not want *her* to think badly of him that she smiled.

'And I want to thank you for the very tactful way you handled the situation. My aunt has been so proud of maintaining her independence from her brothers that the act of asking you for aid now might well have broken her. But she is easy in her mind now, for the first time in months. Because of you.'

'Rubbish!' He stepped back smartly, releasing her hand as though it had stung him. 'I only did what any decent man would do.'

Helen let her own hand fall to her side, humiliatingly aware that she had overstepped the bounds of propriety with him yet again.

'Oh, no,' she insisted, with a shake of her head. 'Some men would have casually crushed her with their condescension. You listened to her. Really listened to what she needed and made it available.'

But he did not look any less troubled.

'It occurred to me, as your aunt was telling me about her plight, that when she lost her fortune you lost your inheritance too. That is why you told me you are now penniless, even though everyone else believes you are an heiress.'

'Well, yes,' she admitted hesitantly. 'Though I do not see that it is any concern of yours.'

'Do you not? Do you not think any man would be concerned to see a young woman, brought up in afflu-ence, suddenly obliged to go out to work for a living?'

It warmed her heart to see him so concerned on her behalf. Though there was nothing he could do for her—not really.

'Miss Forrest,' he said, 'you have no family to speak of. Nobody to whom you can apply for aid. Would it make a difference to your future plans if I were to make it known that I am willing to provide you with a dowry?'

'Wh…what?' Helen could not believe her ears.

'You ought to marry,' he said. 'I know you say you do not want to, but I cannot believe you are completely sin-cere. It is the main ambition of all my female relatives. And of all the ladies of my acquaintance you are the one I could actually see making some man a comfortable sort of wife. You are unselfish. You unfailingly put the welfare of others before your own.'

She went up to bed early with her aunt, missing out on the entertainments the other ladies enjoyed. He had found her sitting, uncomplaining, mending her meagre supply of clothes whilst her aunt was playing cards with another of the matrons. And as for the effect she was having on the children! He had seen little Junia blossom under her kind ministrations, and even the younger Swaledale boy casting off his habitually sulky attitude.

'I have never seen a woman bear misfortune with such fortitude,' he continued. 'You do not pout, or whine that life is unfair. You just take it all on the chin, with that rueful little smile of yours.'

He reached out with one forefinger, running it over her chin, before abruptly snatching it back and saying gruffly, 'You deserve to find happiness. Not to be shut away in some schoolroom for the rest of your life.'

He blinked then, as though he could not believe what he had just done.

And, as for Helen, she could not believe what he had just *said*! He admired her so much that he would insult her by offering her money so that she could go out and marry someone else! She could feel her heart pounding hard in her chest. He thought she would make *some man a comfortable sort of wife*, did he? She clenched her fists.

'How can you still keep on trying to ram your charity down my throat when I have made it quite plain I shall never accept anything from you? Besides, a dowry is the very last thing I need! I shall *never* marry,' she said furiously, as much to herself as to him.

She had learned a lot about herself during the days she had been at Alvanley Hall, and honesty compelled her to admit that the only reason she had never thought much about marriage was because she had never met a man like Lord Bridgemere before! No other man had ever had a strong enough pull to tempt her to break faith with Aunt Bella, who was so very opposed to the institution.

'I could not possibly marry *some man* just so that I might have somebody to keep me in suffocating indolence,' she spat. 'I could have been married by now, you know, without a dowry. There were men in Middleton who were quite keen,' she declared defiantly. *He* might not find her attractive, but others had.

'Even after we lost all our money, if I had given certain gentlemen a little encouragement, they would have been only too happy to take me into their homes and smother me with their generosity.' She laughed bitterly. 'But I was too proud, I suppose *you* would say, to sell myself to some tradesman with greasy skin and hairy knuckles.' She shuddered.

And then, of their own volition, her eyes strayed to his hands. His nails were neatly manicured, his fingers long and lean. She knew there was strength in those hands. He had held her by the shoulders, shaken her in anger.

Held her to his heart and briefly made her feel as though there was nowhere on earth she would rather be...

She tore her eyes from their greedy perusal of his hands, forcing herself to look him in the face even though she feared he would be able to see exactly what was in her heart. What did it matter now? He clearly felt nothing for her beyond a mild sort of admiration of her character. Else he would not have just offered her a dowry so she could go out and find some other man to marry.

'In short, sir, the only reason I would ever marry would be for love. I have absorbed my aunt's belief in independence too much to even consider marrying some man so that he might support me. I would rather provide for myself.'

She flushed and hung her head. She could not maintain eye contact with Lord Bridgemere whilst speaking of love. She was more than halfway to that state with him, she thought, and it felt unbearably humiliating to know he did not return her feelings.

'I see.' His voice sounded particularly hard. 'Then there is no more to be said.'

Why did she always have to fling his offers of help back in his face with such vehemence? It made no difference that she was correct—that it would be improper of her to accept money or indeed any substantial gift from a man who was not related to her. He wanted to help her, dammit! He could tear his hair out with frustration at knowing there was nothing he could do for the most deserving case he had encountered this year. What was the point of having so much wealth if he could not use it to benefit someone he actually *wanted* to help? Not because he felt it was his duty, but because...well, because he just wanted to!

And all she could do was stand there, her eyes flashing angrily, telling him she did not need him at all. She could manage quite well on her own, thank you very much!

He had turned and walked halfway down the corridor before Helen remembered she still had to ask him about transport to her new home.

'Wait!' she cried.

He turned, reluctantly, and looked back at her with barely concealed impatience.

'I *do* need to speak with you,' she said. 'I have something to ask of you.'

'What? You?' He laughed mockingly. 'The proud,

independent woman who wants nothing from any man. Least of all me!'

Her eyes widened in shock and he realised he had been unnecessarily curt with her. He held up his hand and continued on his way.

'Not now, Miss Forrest,' he said, shaking his head. He was not completely in control of his emotions. What he ought to have said was, *yes, Miss Forrest, ask me anything and I shall give it to you.* But she had got him so riled up that he no longer knew what he was saying.

'Oh, but it will not take a minute—'

'I said not now!' he snapped. 'Speak to Cadwallader.' He sighed, running his hand over his head wearily. 'He arranges all my appointments. I will hear your petition,' he said coldly, 'when it is more convenient to me.' When he had regained some vestige of self-control.

Helen frowned at his retreating back, wondering how it was possible to feel so much admiration for a man who was so difficult to understand. Whose moods could change so abruptly.

She sighed and turned back towards the school-room.

It hardly mattered anyway. She would be gone from here in just a few more days. And their paths would never cross again. Gradually, without the stimulus of his presence, these turbulent feelings he stirred up would wither away. Until he became nothing more than a distant memory.

The prospect of becoming a governess had never seemed more dreadful.

Chapter Nine

Lord Bridgemere had organised Christmas Eve so that it would be one continuous round of pleasure for his guests.

Helen started her day by clambering into the cart that conveyed the nursery party into a section of the woods where evergreens were predominant. The children were still rushing about excitedly when Lord Bridgemere himself appeared on horseback, followed by a small party comprised of the younger, unmarried ladies and gentlemen, resplendent in highly fashionable riding habits.

Lady Thrapston's daughter Augustine, who looked as though she was not long out of the schoolroom herself, looked rather wistfully at the children playing tag amongst the trees. Then she darted a furtive look at her companions, as though checking to see if anyone had caught her out, and adopted the same air of languid boredom worn by the other members of the riding party.

Making Helen feel sorry for her.

She was just thinking what a shame it was that Lady

Augustine no longer felt free to be herself now that she wasn't a child, when she caught Lord Bridgemere smiling sadly at his niece. And she knew he was thinking exactly the same thing. When he turned slightly, and their eyes met, it was as though they were of completely one mind. Though they were yards apart, she felt as though they were connected intimately by sharing one and the same thought.

She felt quite a wrench when he looked away.

'I need some of you older boys for a special task,' he said, leaning his forearm across the pommel of his saddle. 'Any volunteers?'

Charles and Peter's hands shot up.

He looked them over critically for a few seconds, before nodding solemnly and saying, 'You will follow me to a copse where I have discovered a holly tree with the biggest, reddest berries you have ever seen.'

'I have found something even better,' Swaledale informed the girls in his party, with a suggestive waggle of his eyebrows. 'Mistletoe.'

Helen could not help casting them a withering look as they rode off after him, giggling and blushing. They would not be so keen on gathering mistletoe with him if they knew how disgusting he could be!

Once more she found Lord Bridgemere watching her when she glanced in his direction, only this time, since her mind was on that encounter on the backstairs, she felt her cheeks heat, and it was she who looked away first.

She heard his horse champ at the bit as he tugged on the reins, wheeling the creature round, and once the boys had darted off after him she permitted herself the luxury of watching him riding away into the forest. Charles and Peter were puffed up with pride at being handpicked for a task which was too difficult for the very little ones. They looked adorable as they trotted off behind him. It was such a pity their parents were not here to see this.

But then there was no reason, really, why their parents should not see this if they wanted to. She sighed and went back to the main group of children, who were pointing out likely-looking branches of fir to the bevy of gardeners who were in charge of the pruning hooks. She knew that there were other entertainments designed for those who preferred to remain within doors, but she could not understand why some of them at least had not come to witness this. What could be more enjoyable than watching their children's happy little faces and sharing in their delight at the magic of Christmas time?

The trouble with this house party was that children were either woefully neglected by parents who regarded them as just one more problem they wished they did not have, or, worse, as in the case of Lord Bridgemere's family, moved about like pawns in the complex power struggle that was raging between the various sets of adult siblings.

Every time the adults came together at mealtimes, or in the withdrawing room afterwards, it turned into yet another skirmish. Lady Thrapston, Helen suddenly realised, was fighting a desperate rearguard action in wearing all that jewellery and flaunting her status by lording it over the foot of the dining table. And whenever Nicholas Swaledale walked into a room, or contributed to the conversation, his mother Lady Craddock was able to shoot her sister a look of spiteful triumph. Though she had only married a baron, and not a very wealthy one at that, she *had* managed to produce two sons, whereas Lady Thrapston had only girls. Poor little Junia was the ultimate disappointment to her mother.

It made Helen's blood boil.

Even more determined that these children should have at least some happy memories of their childhood to look back upon, she flung herself into the task of making the gathering of the greenery as much fun for them as she possibly could.

A brace of footmen, who had travelled to the site in a second cart, loaded the fragrant boughs and the long swathes of ivy they'd pointed out, into a farm wagon. Occasionally members of Lord Bridgemere's riding party returned, with the much prized holly and mistletoe, and soon the cart was piled high with a wonderful assortment of glossy green leaves, bright waxy berries and bristling bluey-green fronds.

In what felt like no time at all they were climbing back into the cart for their homeward journey, the children bubbling over with satisfaction at a job well done.

The riding party followed behind the convoy of open carts, but to her surprise Lord Bridgemere drew up alongside the one that contained the children, just as Reverend Mullen produced a tin whistle from his pocket and began to play Christmas carols. Lord Bridgemere sang out in a fine baritone, the servants in the cart that followed joined in, and then so did the children, with as many of the words as they could remember.

It was an episode Helen knew she would remember for the rest of her life, coming home from gathering in the greenery, with Lord Bridgemere riding alongside.

His powerful voice rose effortlessly above that of the servants following behind, soaring up through the branches even as it reached into the very depths of her being. It put her in mind of the way she had felt that morning when he had taken her to the frost-spangled clearing. There was something about singing hymns outdoors, in nature's own temple, that was particularly moving, she thought. She had certainly never had tears in her eyes when she had sung any of these carols before.

Surreptitiously, because she felt a little foolish, she dabbed away at her tears with the end of her scarf, lifted her chin, and forced a smile to her lips. She kept it fixed there, resolutely, when they returned to the stableyard. Lord Bridgemere dismounted, while she accepted Reverend Mullen's hand to help her out of the cart.

Lord Bridgemere hustled his own party towards the house, while she kept the children together and herded them towards the back door that led through the servants' hall and thence to the stairs up to the nursery wing. He paused in the doorway, watching the children swarming into the house, before giving her an impenetrable look and following his own party indoors.

When they reached the nursery Helen saw that Lord Bridgemere had arranged yet another treat for the youngsters. Not only were a couple of maids waiting, with jugs of steaming hot chocolate and plates of those delectable ginger snaps, but there were several bowls of chestnuts for them to roast over the schoolroom's open fire.

She put Junia, Peter and Charles in charge of roasting the nuts and handing them out to the younger ones. When she knelt on the hearthrug, a little distance away, to make sure there were no burnt fingers or, heaven forbid, singed clothing, a couple of those still in leading strings escaped from their nurses and came to sit on her lap.

It was not long before the warmth of the fire after their outing, coupled with all that hot chocolate and all those biscuits, made them drowsy. Their nurses returned to take them from her and put them down for a nap, and gradually a contented hush settled over the room, punctuated only by the crackle of the fire or a murmured comment from one of the older children, who were now sprawled on their tummies, imagining, Helen surmised from their rapt expressions, dragons, volcanoes, or firework displays amongst the glowing coals.

She had a feeling that Lord Bridgemere would have enjoyed being up here, witnessing this moment of utter peace and harmony, far more than being in the rather contentious atmosphere that would surely be prevailing downstairs.

As her thoughts inevitably turned to him, the remembrance of their last encounter up here, just outside the nursery door, shattered her whimsical mood. Even though she felt as though she was beginning to understand something of his views, he most certainly did not feel the same burning, physical ache for her that she felt for him. Or he would not have offered her a dowry to marry some other man. The fact that he had immediately thought of a financial solution to her problems showed that he did not really separate her in his mind from any of his other guests. Who were his family, after all.

And she was not even that.

She was up here practising being a governess. Thanks to Lord Bridgemere, she had grown more confident that she would be able to cope within the sphere of her new life. She had grown fond of these children, and fiercely protective of them, in the short time she had become part of their world.

But it was not her world. And Lord Bridgemere's offer to pay her off showed her that she did not have so much as a toehold in it.

There was to be dancing after an early dinner that evening, in honour of the day. She was sure most of the other ladies would spend the entire afternoon beautifying themselves. But—she smiled wryly to herself—*she* would much rather be doing something useful than wasting hours in front of a mirror. She would have quite enjoyed joining the team who would be making the greenery up into garlands and wreaths, and helping Mrs Dent decorate the ballroom. But on the whole she thought she would get most pleasure from just staying up here with the children. They would be rehearsing their play again later, and she wanted to be on hand to put finishing touches to their costumes. And just be there, to support them as they got to grips with their parts. Junia was word-perfect already, but Charles, who was playing Gabriel, was still nervous enough to need all the encouragement he could get.

It took her, just as she had suspected, less than an hour to wash and change into her best gown, brush her hair and pin it up in the simple style she had perfected when they'd had to dismiss their maid. All she had to do then was fasten her mother's amber beads around her neck, drape her evening shawl over her elbows, and she was as ready as she would ever be.

Which was not all *that* ready, she reflected upon entering the blue saloon. Everywhere she looked there were crisp ringlets, sumptuous satins and glittering jewels, casting her own plain bronze gown and simple string of beads into the shade. Making her even more aware that she did not belong here.

But it struck her, once they had all sat down to dine, that the amount of personal wealth on display had not brought any one of these people happiness. All round the table she could see one discontented face after another. Most of them never seemed to stop grumbling. It was as though whatever they had was never quite enough to satisfy them.

And the battle which raged between Lady Thrapston and her sister Lady Craddock created a maelstrom of tensions. Maintaining neutrality was hard, but since both ladies were influential in their own ways, risking making either of them an enemy by openly befriending the other made it by far the safest course to steer.

And that was quite apart from the rift that existed between Aunt Bella and her brother General Forrest, which had created still more eddies.

After dinner everyone went to the ballroom, which had been opened up and decorated for the occasion. It really looked magnificent, Helen mused. The floor had been polished to a high sheen, and every chandelier and wall sconce was festooned with ivy, while garlands of pine and fir had been draped over picture frames and mantelpieces. The staff must have worked really hard to achieve so much in such a short space of time. Particularly since there was to be a sumptuous supper later, to round off the evening.

The orchestra which had been hired for the event was still tuning up when Helen walked in. After swiftly examining the seating arrangements, she and her aunt went and took seats in a quiet corner, rather than on the front row of chairs which ringed the dance floor. She did not expect anyone would ask her to dance. The other guests either regarded her as one of the serving classes or somebody's love child. Lady Thrapston, she suspected, given the way she studiously looked straight through her as she glided past, thought she ought not to be there at all.

Well, she was not going to stay for very long. Her aunt would probably move into the card room with Lady Norton as soon as they had watched the opening few sets, and when they made their move she would get to her feet too, say she was tired after the exertions of the day, and claim she needed an early night. There was no way she was going to sit here like a wallflower, watching other, more socially acceptable ladies dance!

The first set was drawing to a close, and her aunt and Lady Norton were shifting in their seats, plucking at their shawls and generally getting ready to leave the dancing for the younger ones, when to Helen's surprise Lord Bridgemere threaded his way through the chairs until he came to a halt right in front of her.

'The next dance,' he said without preamble, 'is to be a waltz. Do you know the steps?'

'I...I do,' she stuttered, her heart bouncing around inside her chest at the possibility he might be going to invite her to dance.

For a moment she wondered if he regretted whatever impulse had brought him over, as he just stood there, gazing down at her with a slight frown on his brow. But then he seemed to make up his mind. He held out his hand, and said, somewhat impatiently, 'Come on, then!'

Both her aunt and Lady Norton dropped straight back down into their seats when she rose and followed him onto the dance floor. Though they could hardly be more surprised than she was!

Or anyone else.

She was very conscious of the hush that fell over the assembled guests as they stood in the very centre of the dance floor, waiting for the music to begin. She was convinced that everyone must be watching her with disapproval, though how they thought she had managed to get Lord Bridgemere to invite her to waltz with him was beyond her!

But she was blowed if she was going to let anyone, or anything, spoil this moment. Resolutely lifting her chin, she looked up into his face, willing the rest of the room to the edges of her notice.

A smile pulled at the corner of his mouth as he saw what she was doing.

'That's it, Miss Forrest,' he said, very softly. 'Look at me, not at them.'

And, as if holding her to the challenge, he kept his own eyes fixed upon hers as the music began and he guided her into a set of basic steps.

She had never danced the waltz whilst looking deep into her partner's eyes before. It was unlike anything she had ever experienced. He filled her consciousness to the exclusion of almost everything else. The music seemed to come from very far away. It was the subtle direction of his hands, the angle of his body, that guided her through the figures of the dance. Once he had ascertained the level of her skill he began to introduce ever more complicated figures, smiling at her every time she rose to the occasion. It was exhilarating to find they were so perfectly matched. Before long she could anticipate his next move, so that she felt as though he was not leading her and she following, but that they were moving as one.

By the time the dance ended there were several other couples on the floor, though she had not noticed them joining in. She had been aware of nothing but the feel of his hand at her waist, the scent of his cologne filling her nostrils, and the steady regard of his eyes, holding her to him with a power that felt stronger than bands of steel.

Lord, she would remember this night, this magical waltz, for the rest of her life! This whole day, in fact, would have a special place in her memory. For he had been at the centre of everything. Even when he had not been in the room with her she had felt his influence holding sway over all her pleasures.

She moved away from him with reluctance when he stood still, removed his hand from her waist, and bowed to her. The music had ended, she realised, and with it the magic. He turned to lead her back to her seat, breaking the eye contact which had held her in thrall throughout the waltz.

And then he brought her right back down to earth with a bump by saying, 'I have made it a tradition to answer the petitions of my family by means of a note which they receive at the breakfast table on Christmas morning. But in your case, since I do not yet know what you want of me, I have requested that Cadwallader free up a quarter of an hour *after* breakfast tomorrow. I hope that will be convenient?'

Her heart abruptly plunged. The interview would truly mark the end of her time here. While she was helping with the children, or dancing in his arms, she could make herself forget for just a few moments that she did not truly belong here. That their time together was only temporary.

'Of course,' she replied, dropping like a stone onto her chair.

'Until tomorrow, then,' he said, and strolled away without a backward look.

Her aunt laid a hand on her sleeve and whispered, 'Well, that was a surprise. You should have seen the look on Lady Thrapston's face! The only person who looked more affronted was Lady Craddock!'

'You have set the cat among the pigeons, Miss Forrest,' said Lady Norton with glee from behind her fluttering fan.

Her suggestive smile made Helen feel horribly exposed. Did everyone here know she was completely infatuated with a man beyond her reach? What a fool she must look!

'Oh, no, I am sure it was just a duty dance,' Helen replied hastily. 'He is the sort of man who would take pity on any unattached female who is not likely to have many partners. Even one who is destined to become a governess.'

'Oh,' said her aunt, her puzzled expression clearing. 'Yes, I expect that must be it. In which case, since you will not be needing me to act as chaperon—' she cast a quelling look at Lady Norton '—I shall be off to the card room. Will you come too?'

'No, thank you,' Helen said, drawing on the ready-made excuse she had prepared. 'I was up very early this morning…'

It was more important than ever that she escape to her room. Waltzing with Lord Bridgemere had been delightful, but it must only have confirmed to the onlookers what they had already suspected.

She could not face anyone now! She wanted to slip away and go over every second of that dance—commit it all to memory, so that she could take it out and re-examine it at her leisure in years to come.

She gave her aunt a swift peck on the cheek, and quietly slipped away to the exit.

But Lady Thrapston had somehow managed to guess what she meant to do. When Helen left the ballroom, she was waiting for her in the corridor.

Laying her fan on Helen's forearm, she said, 'I warned you about making up to my brother. But I can see you have not paid any heed. Every person watching that dance must have seen that you have so far forgotten your station you have fallen headlong in love with him!'

'Unfortunately, my lady,' Helen said sadly, 'my heart does not seem to have heeded the warning either you or I have tried to give it.' She knew her case was hopeless. He could not feel much for her if he was prepared to pay some other man to marry her—which was what his offer of a dowry amounted to.

'Then I pity you,' said Lady Thrapston coldly. 'For he will break it.'

'Oh,' said Helen with a wry smile, 'you do not need to tell me that he is impervious to me as a woman...'

'Far from it,' said Lady Thrapston, with a shake of her head. 'If I thought that, I would not have taken the trouble to try and warn you. It is my belief that he is, in his own way, quite taken with you. He has singled you out for the sort of attention he has not granted another woman for years.'

Had he? Helen's heart, which had been so heavy ever since he had told her she ought to marry *some other man* promptly soared. And with it her self-esteem. She had *not* misinterpreted the heat she had sometimes thought she saw in his eyes. Especially just now, on the dance floor.

'And if you continue to encourage him, you might even persuade him into indulging in an affair. I dare say,' Lady Thrapston said with a contemptuous sniff, 'he is ripe for one!'

Helen's hopes plunged back down to earth. An affair. That was all a girl like her was good for. She had suspected the same thing herself at one point, before she had begun to think he did not reciprocate the physical attraction she felt for him at all.

'But I do not think you are the kind of girl who would survive such an encounter. So I urge you to beware. For you will not succeed in dragging a proposal from him, no matter what you do!'

No, a man who had any honourable intentions towards a woman could not possibly offer to sell her on to another man.

Lady Thrapston went on. 'Believe me, there is nothing I would like more than to see him married again and setting up his nursery. And to that end I have introduced a succession of gels to him who are far prettier and much more suitable than you—without success. Of late I have come to the sorry conclusion that his heart is buried in the grave with Lucinda.'

'L...Lucinda? Who is...was she?'

'His wife.'

The words sank into her brain like a stone dropped into a pond, sending ripples of shock vibrating through her. He had been married? And widowed? Why had her aunt never mentioned this?

'When she died,' Lady Thrapston continued mercilessly, 'he was so heartbroken that he shut himself away from the world, and even now, all these years later, he can hardly bear to live without her. I have watched him year upon year, and I have to tell you that even when he forces himself to come out of his self-imposed seclusion in honour of this season he can hardly bear the celebrations without her.'

Now his behaviour made so much sense! She had wondered how he had got the reputation of being a surly recluse, but she could see it all now. He was a broken-hearted widower, who had only slowly and painfully pieced his life back together after the love of his life had died.

And as for Lady Thrapston's attempts to get him to remarry! Well! She had probably been thrusting marital prospects under his nose with total insensitivity to his pain well before he was ready to take such a step. And not out of concern for him, either! No, it would all have been part of her ongoing battle with Lady Craddock. All Lady Thrapston was keen for him to do was—how had she put it?—set up his own nursery. So that Lady Craddock's son would be cut out of the succession.

But if he really was attracted to her, as Lady Thrapston seemed to think... A sharp pain seared through her. She could understand now why at times he seemed to enjoy her company and then abruptly withdrew into stony hostility. Any tender feelings he might have would seem like a betrayal of his first love! He would resent them. He would resent *her* for making him feel them.

'Thank you for telling me this, My Lady,' said Helen jerkily, dropping an abrupt curtsey. 'Unfortunately for me,' she said with a grimace, 'it comes a little late. Oh, do not worry—I have no intention of becoming his mistress. I have too much pride to allow *any* man to use me in such a fashion! I have honest work to go to. In fact I shall be leaving to take up my job in just a few days. I am sure,' she said bitterly, 'that once I have gone he will forget all about me.'

'But you will not forget him, will you?' Lady Thrapston's face softened into an expression of pity.

'No,' replied Helen. 'Never.'

That night she cried herself to sleep. The more she learned about Lord Bridgemere, the more he tugged at her heart. And the further out of her reach he receded. She might have tempted him out of his customary isolation into a solitary walk, and a waltz which had shocked his family, but only the day before he had offered to buy her a husband. He evidently found her attractive, but would rather see her married to some other man than risk furthering their relationship in any way whatever. What more evidence did she need to prove that his heart was buried in the grave with his late wife? Oh, Lord, but there was nothing more painful than unrequited love. She sobbed. She hurt. She physically hurt inside at the knowledge that he did not, could not, return her feelings. That she had no hope.

She woke with a heavy heart on Christmas Day. She was dreading her interview with Lord Bridgemere, when she would ask for his assistance with her travels. When she would bid him farewell for ever. He might feel a little sorry she was leaving, if he *had* begun to feel some slight attraction towards her, but on the whole he would be relieved that the temptation she represented would be permanently removed from his life.

On Christmas morning it was the custom, she had been told, for everyone to gather for breakfast together. In years past she and her aunt had always exchanged gifts at the breakfast table too, so the day before she had given her gifts to Mrs Dent to place at the correct table setting.

When she reached the dining room she saw that there was a small packet beside each place setting. She felt a little perplexed as she sat down. Lord Bridgemere had told her that he gave everyone a note informing them of his decision regarding whatever petition they had made. But not that he enclosed with it a small gift.

Beside her, Aunt Bella suddenly burst out laughing. She had opened the present Helen had given her, which was a quarter of peppermint drops twisted into the set of handkerchiefs Helen had embroidered for her.

Helen was a little put out. They had agreed that they would only give each other small token gifts this year, considering the state of their finances. She had known peppermint drops were a particular favourite of her aunt's and had thought the gift would please her. Not make her laugh out loud!

Aunt Bella prodded her in the side between whoops of laughter.

'Open yours, open yours!' she chortled.

The moment Helen complied she saw the joke. Aunt Bella had made her a reticule and stuffed it to the brim with those self-same sweets.

They were both giggling like a pair of giddy schoolgirls when Lord Bridgemere came to the table.

He gazed coldly round at the occupants of the table, instantly sobering Helen and her aunt, then took his seat and flicked open his napkin. The butler hastened to his side and poured coffee, whilst everyone else, as though at some hidden signal, began to open the present that lay beside their plate.

Everyone had received something from Lord Bridgemere. Even her. And, while it had been impossible to accept any gift from him on any other day, it was not as though he was singling her out today. She reached for her parcel with trembling fingers.

Inside was a beautiful silk damask shawl. One side had a rose ground and the other gold, so that it could be worn either way to go with different outfits. She felt quite touched by the thoughtfulness of the gift, since one of the shawls she had brought with her had been ruined by a combination of her encounter with Esau in the garden, when it had been trampled into the mud, and Swaledale on the staircase, when his candle had singed it. But her pleasure in Lord Bridgemere's gift dimmed somewhat when she looked up and saw that every other female at table was also in receipt of such a shawl. Just as the men had all received cufflinks along with their promissory note.

At that moment Lady Augustine gave a cry of delight as she unfolded the note which had fallen out of her shawl. Her mother, Lady Thrapston, swiftly quelled her outburst with a withering look, which reduced her to stammering her thanks to Lord Bridgemere with red cheeks. But it was too late. The damage was done. Several of the other guests were looking at her with envy, and when they also thanked Lord Bridgemere for whatever it was he had given them it was stiffly, as though they felt disgruntled.

Apart from Lord Norton, who looked downright relieved.

Then Aunt Bella, as if impervious to the atmosphere of jealousy and resentment that was brewing, beamed at Lord Bridgemere and said, 'Are you not going to open *your* present now?'

Though conversation up to that point had been stilted, Aunt Bella's comment had the effect of stifling it completely.

Lord Bridgemere looked down at his plate, registering surprise to see the small neatly wrapped packet that Helen had asked Mrs Dent to place there for him. Tentatively he pulled on one of the trailing ends to release the bow that held it all together, and frowned down at the pair of embroidered handkerchiefs within.

'Is this from you?' he asked her aunt.

'Oh, no. From Helen,' she informed him.

Lady Thrapston shot her a scandalised look. 'It is not

the done thing, Miss Forrest,' she said. 'Everyone knows that it is not the thing at all.'

'Nevertheless,' he said, as Helen's face flamed with mortification, 'I am touched by Miss Forrest's gesture. She is the only one who thought to give me anything.'

Helen caught General Forrest glaring at her, his cheeks growing ruddy with suppressed fury. She guessed he was among those who had not received all he had hoped for, and by the look on his face, after the way Lord Bridgemere had publicly defended her for committing what was clearly a social *faux pas*, he was inclined to lay the blame on her.

'You always say you have need of nothing!' snapped Lady Thrapston.

'You are correct, as always,' he replied coldly, getting to his feet. 'Miss Forrest? A word in private?'

Oh, yes. The interview. Head lowered, so that she did not have to see the way everyone must be staring at her, she left the table and made for the exit.

'Please—come in and take a seat,' he said, opening the door for her and ushering her into his study.

She walked carefully to the chair he had indicated beside his desk, since her knees were somewhat shaky, and sank onto it as gracefully as her emotional state permitted.

In the few moments it took for him to shut the door, walk round the desk and take his own seat, she drank him in.

She already had a treasure trove of precious memories she could examine in the years ahead. On long, dull evenings she would be able to look back upon their walk through the wintry woodland. Smile at the time his dog had almost knocked her down, scattering his female relatives with his exuberant greeting. Picture him sitting astride his horse, his hound at his side, watching the children sliding around the ice lake he had created just for them. And, best of all, that waltz. Those magical few moments when he had held her in his arms and the rest of the world had ceased to exist.

But this would be the last time she would have a few moments of privacy with him. And she wanted to be able to remember every single second of this, their last encounter, bittersweet though it must inevitably be.

His clothing was understated, as usual. Over the days she had been at Alvanley Hall she had come to see that it was his quiet, self-assured presence that made people take notice of him. He had no need to wear elaborate waistcoats or deck himself with jewels to draw attention to himself. He was confident in who he was and what he was. She had mistaken that very confidence at first for arrogance. Other people, she knew, saw that same demeanour and whispered that he was cold and insular.

But how could he be anything else when he was fulfilling all his duties, caring for the needs of all his dependants, whilst nursing a broken heart?

'I wonder, Miss Forrest,' he said, tossing the offending handkerchiefs onto his desk, 'how you managed to find the time to embroider these for me. You always *seemed* so busy. If you were not running errands for your aunt, you were helping entertain other people's children. And yet I know you must have stitched these since you came here. You copied the emblems from the heraldic glass in the library windows, did you not?'

'Yes. But it did not take me as long as you might suppose.' She'd had no idea that giving him such a trifling gift would cause such a stir. If she could downplay the time it had taken her to do the embroidery, perhaps he would not make so much of it! 'Though the design looks complicated, it was actually quite simple to prick out the outline and fill it in with satin stitch. As for your initials—why, they are only done in chain stitch, after all, which is mere child's play.'

'I fail to see why you thought it was necessary to give me anything at all,' he said angrily. 'What was your motive? Were you trying to impress me? Is that it? I can assure you there was no need.'

He could not believe how angry it had made him to think that she felt free to give him a gift she had laboured over with her own hands but was always so reluctant to accept anything from *him*!

He was angry, too, at the knowledge that every time he touched these small squares of cloth he would see her, sitting in the library with the sun gilding her hair. Or trying out the skating pond he had fabricated for the children, shrieking with laughter as she careened across the ice. Then taking Junia kindly by the hand and reassuring her that there was nothing to fear when he knew she would have had more fun racing with the older boys.

Angry, most of all, at how easily she could touch him. Move him. Make him feel…things he had not felt, not wanted to feel, for years!

And, worse, though he had accused her of trying to impress him—which was what he knew such a gift would signify from any other woman—Miss Forrest saw no need to make the attempt.

He had grown cynical, he realised, over the years. To even think that Miss Forrest would act as so many others had done... Why, he only had to look at her open, honest face, see the affront flashing from her eyes... No, Miss Forrest had not been trying to ingratiate herself with him.

She never would.

By the looks of her, she was about to give him what for even for suggesting it!

Helen took a deep breath. 'I was doing no such thing,' she retorted, sick of everyone attributing the worst interpretation to her behaviour. 'It is common courtesy to give one's host a small gift! And it has always been the custom for my aunt and I to exchange presents upon Christmas Day. I gave *her* handkerchiefs I had embroidered, too. Just as you gave identical gifts to each of your female guests. Honestly,' she huffed, 'I had no notion that extending that custom to you would cause anyone offence!'

He leaned back in his chair, half closing his eyes and taking a deep breath. Being on the receiving end of one of Miss Forrest's tirades was refreshing. Almost like coming upon a hidden spring whilst taking a ride on a hot summer day, and feeling all the dust being washed away by even the briefest of dips into it.

Helen shifted uncomfortably in her chair. He had been regarding her steadily for such a long time that she felt like some kind of exhibit in a museum. She had never been able to understand his abrupt changes of mood. But at least now that Lady Thrapston's revelation had made her face the fact that she had fallen in love with him she knew why it did not make her like him any less. On the contrary, seeing he was in a bad mood just made her wish she could do something to cheer him up. To wipe away that disgruntled expression and see him smile again.

Which was, of course, quite impossible. He did not need her. He did not need anyone. Had he not just said so?

'Are you having some difficulty,' he asked eventually, with a wry smile, 'in making your request known to me now that it comes to the point?'

Oh, yes! Of course! She had almost forgotten the whole point of coming in here. Seeing his mouth hitch at one side into that little smile had put everything right out of her head.

So now she felt like an idiot on top of everything else.

What had he said? Was she finding this difficult? 'Oh, yes.' Because this was it. The beginning of the end.

The end? She mocked herself. Nothing had really started except in her own fevered imagination!

'What I wish to ask for might sound a bit presumptuous,' she began nervously. 'After all, I know I have no claim on your generosity…'

'It never stops anyone else,' he said bitterly.

She got to her feet. The last thing she wanted was for him to regard her in the same light as he did the rest of his troublesome guests, who only came to Alvanley because they wanted something. The only thing she wanted from him was his heart. Though, since it was impossible for him to give her that, she could at least command his respect.

'It does not matter, then. If you are so averse to helping me I shall see to it myself.'

'Sit down!' he barked. 'If you have something you want, just *ask* me, dammit!' Whatever she wanted, if it made her less hostile towards him, he would give it, he realised. Could you buy someone's regard?

Not Miss Forrest's. No, she would toss her hair and, eyes flashing, inform him that she was not to be bought…

But at least she was subsiding onto her chair, twisting her fingers together nervously on her lap. Nervously? Then whatever she wanted to ask him must not be the trivial thing he had assumed was all she would ever bring herself to request of him. He sat forward, every sense on the alert.

Helen had never imagined it would be this hard to ask for his help. She was, she discovered, every bit as proud and prickly as her aunt. Though at least half the trouble was that she simply did not really want to leave.

This experience would be good for her, she decided, lips firming with determination. She would be always having to ask employers for time off, or permission to do one thing or another. Asking him for the loan of one of his carriages would humble her in a way that would make later slights and slurs seem like nothing.

'It was my aunt's idea,' she began. 'She said you would not begrudge me the use of one of your carriages. She seemed to think you would have me taken the entire way, but if you could just arrange for me to reach the nearest staging post I have enough money for my ticket.

Or if not it really does not matter. I can quite easily walk. Only there are my trunks…' she mused with a frown.

'What the blazes are you talking about? Take the stage? When?'

'Tomorrow. I—'

'Out of the question!' He slapped his hand palm down on the tabletop. She could not leave! He had known, of course, that once this house party broke up she would be going to work for a family somewhere—but that was at least a week away!

'You have promised to help the children prepare for their nativity play,' he said, a sense of desperation making him grasp at the first excuse he could come up with that was sure to touch her. 'You cannot break your word to a child!'

'I have no choice. My employers have sent a letter demanding I go to them at once.'

'Nonsense! You are staying here as my guest. Nobody leaves until Twelfth Night!' His heart was pounding. He felt slightly sick. Unless he could stop her somehow, tomorrow she would walk out of his life and…

He would never see her again. It was one thing spending time with a guest under his roof. Quite impossible for an earl to go seeking out a lowly employee of some family he did not even know and begging for an hour or two in her company!

If he let her leave tomorrow she would be lost to him.

'Do you dislike it here that much?'

He knew his relatives were insufferable, but she had always seemed so cheerful in spite of it all. Nothing seemed to get her down for long. Yet now she was talking about leaving. As soon as she possibly could.

'Have you not enjoyed your stay here?'

He felt as though someone had punched him. Perhaps it was him, specifically, she wished to get away from? She had slapped him once. And last night he had brought down upon her the censure of the entire assembly by singling her out as the only female he'd danced with all evening. Had he pushed her too far? It had been selfish of him, he knew. But she had looked so enchanting, sitting there tapping her foot in time to the music. He had been sure she wanted to dance. And none of the others would have asked her! Besides, he had wanted the excuse to hold her in his arms without having to wait until she was in floods of tears again.

'It is not that,' she sighed. 'I was supposed to start working for the Harcourts on the fifteenth of December. They let me have a few days' grace when I explained about my aunt and how I needed to see her settled. They said I could have until the New Year, but now that I know you will be looking after my aunt there is no reason for me to delay even that long. Especially not now they have written to say they cannot do without me any longer.'

'Well, nor can I, dammit!'

'What?'

Helen gazed at him in shock, doubting she could have heard him aright. By the look on his face, *he* could hardly believe what he had said, either.

He clenched his hands into fists on the desktop.

'You heard me. I said I don't want you to leave. Miss Forrest, the only thing that is making this house party bearable this year is the thought of running into you as

I go about my daily business. Playing with the children. Busily sewing away in my library. Or putting my blasted sister to the rightabout!'

He dragged in a deep breath and got to his feet, pacing away from her to the hearth, then whirling round. 'I know we do not always speak. But that is just it. We do not have to. Everything you think is written on your face.'

He loved watching her. Not just because she was pretty—although she was, exceptionally so. It was because more often than not she was like a visual echo of what he was already thinking. And it soothed him.

'I know exactly what you think of General Forrest's boorish manners,' he continued, 'and his incredible insensitivity to his sister. I know what an overbearing snob you think my sister. I see you wondering how on earth I can stand to have such a complete and utter tick as Nicholas Swaledale as my heir, and for the first time in my life I feel...' He turned and took a few paces, before saying, 'I feel as though I have an ally in the midst of an enemy camp.'

And if she left he would be utterly alone.

'And now you say you intend to desert me! Well, I won't have it—do you hear?' He marched up to her and stood, hands on hips, glaring down at her. 'I forbid you to leave!'

'You have no right,' she said, tears springing to her eyes.

For one moment he had seemed so agitated at the thought of her leaving that she had almost started to hope he might be going to tell her that he had feelings for her. And then he'd ruined it all by saying he forbade her to go! Giving her a direct order as though she was a member of his staff!

Which was how, she reflected bitterly, he had always thought of her. A useful person to have about, but nowhere near his equal!

She got to her feet, quivering with indignation. 'No right to forbid me from doing anything I want, sir! Just as I have no right to refuse my employer's summons. They have already been more than lenient with me...'

'I will write to them for you, then.' He grabbed her upper arms. 'Tell them I cannot spare you. That they must do without you until the celebrations here are at an end.'

She felt a clutch of panic. 'Oh, please do not do that! I will lose my job, and then what would become of me?'

'Does your job mean so much to you?'

'Of course it does! If I lose this post I must seek another, and it was difficult enough to secure this one...'

Of course. She had no money. And it was unfair of him to ask her to jeopardise her whole future without some concomitant sacrifice from him.

He slid his hands down her arms until they were loosely clasping hers. He looked down at them, head bowed. The only person who would have the right to help Helen whether she wanted him to or not would be her husband. He had never thought he would put his head in that particular noose again...but had he not already told her that he thought she would make some man a comfortable sort of wife?

He looked into her eyes, which were troubled,

almost afraid, and felt a rush of resolution surge up within him.

At least he would not spend any more sleepless nights wondering what sort of people she was going to work for. Imagining her being accosted by some drunken buck on some other set of backstairs because she was too damned innocent to know girls could not go wandering about a house at night half dressed! Fearing that next time there might not be anybody around to rescue her.

The sacrifice would be worth it if it meant knowing she was being properly looked after.

'Do you really want to leave?' he asked her gently. 'Do you dislike Alvanley Hall so much that you would rather go elsewhere?'

'No.'

He took a deep breath. 'Is it me, then? Have you taken me in dislike? Do you wish to put some distance between us?' If that was the case he was not going to make himself look ridiculous by offering her his name!

'No! Oh, *no*,' she said with feeling.

'Then I will offer you a position here,' he said, gripping her hands a little tighter. 'How about that?'

'What sort of a position?' she asked, bewildered. 'You do not have any children…'

'More's the pity! My sister's boy is proving to be more and more of a disappointment to me the older he grows. After that incident on the stairs I am beginning to feel quite perturbed at the thought of leaving the estate and the people for whom I am responsible in such careless hands. If I had my own son,' he said, 'I could train him up from the day of his birth. I am only in my thirties— the age at which most men consider marriage for the first time. With luck I might live long enough to bring him safely through the troubling years of growing to maturity, and go to my grave with a clear conscience.'

'What are you saying? You want me to kick my heels here, with my aunt, while you find a wife and then breed a son so that I can educate him?'

'No, you little idiot!' he shouted angrily. 'I am not saying that at all! I am asking you to marry me!'

Chapter Ten

'M...marry you?' She tugged her hands free and felt behind her for the chair. She had to sit down. She could not believe he was really asking her. She had cried herself to sleep the night before because she'd been so sure he would never, ever propose to her. Apart from the fact he was still mourning for his late wife, she was a nobody. Nothing. If this time at Alvanley Hall had taught her anything it was that she did not know how to move in the upper echelons of society. She had no idea how to be a wife to a man like him.

He could not possibly mean it!

A strange spasm passed across his face as he eyed the way she clasped her trembling hands together in her lap.

'May I point out that I have neither hairy knuckles nor greasy skin?' He held his hands out to her, palm down.

For a moment she could not understand why he was holding out his hands to her like that. Was he making some kind of jest? But when he turned them over, so that she could inspect them thoroughly, it came to her that he was referring to the conversation they'd had about marriage before. When he'd offered her a dowry and she had thought he wanted to be rid of her.

'I own I am much older than you, but you did not specify at what age a suitor would become unpalatable.'

She looked up into his face and frowned.

'Are you being serious?'

'Yes. Will you have me, Helen? You...you have already given me one gift this Christmas. Agreeing to become my wife would be the greatest gift of all.'

He looked so sincere her heart skipped a beat. But she did wish he had not spoken of *having* her. It made her think of bedrooms. Her entire body blushed. Would she have him? Oh, yes—in that respect in a heartbeat!

She wanted to go to bed with him and know what it felt like to become completely one flesh with him. That dance last night, she realised, had sensitised her whole body to his. As they had moved about the room, scarce an inch separating them from chest to thigh, she had resented even that inch.

Her face flooded with heat. She had told Lady Thrapston in no uncertain terms that she would not become any man's mistress. So why had she not leapt up and shouted, *Yes, yes, I will marry you!* and flung her arms round him and kissed him? What kind of woman was she?

'I d...don't know,' she said, hanging her head. 'I never thought...'

'For God's sake don't say, *Oh, dear, this is so unexpected*!' He laughed bitterly.

His proposal could not have surprised her any more than it had surprised him! But that was always how it was around Helen. She got under his skin to the extent that he never knew what he was going to do or say next. And he really disliked the feeling of uncertainty she was engendering. He had known who he was before she came along.

'Well, it *is* unexpected!' she retorted, lifting her head to glare at him. Especially since his proposal had come without a single word of affection, let alone a hint that he might perhaps, in some way, love her. Even just a little.

'Look,' he said, running the palm of his hand over his head, 'perhaps you had better go away and think it over.' A cold, sick feeling gripped him at the prospect she might refuse. She was not like other women, who regarded him as a prize. There was no telling what she would decide. Certainly, by the looks of her, his proposal was not filling her with rapturous joy.

'You have nothing to fear from me if you refuse. I shall not make things difficult for you. I would appreciate it, though, if you would let me have your answer by this evening,' he said, going to his desk and sitting down on the other side of it.

That was better. Putting a barrier between them helped him to revert to his sane, rational self. Because for a moment there he had experienced an almost overwhelming urge to get down on his knees and beg her not to leave. It shook him. He hardly knew her, and already she had reduced him to that!

'There will be arrangements to make for your departure. I shall, of course, put my carriage and a driver at your disposal should you decide against the match,' he said, forcing himself to focus on practicalities. 'But travelling tomorrow is out of the question. Apart from your promise to the children, I make Boxing Day a holiday for all my staff. I will not have them put out.'

That was better. He was calm, cool, and in control of himself. There was no more risk of an inappropriate descent into some kind of emotional outburst.

And if she left that was what he would go back to. No swift surges of joy, but no risk of pain either. Just the safe, orderly, contained life he had made himself live since Lucinda's death.

The coldness of his eyes, the clinical way in which he addressed her, struck a chill through Helen. It was not just that he did not behave like a lovestruck suitor. It was far worse. He looked to her very much like a man who had just said something that on reflection he wished he had not said at all.

'Of course not,' she said, wounded. 'I would not wish to put anyone out.'

With that, Helen stumbled from the room, staggered a few feet along the corridor, and collapsed onto the nearest chair. For she was shaking. She did not think she had ever felt so confused.

Oh, not about her own feelings. She loved him. From the moment they had met he had affected her as no other man had ever done. And, in spite of that moment of self-doubt just then, it was *not* just a physical attraction. The more she learned about him, the more he drew her to him.

But what did *he* think of *her*? Apart from mentioning that they thought alike on a number of issues, that proposal had given her no clue. No, wait—he had said he thought of her as an ally against his family. Well, that was not saying very much, was it? Nobody with a shred of decency could fail to take his part against them!

Though how could she possibly refuse the one thing he had asked of her? At breakfast she had heard him agree that he needed nothing. That he never asked anybody for anything.

But he had asked *her* to mother his children, so that he could raise up a son he could be proud of.

Dared she reach out and take the little that he seemed to be offering her? Since that talk with Lady Thrapston she knew that loving *any* woman was completely beyond him. For one wild moment she was filled with the desire to pour out her own heart on his wounded soul. To love him and love him! She might not be able to heal his broken heart, but he had asked her to provide some measure of comfort by giving him children of his own, so that he would at least not have to dread leaving his tenants to Swaledale's tender mercies. Could she really do that? Dedicate the rest of her life to bringing some sunshine back into his dark, lonely existence?

It was the only Christmas present he wanted. And did he not deserve it? He was the best of men. The very best. Surrounded by a pack of greedy, grasping relatives who had been, and still were, totally insensitive to his pain.

It would take some getting used to, this inequality in their feelings for each other, but in time he was bound to grow fond of her at least.

Wasn't he?

She rubbed at a tension spot on her forehead. He

might not feel any great affection for her, but he had certainly demonstrated that he had a great deal of respect for her. A man did not ask a woman to marry him unless he felt…

Oh, what was the use? She had no idea what was going on in the aggravating man's head! And even when she thought she might be getting a glimpse of what he was thinking, his mood could change in the blink of an eye.

She got to her feet and strode along the corridors and up to her room to dress for church. If she dithered about down here any longer she would be late.

From her pew, she kept sneaking peeks at Lord Bridgemere. He did not look a bit like a man who was waiting for an answer to a marriage proposal. He seemed so calm and collected as he stood and knelt and sat through the service. While she was still a mass of quivering nerves. Had that proposal really meant anything? By the look of him he would just shrug and go on with his life as though nothing untoward had occurred if she turned him down.

That was why, it suddenly struck her, she had not leapt at his proposal. Because he had not spoken of love. He had only given her a *practical* list of reasons why they should marry.

Very well—she would look at it from a practical point of view herself. She had never really thought seriously about marriage as an option. She cared too much for Aunt Bella to question her strongly held views upon the subject and, because no man had tempted her to abandoning her comfortable single state, she had never given the matter any deeper thought.

But Aunt Bella and she were going to have to go their separate ways now anyway. She would, in fact, be likely to have less contact with Aunt Bella if she went to live the proscribed life of a governess than she would if she married Lord Bridgemere. And she did not think that her aunt would disapprove of the match all that much, considering how highly she had spoken of him after that interview.

If she had met him and fallen for him when they had been living in Middleton things might have been very different, but as they were…

Very well. There was no risk of offending Aunt Bella.

But what else would marriage mean? Well, she would become a countess, for one thing, with unassailable status and untold wealth. She would never have to worry about finding the money to settle outstanding bills, or sell off her gowns to put food on the table.

Most girls would jump at the chance to marry an earl. Any earl. Let alone one who was so handsome. And with whom she had grown so infatuated. She ought to regard getting a proposal from a man who was renowned for being a recluse as a triumph. Especially since his own sister had despaired of ever getting him to take such a radical step.

She glanced round the packed pews at the other members of his family. They would all say she was not good enough for him. And yet he had seen something about her he liked enough to tempt him from his single state. Yes, there was no doubt about it: he was quite a catch.

So why did she not feel triumphant?

In the pew beside her, Aunt Bella stifled a yawn as the local vicar mounted the pulpit to deliver his Christmas sermon.

Here was another factor to consider. If she were to become Lady Bridgemere, she could make sure that her aunt would never have to worry about money again. By golly, how she would enjoy ensuring Aunt Bella had every luxury her heart could crave! Never mind finding some small nook amongst Lord Bridgemere's vast holdings in which she could eke out her declining years. Or palming her off on one of his other relatives in return for bailing them out of their financial embarrassments! It would be wonderful to pamper the darling who had taken her in and comforted and cared for her when she had been just a forlorn little girl.

Yes, there were plenty of solid, practical reasons for accepting his proposal.

So why hadn't she? What was holding her back?

If all these very practical reasons were not making her thrill to the idea, what would convince her to marry a man she knew didn't love her?

When they returned from church, everyone went to the great hall for mulled wine and spiced cake.

The hall, like the ballroom, was festooned with greenery brought in from the woods. One of the suits of armour, Helen noted with amusement, now sported a crown of holly, bright with berries, his upraised gauntleted hand clutching a bunch of mistletoe.

Chairs had been set out in a semi-circle, and gradually everyone took their places. Except the children and Lord

Bridgemere, who were all gathered up in the minstrels' gallery. He must have gone straight up to the nursery wing on returning from church, to make sure they would have the best view of the mummers who had come over from the village.

One of the villagers banged on the drum he was carrying, and everyone stopped talking. The man with the drum stepped forward, tilted his face up towards the minstrels' gallery, and said, 'We come to perform for you, Your Lordship, to thank you for the way you always look after us, whether you're here or busy elsewhere. We know there's unrest in some parts, but as for us we give thanks daily that God has seen fit to grant us such a fair and charitable master as you.'

Lord Bridgemere's face took on that wooden cast Helen had seen him adopt on several occasions. For the first time she realised he was struggling with strong emotion. For a moment her mind went back to the way he had looked immediately after proposing to her. She had thought he looked completely cold then, but that was not it at all. He'd looked just as he did now! Her heart sped up. Did that mean his feelings *were* engaged? Perhaps so strongly that he felt the need to conceal them?

Perhaps there was hope. Perhaps he might come to care for her in time…

He made a slashing motion through the air with one hand, as though he did not want to hear any more, which made him look harsh. Yet it did not stop the villagers from beaming up at him.

They knew him. Had known him and his moods for years. They could see straight through that cold, forbidding exterior to the man he was beneath. And they loved him for what he was. That flicker of hope grew bright enough to drive away some of her fears and doubts. Lord Bridgemere was a good man. It was why they loved him. Why *she* loved him.

Though *her* love for *him* was not the issue.

To the accompaniment of a fiddle and drum, the villagers in their garish costumes then performed a rollicking version of *Saint George and the Dragon*, which ended with a rousing song about shepherds increasing their flocks.

When they'd finished, the assembled house guests clapped politely. Then Lord Bridgemere cleared his throat and said, 'Singing so loud is thirsty work. The traditional wassail cup is over there.' He indicated the table round which they had been clustering earlier. 'I would advise the Methodists amongst you to partake only from the jugs at either end of the table. Not the punchbowl.'

They gave him three rousing cheers. Though, judging from the enthusiasm with which most of the men made straight for the punchbowl, not many of them belonged to the abstemious new religious sect.

'We'll drink to your good health, then, My Lord,' piped up the drummer, who had been among the first to get to the punchbowl.

'Drink rather to the season,' he replied.

'To Christmas!' they roared.

He stood there for a few moments, watching the villagers enjoying themselves with a satisfied smile hovering about his mouth. She had heard that he only came here at Christmas to preside over the festivities for his tenants, but somehow she had always assumed it was a matter of duty. Of keeping faith with the generations of tradition he had to uphold as lord of the manor here. But now she was of the opinion that it was far more than that. He really cared about these people.

Could she settle for that much? As his wife, the mother of his children, of course he would care for her—at least as much as he cared for these people.

Wouldn't he?

She did not feel up to following the rest of the guests to the dining room and taking luncheon when they began to file out of the great hall. It was too much to expect her to make appropriate responses to the barbed insults and snide comments that passed for conversation around that table. Not while her own mind was in such turmoil.

So she informed her aunt she would spend the rest of the day with the nursery party, and set off up the stairs.

She dawdled on the landings, since she was not quite ready even to deal with children in her given state. She gazed out of the windows that lit the deserted stairwell, basking in the absence of other people. She needed space to think. She had only until tonight to make her decision.

She sighed, rubbing at a dirty spot on the window with her cuff so that she could see out more clearly. She only wished it were that easy to clarify her thoughts.

She'd had her life mapped out before coming to Alvanley Hall. That was why his proposal had thrown her into such turmoil. If she married him, her whole life would undergo a radical change.

Most women would think the changes all for the better, but they would be women who thought of marriage as the height of their ambition. Whatever her circumstances, marriage had *never* been part of her plans. This was the first time in her life she had ever really had to examine what she thought about the institution.

When she had thought herself financially secure she'd believed she would be content to live exactly as her aunt had done. Alone, or with a companion, finding fulfilment in the simple life of a country town. Even when all their money had vanished overnight it had never occurred to her to look to a man to take care of her.

Or that she would fall in love.

That fact alone ought to have made her accept him like a shot.

Instead, it was that very fact which made marrying him such a scary prospect. When she had told him she would only marry for love, it was the first thing that had come into her head, she realised. And even then she had been vaguely thinking about an *equal* love. A man and a woman falling in love with each other, as her parents had done, and then finding they could not bear to be apart. Marriage naturally flowed from such strong feelings. She could see exactly why marrying, in their case, had been so right.

But in this case it was all lopsided. She had fallen headlong in love with him. But he appeared to have looked her over, noted down her admirable qualities as though he had some kind of a mental list, and decided that, yes, she would do very well in the role.

Many women would regard that kind of proposal as a triumph. The kind of women who regarded marriage as the *only* respectable state for a female of good birth. Unfortunately she was just not of their number!

Her breath was steaming up the window, obscuring the view she had dirtied her gown to obtain, just as her infatuation with Lord Bridgemere had clouded her judgement. Before coming here she would never have dreamt of marrying a man who saw her as nothing more than a means to prolong his bloodline. Where had her pride gone? She deserved more than that! More than the kind of marriage she'd had such a clear vision of immediately after his proposal, with her pouring out her heart and him taking it as his due.

Her lips tight with strain, she trudged off up the stairs again. She wanted him—oh, yes, how she wanted him! But could she pay the price? That was the question.

When she reached the schoolroom, she was amazed to see the air thick with glistening soap bubbles. Several of the children were sitting at a table, industriously dipping little clay pipes into dishes of soapy water, while the smaller ones were dancing about madly trying to burst them before they popped of their own accord.

Her mouth relaxed into a smile. It was impossible to remain out of sorts in such an atmosphere.

'Merry Christmas, miss!' said one of the nursery-maids as she scurried past with an empty coal scuttle.

'Merry Christmas to you, Jenny,' Helen replied.

'Miss Forrest!' cried Charles, scampering up to her. 'Look what I got for Christmas!' It was a clasp knife and *exactly*, he stressed, what he had been wanting.

Every child, it appeared, had mysteriously received exactly what they had wanted most. She smiled to think of Lord Bridgemere skilfully yet subtly extracting the information from them over the few days they had been here, and then sending somebody—Cadwallader, probably—to make the purchases in the nearest town.

'There were bunches of grapes hanging from the rocking horse when I woke up this morning,' said Peter, pausing for a moment in his endeavours with his clay pipe. 'And twists of barley sugar and peppermints...'

'I got a doll,' said Junia, holding it up.

Her heart squeezed inside her chest. He was such a darling to do all this for the children. To make sure Christmas reached to the very furthest corners of his domain—be it to the neglected children, thrust out of sight of their selfish parents, or to the meanest cottager inhabiting his estates.

He was a man who ought to have his own children. He wanted a son and heir. She had already noticed that he seemed to approve of the way she was with other people's children, and now something had made him decide he wanted that for his own.

And if they were hers, too...

Already she had grown fond of this group. It would be quite a wrench to leave them. If she really did become a governess her life would become a continual round of growing fond of children who were not hers and then having to bid them farewell when they outgrew her and she had to move to a new post. If she married Lord Bridgemere it would save her from all that heartache. She could have her own children. Raise them exactly as she pleased. Love them unreservedly.

Whatever problems she might have with their father.

But was it enough?

It was not long after a joyful and rather chaotic

Christmas lunch, which had started with ham and sausage and finished with jellies and creams, that the door opened and to her utter astonishment Nicholas Swaledale and Lady Augustine came in.

The maids glanced at them and dropped curtsies, but did not greet either of them warmly, as they had done Helen. Because they were gentry, she realised, whilst over the week she had been there she had almost become one of them.

She had to lower her head to conceal a smile when Swaledale waved his hand regally, as though granting them permission to carry on.

Then Junia squirmed down from her chair and ran over to them.

'Gussy, look!' she cried, her eyes alight with happiness as she held up the doll to show her sister. 'Look what I got for Christmas!'

Swaledale took a hasty step back. 'For the Lord's sake, make sure that child keeps her sticky hands off my clothing, if you please.'

Lady Augustine cast him a look of irritation, then hunkered down and put her arm round Junia's shoulders.

'Oh, what a lovely doll,' she said. 'I *do* like her dress!'

'Would still rather be playing with them, wouldn't you,' Swaledale drawled, 'than partaking of more adult pursuits?'

'I just wanted to see what they'd all got for Christmas,' snapped Augustine. 'And you needn't have come with me if you dislike children so much. In fact,' she said, getting to her feet, 'I wish you had not if you are just going to be nasty.'

'But how else was I to manage to get a few words with Miss Forrest?' he replied glibly. 'Now that she has taken to hiding herself away up here?'

'We have nothing to say to each other, sir,' said Helen.

'Oh, but I disagree,' he replied. 'Run along, Gussy, do. What I am about to say to this person is not for your ears.'

Helen was the one who tried to move away but, like a snake striking, his hand shot out and grabbed her arm. His grip was so tight that she knew if she resisted the way he was tugging her to a quiet corner his fingers would leave a bruise.

'Think you are very clever, don't you?' he breathed, once they were out of earshot of anyone else. 'I saw you dancing with him last night. You think you have him eating out of your hand. Though I can't say I blame him for making the most of what you're offering. One taste of you was enough to make me want more. And you looked very beddable in that nightgown, with your hair all down your back, from what I can recall. Was pretty castaway, was I not?' He sniggered, as though they were sharing some dirty secret.

Helen felt the bile rise in her throat as his proximity brought the whole episode rushing back to her so vividly that she could almost feel his tongue sliding across her face. Instinctively she tugged her hand free and put it to her cheek, as though erasing the very memory of his intrusive kisses.

'You know, flinging yourself at him won't get you anywhere. Even if you've gone so far as sacrificing your virginity you won't get a marriage proposal from him.

He will cast you off without a backward glance when he's done with you!'

'How dare you?' she gasped. Lord Bridgemere had already offered her marriage—and how could this toad imply that his uncle would seduce a female living under his roof? It would be completely out of character! Naturally she was not going to tell Swaledale about the proposal. That was strictly between her and His Lordship! But one thing she *could* refute.

'Lord Bridgemere is an honourable man. He would never take advantage of an innocent woman then discard her!'

'My, my, you *are* hot in his defence. He must have really turned on the charm. He can be charming, so I believe. But you would change your tune if you knew what he is really like.'

'I *do* know what he's really like.'

'Oh, do you?' He smiled nastily, leaned closer and murmured, 'Do you, perchance, happen to know exactly what became of his first wife?'

'What do you mean?'

'It is strange, but nobody who was around at the time is at all willing to talk about it. Suspicious, wouldn't you say—the way they all clam up and look shifty, saying the accident was nobody's fault? It is almost as if nobody dares to lay the blame at his door. But then the people round here need to keep on his good side. You have seen the power he wields over them.' He smirked. 'But my mother has told me there is quite a scandal there. If you know him as well as you say you do,' he said suggestively, leaning closer still and lowering his voice, 'then you will already have discovered he has the devil's own temper when roused. And Lucinda roused him all right…from what I hear.'

Helen could not help flinching to hear yet another person speak of the very great love Lord Bridgemere had had for his first wife. When he saw *her* as little more than a potential mother for his children.

Swaledale must have seen the hurt flicker across her face and decided he had achieved what he had set out to do, because with one more smirk he turned and stalked over to where Lady Augustine was dipping a clay pipe into a dish of bubbles.

'Playtime over, Gussy,' he said. 'Time to return to the world of adults.'

Her face red, Lady Augustine handed the pipe back to his younger brother, whom he had completely ignored, and they left.

Junia stuck her tongue out as the door closed behind him, and Helen couldn't blame her. What a toad he was!

What a liar!

Lord Bridgemere would never hurt a lady! And as for implying he could fly into some sort of rage. Hah! Were they talking about the same man? Lord Bridgemere was always fully in control of himself.

She felt a small hand tugging her fingers out of the fist she had unconsciously clenched them into. She looked down as Junia looked up. 'He always makes me want to hit him as well,' she said.

Helen knelt down and gave her a swift hug. He would make a *saint* want to hit him. In fact, even though she could not imagine Lord Bridgemere ever raising his hand to a lady, she could see him becoming so angry with Swaledale that he would do whatever it took to prevent him inheriting his title.

She went cold inside. He would even enter a loveless marriage, provided the woman in question could make him *comfortable*. That was what he thought of her, was it not? That she would make some man a comfortable sort of wife?

And perhaps, if loving his first wife so much had made him grieve for so many years, he would only risk marrying again if he could be sure he would never experience the same sort of hurt.

He obviously thought *she* would not give him a moment's worry or heartache because he felt certain that his heart would never be deeply touched by her. How could it be? It was buried in the grave with his first wife!

Her hands went to her beads, which she had put on in honour of Christmas Day, even though she did not usually wear jewellery during the daytime, and she thought again of her parents, who had married for love. Their love for one another had carried them through the opposition of both their families, various financial hardships—oh, all their difficulties. She had not seen it as a child, but now she perceived that it had been the best for them, that they had died together. Neither would have wanted to outlive the other.

They'd been as essential to each other as the air they'd breathed.

And was she, their daughter, seriously contemplating marrying a man who, though he had shut himself away in mourning for years after the death of his first wife, would regard her as *comfortable*?

Comfortable for him, perhaps. But what would such a match be like for her? She had already imagined herself pouring her love into his wounded soul. But if his heart remained closed, as was clearly his intent, then how long would it be before loving him without hope proved too much for her? She was not a saint! Far from it. She had only a very limited supply of patience. And a great deal of pride. And a temper that she often had a struggle to contain.

It would not be very long before she became disgruntled. She would shout at him. He would coldly withdraw.

Eventually, from being merely cool towards her, he would grow increasingly irritated by her outbursts. Which would hurt her terribly.

Before much longer they would become one of those couples who lived in a state of cordial dislike. Given his propensity to remove himself from unwelcome society, he would probably disappear to the estate furthest flung from wherever she was, and she did not want to be reduced to the kind of woman who followed around after a man, begging for scraps of attention like some… spaniel! She would not do it. She had too much pride to beg anyone for anything!

No, she would stay exactly where she was, proudly refusing to show how much he hurt her.

It would be hell on earth!

She hugged Junia swiftly, got to her feet and, after waving goodbye to the children and wishing them a happy Christmas, left the nursery to go and find Lord Bridgemere.

She was going to tell him she could not marry him. The prospect of living like that was too dreadful.

Chapter Eleven

For a man who wanted an answer to his proposal before nighttime he was being extremely elusive. But at length, just before dinner, she ran him to ground in his study.

'Please take a seat,' he said, when she hesitated just inside the doorway, her heart in her mouth. He was dressed for dinner, as was she by now. His face was shuttered. He had never looked more unapproachable.

She took a seat. She bowed her head. She was on the verge of tears. Was she doing the right thing? Was she walking away from what could be her heart's desire?

No. She swallowed down an incipient sob. The vision she'd had of marriage to Lord Bridgemere had convinced her he would utterly destroy her. This brief interview would be painful, but at least all her memories of him would be good ones. She would not grow bitter with resentment. Turn into a shrew that no man could like, never mind love.

She took a deep breath, raised her head and looked at him.

'I am conscious you have paid me a great compliment by asking me to marry you,' she began, using the phrases she had rehearsed so many times in her head. 'I am flattered by your proposal. But on reflection I am afraid that I m…must…' *Oh, no! She could not burst into tears. How undignified that would be.* She took another deep breath, clenching her hands into fists on her lap. 'I am sorry, but I c…cannot m…marry you.'

There! She had done it.

Oh, God. It felt as though her heart was going to break. It hurt to breathe.

'I see.' For a moment he looked completely blank. Then he frowned slightly at her, as though she were something of a puzzle, got to his feet and walked past her to the door. 'There is no more to be said,' he said tonelessly, opening the door. 'I trust you enjoy the rest of your stay. I will make the necessary arrangements for your departure on the twenty-seventh.'

He made a gesture with his arm to indicate she should leave.

And she no longer felt as though she might burst into tears.

She had suspected that he would simply shrug and get on with his life if she refused him. And just look at him! That was exactly what he was doing. Calmly ordering her from his study—from his life.

Oh, how right she had been to refuse him.

She leapt from the chair and stalked past him, her head held high. Since he was holding the door open for her he did not even afford her the satisfaction of slamming it in his face.

She was halfway along the corridor before the breath

got stuck behind the hard lump of misery in her chest and she had to sit down swiftly on one of the chairs that were ranged along the walls. Oh, what a fool she was! She knew she had made the right choice, to avoid exposing herself to a lifetime of pain, and yet it still hurt.

She suspected it would hurt for quite some time.

But in the distance she heard the dinner gong sound, and knew she must somehow put on a brave face and go and find her Aunt Bella. If she did not turn up for dinner, her aunt would worry about her and demand to know what was wrong with her. And she did not feel up to speaking about it. Not even with her.

This cut too deep. And somehow she did not think Aunt Bella would understand. She had never had any time for men. She might applaud Helen's decision to reject a proposal of marriage, but it was highly unlikely she would understand the pain it had caused her to do it.

She paused just inside the doorway of the blue saloon, wondering how on earth she would survive another evening closed in with Lord Bridgemere's extended family.

One or two glanced her way, before turning away abruptly in dismissal. Aunt Bella smiled vaguely in her direction, but she was deeply engrossed in conversation with her friend Lady Norton.

Helen had never felt so alone. So utterly, hopelessly lost.

And then Reverend Mullen approached her. 'Good evening,' he said with a friendly smile. 'I have the honour to escort you in to dine tonight,' he said, taking her by the arm and drawing her into the room. 'And may I say what a pleasure it will be to have a like-minded person with whom to converse…'

In a daze, she watched his mouth moving as he no doubt said a lot of very kind things to her. But Lord Bridgemere had just at that moment entered by the far door, and he was walking across the room. Nobody else existed.

He looked, she thought on a fresh wave of misery, just as he always did. Calm, controlled. Perhaps just slightly irritated. Just very slightly.

As he might have been by any minor setback that had occurred during the course of his busy day.

Nobody, but nobody, would be able to tell from his demeanour that he was a spurned suitor.

But then he was not. He had not courted her as a suitor would a woman he cared for deeply. He must have proposed to her on some kind of a whim!

'I say, Miss Forrest, are you quite well?' The Reverend Mullen's voice swam to the forefront of her consciousness briefly. She saw his concerned face, peering intently at her.

'No…no. Actually, I do feel a little unwell,' she said. 'I think that perhaps I shall go to my room…'

There was certainly no way she could sit through dinner, watching him carry on as though nothing had happened between them, when she felt as though… Oh, the only way to describe it was as though she was dying inside.

It was not long before her aunt came to join her. Helen had undressed and got into bed, though she was not sleepy. She saw no point in sitting up, brooding. She wanted to pull the blankets over her head and will the day to end. It was sure to hurt less in the morning.

Wasn't it?

'What is the matter, dear?' her aunt enquired, laying her hand upon her forehead. 'You do not seem to have a fever.'

'No, it is not a fever,' she sighed.

'Then what is it? What can I do to make you feel better?'

There was nothing anyone could do to make her feel better. She suspected she was not going to feel any better for some considerable time. She had thought earlier on that she could not possibly open her heart to Aunt Bella, but there *was* nobody else. And her aunt deserved some sort of explanation for why she was missing her dinner.

'Aunt Bella, have you ever been in love?'

Her aunt looked at her sharply. 'Ah, so that is it after all. Sally said you had fallen for Lord Bridgemere. The fellow has played fast and loose with your feelings, has he?'

'No,' sighed Helen. 'He asked me to marry him. And I refused.'

Aunt Bella looked completely confused. As well she might.

'Have I done the right thing?'

Aunt Bella pulled up a chair and sat down beside the bed. 'I do not know, Helen. I am not the best person to talk about romantic love between a man and woman, if that is what ails you. I have no experience of it myself. And from what I have observed in others it brings nothing but pain and disillusion.'

'So you would say it is better not to marry if you are not sure…?'

'Oh, unquestionably. A woman is better alone.'

Alone. The word tolled like a death knell in Helen's heart. She would always be alone. She would never meet another man who would match up to Lord Bridgemere.

'That is what I thought. Only it does hurt so…'

And finally Helen burst into tears. Tears she had been holding back since the moment she had reached her decision.

'H…he does not l…love me, you s…see,' she sobbed. 'So of course I c…could not marry him, c…could I?'

'Not if you have any sense of self-worth, no,' said Aunt Bella prosaically.

For a while Helen just wept, while her aunt patted her on the back.

'In time I expect the pain will ease,' said Aunt Bella, offering her a handkerchief when Helen began to weep a little less bitterly. 'People do not really die of broken hearts. Not sensible people, at any rate. I could tell, really, I suppose,' she admitted, 'that you fell hard for him the moment you clapped eyes on him. You have never been able to hide what you are feeling,' she said, gently brushing a strand of hair from Helen's tearstained cheek. 'Did he try to take advantage of you? Is that what upsets you so?'

Helen shook her head furiously. 'No! It is because he said I should be a comfortable wife!'

Aunt Bella's brows shot up. 'You? Comfortable? Are you sure?'

When Helen nodded, Bella clicked her tongue. 'The

man's an idiot. Only a grand passion would induce *you* to marry. And there is nothing comfortable about that sort of relationship, I should not think.' She frowned. 'You would not have wanted to upset me by marrying for anything less. I have always been so scathing about the institution, have I not? Have I been utterly selfish? I have worried recently that I did you a great wrong by not taking you to London and introducing you to some eligible men. Just because I never wished to marry, there was no reason to assume that you would not.'

'Oh, Aunt Bella, no! Please do not think that. I never wanted a Season. Besides, I am certain that had I said I wanted one you would have gone along with my wishes. You always let me have whatever I wanted.'

Aunt Bella looked a little mollified.

'And,' Helen continued, 'this week, mixing with the kind of people we would have run into in London, has shown me that I should not have enjoyed it all that much. I do not regret anything about the way you brought me up, Aunt Bella. Please do not think so!'

Aunt Bella produced another handkerchief and blew her own nose on it. 'And yet if you had married someone you would not now be obliged to go and work as a governess. Be reliant upon strangers. We know nothing of these Harcourts. I worry that—' She broke off and dabbed at her eyes. 'You have been so brave about it, but this week I confess I have often felt so uncomfortable about the way things have turned out that I have actually been avoiding you. Sticking my head in the sand, I suppose you would say. Because every time I am with you I—' She broke off again, on a little sob.

Helen knelt up in bed and put her arms about her

aunt. 'Please do not worry about me. You have taught me to be strong and resourceful. I have appreciated the way you have brought me up even more this week, after renewing my acquaintance with General Forrest and his wife. I shudder to think what I would have ended up like had I stayed with them!'

'And yet you refused Lord Bridgemere. When most women would think marrying him would be far preferable to going out to work for a living. Helen, what have I done to you?'

'Taught me to have pride,' she said. 'The man is still in love with his first wife, Lucinda. If I married him he would expect me to simply accept what is left over—like a beggar taking crumbs from his table!'

Aunt Bella frowned. 'Lucinda? In love with her, was he? I should not have thought it myself.'

'Wh…what do you mean? Lady Thrapston said—'

'That woman! Twists the facts to suit herself, she does. Lord Bridgemere could not have been much more than seventeen when he married Lucinda Ellingham. She was of much the same age. The match was arranged by their families.'

'Oh?' Helen had a peculiar cold sensation in her insides. Had she just made the most colossal error? 'B…but why did he shut himself away from everyone after she died? Lady Thrapston said his heart was buried with her in her grave.'

Aunt Bella flung up her hands in annoyance. 'What a piece of melodramatic nonsense! Honestly! Does he strike you as the sort of man who would care that much about any woman?'

That remark did not help Helen as much as her aunt

had probably intended. Though it might be some consolation to hear he had not been so enamoured of his first wife as she had been led to believe, it still did not bode well for any relationship they might have had.

'S…Swaledale said—'

'Helen, if you have been listening to the tales those two have been telling, then I despair of you. Surely they contradicted each other on every conceivable point?'

Now she came to think of it, they had. Lady Thrapston had said Lord Bridgemere was a man with a broken heart. Whilst Swaledale had implied he had a guilty conscience.

'So…are you saying he did not love her?'

Aunt Bella shrugged. 'That I cannot tell you. It was a long time ago, and I have never been that close to him. Does it make so much difference?'

Helen's shoulders slumped. 'Probably not. He does not love *me*, and that is the main reason I could not accept. I sat down and really thought about marriage for the first time today. And I saw that the kind of match I want would be the kind my parents had. The grand passion, as you so rightly said. They were so very much in love, my mother and father.' She shook her head sadly. 'Bridgemere I think admires me a little. But he does not love me the way I need to be loved. He would have made me miserable.'

'I expect so,' said Aunt Bella tartly. 'That is what men are best at. Making women miserable.'

Helen could not help smiling weakly at that remark.

'That is what Swaledale said. That Lord Bridgemere would make me miserable. According to him, Lord

Bridgemere has a dreadful temper. And, what is more, he implied his first wife's death might not have been an accident. He said that nobody ever dared question Lord Bridgemere too closely about the incident, as though there was something sinister about her death that he wished to keep quiet.'

Aunt Bella snorted contemptuously. 'Well, from what I recall of that time it would have been no surprise if Bridgemere *had* lost his temper with Lucinda. She acted like a spoiled child instead of a wife with a position in society to live up to. But as for implying he had anything to do with her death—why, that is absolute nonsense! He may have blamed himself for not being here to curb her excesses perhaps…'

'It happened here?'

'Yes. She fell down the grand staircase and broke her neck. During one of the riotous parties she liked to throw. The rumours that came my way were to the effect that she was intoxicated. *Not* that Bridgemere had anything to do with it. And if Swaledale implied otherwise I should say that it stems from spite, because he feared what he could see was going on between you and His Lordship. That young man must be terrified of being cut from the succession.'

'I…I never thought of that…' Helen whispered. Oh, Lord, what had she done? She shut her eyes and wrapped her arms round her waist.

But it did not take her long to realise that it made no difference what had gone on in that first long-ago marriage, even though it had cast such long shadows over his life. The reason she had not accepted Lord Bridgemere's proposal was that he did not love her now, today. Not because of anything that might or might not have happened in his youth.

'Shall I send for a supper tray?' said Aunt Bella, dabbing at her eyes and sitting up straight. 'It is bad enough that the wretched man has upset you so much. I see no reason why we both need to go hungry on his account as well.'

They were not going to discuss the matter any further, Helen could see that. Aunt Bella disliked emotional scenes of this sort. They had made their peace with each other, dealt with Lord Bridgemere's proposal, and that was the end of that.

Helen blew her nose one last time, knowing the subject was closed. When Aunt Bella drew a line under any topic there was no point in trying to revisit it.

Helen woke next morning with a throat that felt raw from weeping quietly into her pillow and eyes that were heavy from lack of sleep.

It was her last day at Alvanley Hall. And she did not know how she was going to get through it. He would be somewhere near all the time. She might see him unexpectedly at any moment. And every time she saw him it would be a like a fresh blow. To know she might have married him if she'd had less pride. To know that because of it she would likely never see him again.

Oh, how she longed for the day to be over, so that she could leave tomorrow and start to get on with the rest of her life without him. To begin to allow her wounded heart to heal.

This must be what purgatory was like. Neither one thing nor the other. Just enduring the present punishment for a decision she was bitterly regretting even though she knew it had been the right one.

For once she had no wish to go up to the nursery. Children were perceptive. They would be bound to ask her what was the matter. Or Reverend Mullen would enquire after her health. She was afraid that she might start to cry again, and upset them. As well as drawing the kind of attention to herself she desperately wished to avoid.

But she had no wish to sit in her room moping all day, either.

Fortunately she knew exactly where another pair of willing hands would be welcome, and that was at the barn on the home farm, where the tenants' ball was to be held tonight.

As she had suspected, Mrs Dent welcomed her with open arms, and promptly handed her a broom. Once Helen had finished helping sweep the floor she went and stood with the village girls who had also come up to help, and had a drink while they all watched the men setting up trestle tables along one wall. From then on her feet hardly touched the ground. There were cloths to spread, garlands to make, wreaths to hang and, to the accompaniment of much giggling, kissing balls to fashion from mistletoe and hang in as many strategic locations as possible.

Much later she went to the nursery, to take an early tea with the children since she was feeling a little shaky. She could not say she wanted to eat anything, but she knew there was a lot of the day left to get through, and the last thing she wanted to do was faint away and ruin the children's big moment on stage.

She helped them into their costumes and handed Charles, swathed in silk as the angel Gabriel, the supply of ginger snaps which she had fetched on her way up through the kitchens, so that he could bribe the little angels to behave themselves. Then she helped Reverend Mullen and the nurserymaids to get them all downstairs and into their cart for the short drive over to the barn.

Their party was the last to arrive. The house guests were sitting on benches directly in front of the raised platform on which the band would later play music for the dance, and the villagers, dressed up in their Sunday best, were standing behind them.

There was an empty seat next to Lord Bridgemere, on the front row. He got to his feet the moment he saw her and indicated that she should come and sit beside him.

Helen's heart sank. It was further proof, as if she needed any, that he had not a grain of sensitivity. How could he think she would want to sit so close to him when her whole being was grazed red raw from rejecting his proposal?

Yet how could she refuse his invitation with everyone watching? It would look as though… She grappled with the possible interpretations the others would put on her actions, then gave up, too weary to take any thought to its logical conclusion, and sank onto the seat beside him.

'Are you feeling any better?' he murmured as she took her seat. 'You did not take dinner last night.'

How could he think she could have sat through another interminable meal with his family when her heart had felt as though it was breaking?

'I feel…'

She felt dreadful. And sitting so close to him was not helping. If she should reach out, just a little, she would be able to touch him. When she knew that really he was forever out of her reach. For two pins she could throw back her head and howl with misery. She had to bite down hard on her lower lip, to stop it quivering.

'Hush,' she said, keeping her face fixed straight ahead, for she dared not look at him lest he see exactly how much she was hurting. 'The children are about to start.'

Something inside Lord Bridgemere had settled when she took her place beside him. He had been worried about her all day. He had upset her somehow by proposing marriage. Though he could not tell why. He had thought she liked him. But last night in his study she had looked as though she could not wait to get as far from him as possible. She had not been able to look him in the face from the moment she'd entered. Had run from the room positively bristling with indignation when he had decided he might as well put a period to that embarrassing little scene.

But at least she did not have such a disgust of him that she could not even bear to sit beside him now.

Strange how badly he had misinterpreted her. He had thought he could always tell exactly what she was feeling. He had caught her looking at him sometimes with what he had thought was her heart in her eyes. He would have sworn she would leap at the chance to marry him.

Instead she had turned him down. Had run from the dining room the second he'd entered it as though

she could not bear to so much as look at him and gone
without dinner rather than endure another second in
his presence. And she had clearly been avoiding him
all day. He'd respected her wishes, leaving her to her
own devices though he would much rather have made
the most of this last day they would ever have together.
But he was too much the gentleman to trample all over
her feelings.

Whatever they were. He glanced at her out of the
corner of his eye. She looked as though she had slept
as poorly as he had done. The feeling of numbness that
had descended over him when she had turned down
his proposal had stayed with him through the night.
He just could not believe she would walk away from
him when she could be his wife. *Why?* he had wanted
to shout when she had stammered through that painful
little rejection speech. Why could she not stay with him?
Did he mean nothing to her at all? He had lain in bed
all night feeling…empty. Completely empty.

But she was sitting next to him now.

He barely restrained the urge to reach out and take
hold of her hand.

Reverend Mullen had done a masterful job of coaching the children, who acted out the story of the nativity
quite beautifully, even if several of the tiniest angels
could clearly be seen munching biscuits throughout. To
end the performance the whole audience joined in with
a heartfelt rendition of 'Hark the Herald Angels Sing',
then the seated guests applauded the children's effort
politely, while the villagers whooped and cheered.

When the applause had died down, all the seated

spectators got up and made their way to the exit, intent on returning to the chilly grandeur of the big house. Instinctively Helen made a move towards the children, intending to help their nurses wrap warm coats over the tops of their costumes for the ride home.

'Miss Forrest,' said Lord Bridgemere, putting his hand on her arm to stay her.

'Please, don't go.' His heart was hammering so hard it was a wonder she could not hear it. There was so little time left. Mere hours before the coach would come round and carry her away. How could they waste them sleeping? Or in his case pacing his room, wondering what he could have done to make her accept rather than reject him.

Her heart leapt within her breast. Was he asking her to reconsider? Had he, on reflection, decided he could not bear the thought that she was leaving tomorrow?

'It is your last night here,' he said. 'Your last night of freedom before you have to try to behave with propriety all the time, as befits a governess.' He tried to make a joke of it, so that she would not hear how close he was to begging her to spend the evening with him.

Her heart plunged. It was not a renewal of his proposal, then. How foolish of her! Why would it be? She'd only ever been supposed to be his 'comfortable' wife.

'There is to be dancing. And I should like you to be my partner for the opening set even if you do not care to stay longer. Will you stay for just one dance? Please?'

He held out his hand to her. The rest of the room was in a bustle as the children were shepherded out of the door. The villagers cleared away the chairs, and musicians mounted the stage and began tuning up.

But where she was standing there was nothing but Lord Bridgemere, holding out his hand to her with an intensity in his expression that produced an echoing yearning deep within her. As he had said, this was her last night. The last time she would ever see him. And he wanted her to spend it with him.

What else could she do? Go up to her room and finish her packing? Sit on her bed and spend the whole night weeping?

Or make the most of this chance—this one last chance to be with him?

She put her hand in his and he smiled.

'Thank you,' he said quietly, and led her to the head of the first set that was now forming to the cheers of the locals.

Helen had never seen Lord Bridgemere looking so carefree as he did that night.

He was dressed fairly casually, so that he did not look so very different from the other young village men in their Sunday best. When the first dance was finished he proceeded to dance with his tenants' wives and daughters, whilst the farmers and their sons swept her up into the merriment. Though even when she was not his partner, she still felt as though she was dancing with him. The nature of the country dances was such that they all continually moved up and down the set, so that she never knew when he might take hold of her hand or swing her round by the waist in performance of one of the figures. So long as she was dancing and he was dancing it was as though they were dancing together, no matter who their nominal partners happened to be.

Which was why she stayed. And kept on dancing.

Until she was so tired that she was forced to go to the refreshments table for a glass of the local cider.

It was only moments before Lord Bridgemere joined her.

'You have enjoyed your last night here, I think,' he said, accepting a drink from the girl who was serving. 'Rather more than you have enjoyed most of the rest of your stay at Alvanley Hall.'

She nodded as they both sipped their cool, refreshing drinks. In spite of everything she was glad she would have the memory of this night to look back on. When she had glimpsed yet another facet of Lord Bridgemere's character.

'I have, too,' he said. He moved a little closer and lowered his head, so that she could hear him above the music that was striking up again. 'We only danced the once, but somehow, because you were here, too, and happy, it made it...very special.' He smiled at her, ruefully.

Helen closed her eyes. Hearing him say that was unbearably poignant. She wanted to savour his words without giving away her state of mind. She was not wearing her best bronze gown tonight, but a simpler dress that she'd thought more appropriate for the activities in which she had envisaged taking part. And he was standing so close that she could feel his body heat through the thin muslin.

Her heart began to pound. Her eyes flew open. And she saw him looking down at her with sadness in his eyes.

'It is almost midnight,' he said. 'I really think we should leave. Some of these men have been partaking of the ale I have provided somewhat too freely and the atmosphere is about to become rather boisterous. I should like to take you back now.'

Take her back. She had not given a thought as to how she would get back to the house. But the prospect of leaving did not sound quite so terrible now she knew he meant to escort her. The dancing might be over, but there was still the walk home.

'Thank you,' she said. 'I shall fetch my coat and bonnet.'

Lord Bridgemere waited for her by the door, leaning against the frame with his arms crossed over his chest. She had not liked it when he'd spoken to her of his feelings. From being relaxed and seemingly happy in his company she had completely withdrawn. And when he had suggested they leave her relief had been palpable.

She really did not want to marry him.

Helen thought Lord Bridgemere had never looked more isolated as he lounged against the doorpost, watching his tenants enjoying the festivities. It was as though a great gulf separated him from other, lesser beings.

As if to confirm her opinion of his exalted status, the moment she joined him the band stopped playing, the villagers stopped dancing, and everyone turned to look at him.

'I usually make a sort of farewell speech when I leave the ball,' he explained to her. 'It will not take a moment…'

But before he had the chance to say anything to his tenants the fiddler, who had been imbibing steadily all night, suddenly yelled, 'Don't leave without giving her a kiss, Your Lordship! Don't let that mistletoe go to waste!'

Everyone was either roaring with laughter or pointing at the kissing ball under which, he now perceived, he and Helen were standing.

She was looking up at it, too, but then she glanced at him, her cheeks turning fiery red.

That reckless spirit that she so often managed to provoke in him surged to life. She might rather become a governess than his wife, but, dammit, this was Christmas. He had every right to kiss the woman he wanted to marry under the mistletoe. Whether she wanted him to or not!

In a spirit of defiance, he reached up and plucked a berry from the already much used bough.

'It would disappoint them if I did not oblige,' he said, tucking it into his waistcoat pocket. Then he took her firmly by the upper arms, and drew her close. 'You do not mind, do you?'

She was staring at him wide-eyed, lips already slightly parted. 'N…no,' she stammered. 'W…we would not want to disappoint anyone, would we?'

'Not at Christmas,' he said, his heart pounding in his chest as he drew her closer still. 'I make a point of giving everyone exactly what they want at Christmas.'

Then he bent down, just slightly, and brushed his mouth against hers. She shut her eyes. He felt a quiver run through her body.

He stepped back. She opened her eyes and looked at him. As though what he had done had stunned her.

And then a sheen of tears began to form in her eyes.

He flung his arm about her shoulders and turned her to shield her from view. Waving his arm at the revellers, he pulled her out of the barn and into the yard, to the accompaniment of cheers and applause.

How little his tenants knew! They thought he was going to have a romantic walk home with his sweetheart by starlight. Not escort a reluctant and probably highly offended female back to the Hall.

'Miss Forrest—' He pulled himself up short. He was not going to apologise for kissing her. He had asked her if she minded, and she had not refused. If she had disliked it so much it had made her cry...

Dammit, he had never meant to ride roughshod over her feelings. Just because he wanted her it was quite wrong of him to conveniently forget the fact she did not want to marry him!

Beside him in the dark he heard her give a little sniff, as though she was trying hard not to weep.

'Hell,' he growled, coming to a complete halt and pulling her into his arms. 'I never meant to make you cry. I would not have kissed you if I had known you would dislike it so much. You should not have said you did not mind if you did!' he finished, confusion and frustration making him spit the words at her angrily.

She raised her head and looked up at him. 'I d...did not mind at all!' she said, confusing him even more.

'Then why the devil are you crying?'

'I am not crying,' she said, averting her face.

He took hold of her chin and turned her face up to his, so that he could see quite clearly the silvery tracks glinting on her cheeks that exposed her lie.

'Then what are these?' he said, brushing his thumbs

across the tearstains. 'Miss Forrest, what is the matter with you? If you do not explain, then how am I to make it right for you?'

She took a breath, as though she was going to speak, but then shook her head, looking so woebegone it tore him up inside.

'You cannot make it right for me, Lord Bridgemere. The reason I am crying is something you can never mend for me.' She reached up and placed her palm against his cheek. 'Though I wish with all my heart that you could.'

Chapter Twelve

It was no use wishing, though, was it? He did not love her. And that was that.

Reluctantly she removed her hand from his cheek and let it hang at her side.

'Tell me what I can do to make you happy,' he said.

Her mind went back to the way she had felt when he had kissed her under the mistletoe. She had known he was only kissing her to amuse his tenants. She had known she had to keep that thought very clear in her head and not permit herself to indulge in any kind of romantic fantasy. And, as if to reinforce her strict warning, he had barely brushed his lips across hers.

So briefly, and yet it had felt so sweet. Like a benediction which she had felt all the way down to her toes.

And so powerful that it had completely erased the shame she had felt after Swaledale assaulted her.

What would make her happy would be another kiss just like that one. Only given because he wanted to give it, not because she or anyone else had asked for it. She smiled sadly.

'There is nothing you can do, truly.' She had finally, she reflected ruefully, had her curiosity satisfied in regards to Lord Bridgemere's mouth. And the memory of that kiss would be something she would treasure for the remainder of her life.

She shivered, suddenly picturing all those cold, lonely years without him.

'We should not be standing here like this,' said Lord Bridgemere. They had paused beside the gate after he had closed it behind them. They were still only a few yards from the barn. Helen could hear the sounds of merriment spilling through the gaps in the barn door, along with the light from the lanterns.

'You are getting cold,' he said with concern.

Helen had been driven over in the cart, with a thick rug tucked over her lap and the bodies of all the children squeezed up against her to keep her warm. It was much colder now than it had been earlier. The clouds that had made the day so dull had cleared and frost coated every surface, so that every branch and twig and blade of grass, even the old farmyard gate, glittered brightly in the light of the almost full moon.

Lord Bridgemere began to unbutton his coat.

'No,' cried Helen, thinking he meant to take it off and lend it to her. 'If you remove your coat then *you* will be cold. As soon as we start walking again I am sure I shall get warm.'

He paused, but then resolutely went on unfastening his coat. 'I have a better idea,' he said. 'Stand still.' He opened the front of his coat, stepped forward and wrapped his arms about her, enveloping her in the thick folds of material and his own body heat. 'If you turn a little and put your arm about my waist we can share the warmth of my coat as we walk home,' he said. 'So neither of us need feel the cold.'

For a few seconds Helen stood quite still, revelling in the feel of his arms about her. But eventually, when she felt she had absolutely no excuse for stretching the moment out any longer, she said, weakly, 'Y…yes, that is a most practical solution.'

'I thought so,' he said softly. 'Though I don't suppose we will be able to walk very fast like this.'

As she turned he kept both his arms about her, so that his coat completely enfolded her.

'N…not very fast, no,' she agreed, as he attempted to match his stride to accommodate her stumbling steps.

It was highly improper to cling onto Lord Bridgemere as he held his coat about her for warmth, but who was ever going to know? They were the only two people out here tonight. And even if somebody did spot them, what could they do? For once Helen was just going to do exactly as she wished and hang the consequences!

Slowly, entwined like lovers, they picked their way along the frozen rutted lane. As soon as they drew away from the farm buildings the deep silence of a winter's night descended. She was more than ever aware of how utterly alone they were under the vast canopy of stars. And also of how very intimate it felt. Why, even their breath mingled visibly, as it rose above their heads before dissipating into the clear cold air.

Neither of them said a word. Helen was afraid to break the spell that seemed to be holding them suspended in this moment out of ordinary time, and every time she peeped up at him Lord Bridgemere looked as though he was concentrating on where he was putting his feet. Though he did not seem to be in any hurry. And that was good enough for her—for now. She shut her eyes briefly, revelling in the feel of his body flexing beneath her hands with every step he took.

But all too soon they were entering the kitchen court and crossing the slick cobbles. And then he was removing one arm to reach out and open the door. His coat was still round her. He still had one arm about her shoulders as they stepped inside, into the unlit lobby of the servants' hall.

The door creaked shut behind them, blotting out even the moonlight, and as they both stood quite still in complete darkness Lord Bridgemere remarked, 'Nobody seems to have thought of leaving a lantern lit.'

'I expect,' replied Helen, 'the servants know exactly where it is, and can put their hand upon it and get it lit in an instant.'

'No, I do not think that is it. I think it is more likely that there are usually plenty of people about down here and lights all over the place.'

But tonight the servants were all still at the barn, dancing. The gentry were all above stairs, for once fending for themselves. They were utterly alone.

And somehow, even though they were no more alone than they had been on the walk back here, being within doors, with her arm about his waist and his arm about her shoulder, felt a whole lot more intimate. And risqué. Especially since there was now absolutely no excuse for them to be touching each other.

With great reluctance Helen began to slide her arm out from round his waist.

Lord Bridgemere sucked in a sharp breath. She felt his body jerk.

'No,' he said, turning as she moved her arm so that it stayed imprisoned under the fabric of his coat.

They were standing face to face now, although it was still too dark to see. But she could feel the warmth of his breath fanning her cheek, so she knew he was angling his head down towards hers. And then he slid his arm from her shoulder, lower down her back, and exerted a slight pressure. Only a little, but it was all the encouragement she needed to move closer to him and lay her head against his chest. The buttons of his waistcoat stung cold against her cheek, but she did not care. For Lord Bridgemere had given a great sigh and put his other arm around her.

Helen slid her other arm about his waist and held him, too. For a moment or two it seemed to be enough. They stood, clinging together in the dark, as though neither could bear the thought of letting the other go. But then the tenor of his breathing changed.

'Is there mistletoe hanging above this doorway, do you suppose?' he said.

It was far too dark to see. So there was no point in raising her head to look.

'There might be,' she said wistfully.

'If there was, would there be any chance you would let me kiss you again?'

Beneath her cheek Helen could feel his heart beating very fast. And he was breathing hard, as though he had been running, not walking slowly with her cradled in his arms like some precious, fragile piece of porcelain.

And in the dark, with nobody to see them, and the minutes before she had to leave ticking away urgently in her mind, she gave him the only answer possible.

'Yes, I am sure there is mistletoe here. And yes to the other question, too.'

It would be too brazen to actually say *Yes, I want you to kiss me*. But he knew what she meant, because the moment she lifted her head from his chest and raised her face he swooped down and took her mouth.

This time his kiss was not the polite brush of the lips he had given her in the barn, with all his tenants watching. It was too dark here for anyone to see anything— even each other—and it was as if the very darkness freed him from all restraint. His lips moved urgently across her own, nipping and tasting her. He stroked his tongue across the seam and when she gasped he plunged it into her mouth with a groan. It was as if he wanted to devour her.

Helen was in such bliss that she yielded to every prompt he gave her, opening her mouth wider to allow him deeper access, tentatively tasting him as he was tasting her. He tasted sweet, like the cider they had both been drinking. His lips were soft, but the skin of his cheek felt rough, even though he had looked clean-shaven in the moonlight earlier. But she did not dislike the sensation of his jaw abrading her chin. It made her thrillingly conscious of his masculinity.

All her senses seemed particularly acute. She expected it was because she could not see him with her eyes. She was aware, for example, that he smelled slightly different. Or perhaps because he had been dancing the scent of his skin was slightly stronger than usual. For whatever reason, she felt as though she was breathing in the heat of his body, along with the more familiar smell of cologne and clean linen she usually associated with him.

And the darkness freed her from some of the restraint she would have felt in bright light. She felt bold enough to reach up and loop one arm about his neck and press her body closer to his. He encouraged her by holding her harder, as if he wanted to meld their bodies into each other.

Excitement flared through her when his hands slid down to her waist, tracing the shape of her body through her clothing. She did not feel cold any more. In fact she felt warm in the most unlikely places. Not just where his hands were touching her, but in the pit of her stomach, the tips of her breasts and, most shockingly, in the secret folds of skin between her legs.

Under his coat she ran the hand that had been round his waist up his back, then down his side, tracing the tapering shape of his torso. He growled low in his throat and his hands went round her back and down, to cup her bottom, pulling her hard against his body.

She could feel something hard pressing into her stomach. She only wondered what it was for a split second before realising it was his arousal.

She revelled in the knowledge that he wanted her in this most primal, basic way. And the heat that had begun to bloom between her legs became an ache of need.

He flexed against her, his fingers kneading at her

bottom in time with the undulation of his hips. And her legs almost gave way.

She staggered backwards and he came with her, their mouths still fused together, their feet shuffling and dragging as they stumbled across the corridor, locked together in a dance of urgency. As soon as her back hit the wall he let go of her, but only so that he could fumble open the buttons of her coat and delve inside. His hands felt hot as they shaped her breasts.

She felt lost. Confused. But whatever the question that was niggling at the back of her mind she was too caught up in sensation to want to know the answer. Lord Bridgemere was trailing hot kisses down her neck, along her collarbone, and then the upper slopes of her breasts. Her gown had a square-cut neck, and he deftly scooped one breast free so that he could suckle it.

Helen gasped. The pleasure was so intense she hardly knew what she was doing any more. Her fingers kneaded his shoulders as he laved her nipple, while his hand caressed the fullness of her breast. She found that she was writhing against him, her hips gyrating in time with his own undulations.

He kept his mouth at her breast, but his hands slid down her sides, then grasped handfuls of her skirt, hitching up her dress until he could reach beneath. She gasped again when his hands found the bare skin above the tops of her stockings.

He was going to touch her there!

Oh, yes!

But then somewhere in the depths of the house a door slammed.

Lord Bridgemere jerked upright. And swore.

Her skirts fell decorously to her ankles, but one breast was still hanging out of the bodice of her gown.

Her eyes had grown used to the dark by now. She could see him looking down at her breast, which she knew must be glistening with moisture from his tongue. He looked appalled.

'Miss Forrest, forgive me,' he said, stepping back and disappearing into the shadows.

She felt cold and alone—and humiliated. With trembling fingers she straightened her gown, then pulled the edges of her coat together to cover herself up.

'I should not have—' he began.

Oh, this was terrible! Bad enough that she had let him put his hands and mouth all over her. But now his moment of madness was over he was going to make some feeble excuse about having drunk too much, or give some other reason that would negate everything she had felt and reduce it to an impulse he now regretted.

She did not want to hear it!

It had been glorious. Wonderful! And she would not let him destroy it with his words.

Clapping her hands over her ears, she stumbled away from him.

'No, wait—please. I...'

'Don't say it!' she cried, breaking into a run. She knew her way about down here sufficiently to know that so long as she kept to the centre of the corridor there was nothing she could trip over. 'I don't want to know!'

Lord Bridgemere stood stock still, listening to the sounds of her footsteps fading into the distance.

Then he reached out and touched the wall against

which she had been standing. Whilst he had... God! He had practically ravished her! He could not believe he had lost control like that. He had never known such passion. Such driving need. If not for hearing that door slam, which had brought him back to his senses, who knew what might have happened? No wonder she had fled from him! Had refused to listen to his apologies! What he had almost done was beyond forgiveness.

He was no better than Swaledale, preying on an innocent, unprotected female in a deserted corridor.

He closed his eyes and pressed his forehead against the cold, smooth surface, gritting his teeth as he struggled to bring his body back to something resembling normality. But in the dark he could still feel her little hands, clinging to his shoulders. Could still smell her sweet, womanly fragrance hanging in the air. Could taste her in his mouth. Feel her nipple beading under his questing tongue.

He had to move away from this spot. She haunted it!

Muttering a curse, he pushed away from the wall and set out for his bedroom. His valet, like the other servants, would be kicking up his heels over at the barn, so he had no need to maintain any kind of pretence when he got there. He shut the door behind him and leaned against it, bowing his head as a wave of self-loathing swept over him. He was *worse* than Swaledale. At least the youth had the excuse of being so drunk he'd hardly known what he was doing. But he was without excuse. It was desire alone that had made him act like a ravening beast.

The two scenes swam into his mind, overlapping as

he saw himself as the predator and Miss Forrest as his victim. He saw Swaledale slobbering down her neck while she stood rigid, her face averted, sick with terror and not knowing what to do. And then himself, scooping her breast out of her gown to suckle at it while she...

He straightened up abruptly. She had been writhing against him. Clinging to him.

She had been with him every step of the way!

He recalled now her little gasps and moans of pleasure. The way her hands had tentatively begun to explore his body. It had been her eager yet innocent response that had ramped up his own arousal to almost overwhelming proportions.

He walked to the bed and sat down heavily, remembering suddenly that he had not just pounced on her but had asked permission to kiss her.

And she had said yes.

They had *both* imagined mistletoe to give themselves the liberty to do exactly what they wanted, even though they both knew it was wrong.

So...why had she fled from him? Could it possibly be that she did not blame him for the whole episode, but that she, too, had abruptly come back down to earth and been ashamed to have let things go so far? Ashamed, most of all, that it had been he who had called a halt to proceedings. If he had not stopped, he did not think she could have done so!

He gave a great sigh of relief, running the palm of his hand over his hair. That was more like it. That was Miss Forrest all over. She acted on impulse and thought about what she had done afterwards. She had not been able to resist his advances, and the moment they had been interrupted she had been as full of remorse as he had been.

How her pride must have stung to know that any man had the power to make her sigh and moan with desire. Particularly one she had refused to marry.

His sense of relief ebbed away as bitter regret swamped him. Shakily he covered his hands with his face and hunched over.

How could she have let him put his hands all over her when she knew she would be walking away from him in the morning? He had thought she had a deep vein of integrity running through her. She was so proud she would not marry him, even though he was one of the wealthiest men in the country.

What was it about him that made her still want to leave when she had just acted as though she wanted him with every fibre of her being?

He leapt up from the bed and paced across the floor. God in heaven, but he wished he understood her! What was the key that would unlock her mystery? He thumped the windowframe, turned, and paced back towards his bed.

There was no logical reason why she should not marry him if she could respond to him as she had just done downstairs!

No logical reason, no. But when had logic ever played a part in anything Miss Forrest did? She was not a cold, calculating woman. From the first he had thought she was a force of nature. As well try to capture lightning in a bucket as to think Miss Forrest would tamely settle with him when she wanted—

What the hell *did* she want? He turned and stalked

back to the window. She had made it clear she had no ambition to net herself a wealthy, titled husband. What was it she had said about those tradesmen who might have offered for her had she given them any encouragement? He had thought it sounded proud at the time. Had thought she did not want to be demeaned by taking a step that would see her descend the social scale.

But then she had spurned him, too.

Just what did she want from a husband, then, if it was not money, or a title, or even physical gratification?

And then her voice came to him—proud and clear and defiant. *The only reason I would ever marry would be for love.*

He sat down hard on the bed, winded.

He should not have given her a practical list of reasons for marrying him. He should have romanced her!

He thought back to that stilted little speech he had made. To the reluctance he had felt to enter the married state again, which must surely have transmitted itself to her. His cursed pride had made him disguise how much her answer mattered to him. He had let her think he did not care much either way. When the reality was that the thought of living without her was almost unbearable. He groaned out loud. What a fool he had been! He suddenly perceived he had not offered her the one thing that she might have valued.

His heart.

He laid his hand upon his chest, feeling it beating. Pounding. Because he was afraid there was nothing he could do to stop her leaving.

Two days ago he would have said it did not matter. He would have expected to feel some regret, but would have thought it would fade in time, and that as he went back to his orderly existence the routine of carrying out his duty would soothe the passions she had roused.

But that was before he had kissed her.

If he let her slip through his fingers now, without making one last effort to persuade her...

He got to his feet and went to the door. Opened it. Then remembered that she was sharing a suite of rooms with her aunt by adoption. He could not go in there and try to make love to Helen with her aunt watching his every move. If a man invaded her rooms she would probably set up such a squawk that she would set the whole house in an uproar.

He shut the door and stood there, his mind whirling.

He could not let Helen go. Not without putting up a fight.

Then his face set. It was *his* coach she was relying on to take her away in the morning. Driven by *his* coachman. Without his say-so the man would not carry her off his lands.

He flung open his door and strode purposefully along the corridor. To judge by their reaction when he had kissed Miss Forrest in the barn, his tenants would be only too pleased to help him carry out the plan that was forming in his mind. They could all see the impact she'd had on him. And, to a man, they would welcome her as their new countess. She had impressed them all as much as she had impressed him.

He just hoped a sufficient number of them were still sober enough to be able to carry out the work needed to bring his plan to fruition.

Chapter Thirteen

Helen and her aunt ate a very subdued breakfast in their room the next morning. They were both too upset by the prospect of parting to try and speak to each other, lest one of them break down. They just hugged each other fiercely when a couple of under-footmen came to collect her trunks. And both walked down to the coach with their lips firmly pressed together.

Although Helen felt further from tears than her aunt looked. It was as though there were some hurts that just went too deep. She had lain in bed the night before feeling strangely numb. It reminded her a bit of the way she had felt when her parents had died and her future had seemed so vast and terrifyingly empty. She had known then that she would have to be brave to survive. And somehow, last night, she had felt that shedding any more tears over Lord Bridgemere would only weaken her resolve to survive life without him.

She paused before getting into the coach that was to take her away from Alvanley Hall for ever, swiftly glancing along the rows of windows and wondering if *he* stood behind one of them, watching her go. Naturally he could not come and bid her farewell in public. An earl did not condescend to notice the departure of a woman who was destined to become a governess.

A man who had been disappointed in love would not be able to bear the parting, either, she reflected wistfully.

But a man whose emotions were not engaged at all would probably have gone out riding, as was his habit, with his enormous hound loping at his side.

Suddenly Helen's breath hitched in her throat, and she had to duck her head to hide the way her eyes were smarting as she took the footman's extended arm and he helped her climb into the coach.

She understood the difference between passion and love. There were places men could go to in just about every town to slake the kind of need Lord Bridgemere had been exhibiting last night. Which she, to her shame, had not even attempted to deny. To think she had once joked with her aunt about a man's *proclivities*!

Aunt Bella fumbled a handkerchief out of her pocket and, pressing it to her eyes, abruptly turned away and marched swiftly back to the house.

The door slammed shut, the coach lurched, and she was off. And, perhaps because she was finally alone, and nobody would be able to either hear or see her weep, she found she could no longer stem the flood of feelings that pride had kept so firmly held back. She delved into her reticule and held a handkerchief over her face while she released all the misery that had formed into a cold, hard lump in her chest. Lord Bridgemere desired her. Enough to make marrying her and getting her with child no hardship for him. But he had never—not once—spoken of having any feelings for her that would make sacrificing her independence worth the risk. And so now she was leaving behind the only other person in this world that she loved, Aunt Bella, to start a new life alone.

All too soon, it seemed to her, the coach came to a halt. She looked up, stunned, when the driver came and opened the door himself.

'Is there a p…problem?' she asked, hastily wiping her nose. Beyond him she could see trees. They had not even left Alvanley land yet, so far as she could tell.

The driver's face softened at the sight of her red swollen eyes, and the way she was blowing her nose.

'I do not think so,' he said, confusing her still further. 'But it's just that I can't take you no further than this. Coach won't get up the track.'

'Track?' Helen peered past him as he stood back, opening the door wider and gesturing that she should get out.

'You will have to walk the last little bit,' he said, holding out his hand in readiness to steady her. 'That is if you want to speak to His Lordship. He is waiting for you up yonder.' He jerked his head to the right, and quite suddenly Helen recognised where they had stopped. They were at the end of the lane that led to the woods that sheltered the children's skating pond.

'His Lordship wants to speak to me?'

The driver grinned at her. 'Says I wasn't to take no for an answer.'

'There really is nothing more to say to him,' she said aloud. But her heart was pounding. Could she really leave without finding out what he wanted to say to her? It could not, of course, be what she most wanted to hear. 'I should just go on my way,' she said. But if she left, and did not hear him out, she would always wonder what he had wanted to tell her. It would drive her mad with curiosity!

And so, against her better judgement, she found herself taking the driver's hand and getting out of the coach. And standing looking at the narrow path that wound through the thick belt of trees with her heart in her mouth.

And wonder in her eyes.

For strung amidst the dark, oppressive branches were dozens of coloured lanterns, lighting the way. She followed the route they lit for her stumbling feet, emerging in a matter of moments into the clearing where the children had skated. There had been another heavy frost overnight, adding a coating of what looked like swansdown to the pond where the children would no doubt be skating later on. And beyond it the old tumbledown ruins of the watchtower. The door was closed today, but through the arrow slits she could see a golden glow, and she knew Lord Bridgemere was inside, waiting for her, a fire already prepared so that they should not grow cold while they discussed…whatever it was he had summoned her to discuss.

Her heart pounding, she began to pick her way round the edges of the shallow dish of ice. She had still not reached the door before it flew open, and Lord Bridgemere was standing there, a dark silhouette against the golden glow of the fire.

'Miss Forrest, you came!'

She paused, astonished by the eagerness of his greeting and the slight tinge of surprise she could hear in his voice—as though he had not been certain she would come. Had he really thought she could have insisted the driver turn the coach round and take her away?

He was standing to one side now, holding out his hand to her, 'Come into the warm, please,' he said. And she realised she was standing stock still, just gazing at him in surprise. 'I promise you have nothing to fear from me.'

She knew that! It was just surprising to hear uncertainty in the voice of a man who had always seemed to her so very certain about everything.

She stepped over the threshold, and paused again in utter amazement. When he had opened it up for the children's use she had thought it pretty rustic. It had a flagged stone floor and whitewashed walls, against which the fire-blackened beams stood out in stark contrast. There had been a table positioned a safe distance from the generously proportioned hearth from which the maids had dispensed hot drinks, and several mismatched dining chairs had been ranged about the walls, so that the smaller children or the nurserymaids would have somewhere to sit while they warmed themselves.

But today the place looked completely different. There was a sumptuous deep red carpet spread over the flags. The table had gone. And a pair of sofas had been draped with yards of heavy red velvet, heaped with cushions, and situated on either side of the fireplace. From every exposed beam hung garlands of fir and ivy, so that the air within was redolent of the greenwood.

But what struck her most of all was the mistletoe.

There were bunches of it everywhere. There were two over the doorframe, and another hanging from the central rustic candleholder. There were bunches hanging in the arrow slit windows, and dangling from the mantelpiece, and even a small sprig of it, she noted, her cheeks flaming, tucked into Lord Bridgemere's buttonhole.

He saw her looking at it.

'There will be no need for either of us to hope there might be mistletoe around today, Miss Forrest,' he said, shutting the door. 'I have made sure that wherever in this room you stand I will have the right to ask you for a kiss.'

'B…but I am leaving…' she said faintly.

He shook his head. 'I do not think I can permit that.' He turned his back on her to lock the door, then dropped the enormous iron key into the capacious pocket of a coat that was hanging on a peg nearby. He turned back to her, and with his hands on his hips shook his head. 'No, I cannot permit it. If I have to keep you locked up in here for days until you see sense, then so be it!'

He stalked up to her, grim purpose writ all over his face.

Helen did not know what to make of what sounded like a declaration of intent to imprison her. She supposed, fleetingly, that she ought to be afraid. But, perversely, her heart was beating wildly with excitement. All that mistletoe, coupled with the look on his face, made her think he fully intended to kiss her senseless, as he had done last night. And she wanted him to! Wanted him to kiss her until *he* was wild and out of control, too.

But she could not let him do any such thing. It would be madness. She had a job to go to. Her own way to make in the world. Yielding to him just because he felt like kissing her was absolutely out of the question!

As he had been advancing on her she had been steadily retreating, until the backs of her knees hit the sofa, and she dropped far from gracefully onto the soft, velvety surface, her eyes never leaving his intent face.

But, to her surprise, the moment he caught up with her, instead of joining her on the sofa and perhaps flinging her down and behaving like a proper kidnapper, he dropped to his knees before her. Seized her hands and looked up into her face, his eyes pleading.

'Miss Forrest, you were right to refuse me when I asked you to marry me.'

Now Helen was really confused. If he thought she was right not to have accepted his proposal, then why had he bothered abducting her?

Her heart sank. Was he going to ask her to become his mistress? Because she had responded to him with such passion last night, did he think she was more fitted to that kind of position in his life?

She stiffened with anger.

'I know, I know,' he was saying, sensitive to her reaction. 'That proposal was…an insult to a woman like you! It was just that hearing you were going to leave took me by surprise. I could not bear to think of you leaving. But I did not think about *why* I was so upset by the notion of never seeing you again. All I could think of was that I had to prevent you going. Had to do whatever it would take to make you stay and give me the right to care for you. I proposed to you out of panic. And then reeled with shock at having said the words I swore I would never say to any woman again after what happened with Lucinda.'

He paused, an expression of anguish flickering across his face. And Helen's anger cooled in the face of his misery. It appeared Lady Thrapston had been in the right. He *had* loved his first wife. So much that it was causing him agony to so much as mention her name!

'And then last night I behaved like a brute beast. I knew you were leaving, that I had no right to kiss you like that, never mind the other liberties I took with you!'

At the mere mention of those liberties Helen could feel his tongue sweeping over the breast that his hands had freed from its confinement. She remembered the delicious shivers that had racked her whole body when he had bunched up her skirts and slid his hands between her thighs.

'I do not want your apology—' she began.

But he let go of her hands, got to his feet, and said fiercely, 'I have no intention of apologising! I am merely trying to explain things!'

He paced away from her, as though grappling with some internal demons before being able to speak again.

'I suppose I could blame the moonlit walk home with you in my arms. Or claim I drank rather more than I should have at the tenants' ball. But the truth was,' he said, his eyes bleak, 'that you were utterly irresistible. At one point I was almost completely overwhelmed by my desire for you. I think I was on the point of ravishing you up against that wall,' he said bitterly. 'Which is not at all like me. You see, I have not looked at any woman in that way since Lucinda died. I had thought I would never feel desire again. And then you came into my life, and I began to feel again. It has been like coming back to life. Or…or like spring bringing everything into flower after a long, cold winter.'

'Did…did you love her that much?' she blurted. It hurt so much to think he seemed angry with her for making him feel again. As if she had done it to him on purpose!

'Love her? I did not love her! What the devil made you think I loved her?'

'Y…you said it was like winter. That you had not been happy for years or thought of another woman… What am I supposed to think?'

He came back to the sofa, sat down heavily, and reached for her hand. 'I did think I loved Lucinda at first,' he grated. 'When my guardians told me they had chosen her to be my wife I was thrilled. She was so beautiful. So captivating. She dazzled me. But whatever it was I felt for her it was turned completely on its head within a month of marrying her. When I discovered what she was really like. And when it ended I swore I would never let another woman take me for a fool again. Because my first marriage, you see, was an unmitigated disaster.

'Lucinda was a consummate actress,' he continued. 'She pretended to be all sweetness and light, fooling my guardians, fooling me, into thinking she would make the ideal Countess of Bridgemere.'

Helen's mind flew back to what Aunt Bella had said about Lucinda acting like a spoiled child instead of a wife with a position in society to live up to. And how she would not have been surprised if His Lordship *had* lost his temper with her. And wondered whatever she could have done to make him speak of her with such bitterness even after all these years.

'She *was* a virgin when we wed. I'll grant her that,' he said, giving Helen a pretty good idea of what the answer to her unspoken question was going to be. 'I can only suppose she must have thought she ought to bow to the conventions until her position became unassailable. But once I had relieved her of that impediment she saw no more need for discretion. She took her first lover within a month of marrying me...'

Helen gasped. Even in a marriage arranged by families, where no love existed between the parties, convention demanded that a wife stay faithful at least until she had presented her husband with an heir.

'At first I refused to believe the evidence of my own eyes. Until she grew so indiscreet that even I, besotted as I was, could no longer pretend. I went through two years of utter hell, trying to make her change her ways. In the end I realised I was just too dull for her... You see, I had become Earl at only nine years of age. My mother bore my father several daughters, only two of whom survived infancy, but I was the only son. My guardians cosseted and sheltered me. They did not want to risk sending me to school, where I might come into contact with some disease or other, and so they brought in tutors. I had very little contact with any life beyond the environs of Alvanley Hall. *They* selected Lucinda, for her pedigree and wealth, and brought her here. She burst into my life like... I don't know how to describe her. A whirlwind, perhaps. With hindsight, I can see that she needed more than just to live quietly in the countryside. But back then I had no idea how to handle her. She did not respond to threats or begging.'

He ran his hand over the crown of his head. 'I blamed myself, my own lack of experience, for her inability to remain faithful. And so did she,' he said, his mouth twisting with bitterness. 'She told me to my face that I was dull, provincial, not as exciting as her other lovers…'

'Oh, no…' Helen reached out and grasped his hand. How cruel of that Lucinda, to destroy his youthful optimism, his hopes of a happy marriage, his very self-confidence! 'You are not…'

But he placed one finger to her lips, to silence her. 'Please hear me out. I need to tell you all.'

She nodded and he removed his hand, though her lips tingled where his finger had rested, albeit briefly.

'Had I been older, more worldly-wise, I might have handled the situation better. I dare say there are any number of men who have unfaithful wives and manage not to go to pieces.'

'You were just a boy!' she protested.

'And a coward,' he condemned himself bitterly. 'I left her here at Alvanley Hall and began an existence entirely separate from hers. Nursed what I thought was my broken heart…' His face twisted with contempt. 'But you are right. I was just a boy. A green boy. I did not know what love was! I did not know anything!' He gripped her hand so hard it was almost painful.

'When she died, and I came back here to deal with things, even I who thought I knew what she was like was shocked by the things my tenants told me had gone on in my absence. Perhaps the worst thing, though, was to learn that she was pregnant when she died. With a child that could not possibly have been mine. Had she lived, I would have been forced to acknowledge it. That was the worst betrayal of all. And when I learned about that I was glad she was dead. I felt as though I had been released from prison. I watched them shovelling earth onto her coffin and felt nothing but relief. And I swore on her grave that I would never let my family arrange a marriage for me again. I did not care about my so-called duty to produce an heir. I already had a nephew who could step into my shoes should anything happen to me. And so I told them when we got back to the house that I would not be browbeaten into another arranged match. And when they kept on badgering me about doing my duty to the family name I told them that so far as I was concerned the whole family could go to hell!

'Even now I can barely tolerate having any of that generation near me. Only once a year do I permit them into my house, and that is largely because I do, in truth, have a duty to my family as much as to my tenants. And for one season of the year—just one—I do the right thing. Not the thing I want. In honour of the season.'

Helen could have wept. After shunning people for so long, hiding away and recovering from what his first wife had done to him, he had at long last reached out to someone. To her. He had asked her to marry him only a week after they had met. He might not have declared his love for her in the conventional way, but now he had explained why he was the way he was that proposal told her how very much he needed her. And she had refused him. Turned her back on him in his hour of need! Oh, he had not deserved that! If only she had understood!

'I am so sorry I refused you—' she began, but once again he silenced her.

'You did the right thing. I am glad you refused me.'

'What?' Now Helen hurt on her own behalf. For he was telling her that she had destroyed any chance for them to be together!

'Your refusal made me really think. You brought me down to a level I have never visited before. You see, all my life I have been taught that I am my rank. I am Lord Bridgemere. But the rank means nothing to you, does it? I began to see that if I really wanted you to marry me I would have to offer you something more than rank or wealth. Something that would be of value to you. And then last night, after having you in my arms, I knew I would never forgive myself if I let you walk away without offering it to you. Miss Forrest, last time I proposed to you I told you that if you agreed to marry me it would be the best Christmas present anyone could give me. But last night showed me that is simply not true.'

'No?' A pang of dismay shot through her.

He shook his head. 'The greatest gift you could give me would be your heart. As I…' He swallowed, took a deep breath, and then said, 'As I give you mine. I am sorry I was so often cold and distant with you. I kept telling myself I was being a fool to expose myself to the risk of so much hurt again. But when you said you were leaving, and I pictured my entire future without you, that was far worse!'

He dropped to his knees, seized her hand and kissed it.

'Besides, what I feel for you is nothing like what I

felt for Lucinda. She dazzled me. But from the moment you walked in I felt as though you knew me.'

'I thought you were a footman,' she protested weakly.

'You brought me down to earth. You would not let me behave in that pompous, arrogant manner which keeps everyone else so very far from me. And you spoke as I would have spoken, you thought as I think. You made me laugh. Miss Forrest, you once told me you would only marry for love. And love is the reason I have had you brought here and am proposing to you again. I do not fear loving you, Miss Forrest, for I know you will not despise the love I bear you as…as *she* did. Quite simply, I need you. To work alongside me. To make me laugh. Make me weep. To rebuke me when I grow too pompous. To…to complete me. I have been so empty and lonely for so long…'

'Please do not say any more,' she begged him, tears streaming down her cheeks.

A look of utter hopelessness came over his face. 'I know you do not love me yet, but in time do you not think you could learn to? I swear, I will be the most devoted husband any woman has ever had. If you cannot agree to marry me now, then at least stay on at Alvanley longer and grant me the chance to court you, to woo you as you deserve. You have not known me long enough to decide whether or not you can love me…'

'I do not need time to know whether I love you or not. I already do!'

He shook his head. 'You cannot mean that.'

'Why not?'

'Because I have always been a dull fellow. And

marrying Lucinda left me twisted inside. I have become suspicious and insular and moody. Not at all the kind of man to attract a vibrant, passionately warm woman like you…'

She shook her head, her eyes shining with love. 'You are upright and noble and good.'

He was still frowning, as though the notion any woman could love him was preposterous.

'And handsome,' she declared, as though that was the clincher. 'I can see now,' she said, 'that for years you have thought yourself unable to inspire a woman's love. You have been so used to thinking people only come near you when they are desperate for your aid. You don't mix in society enough to see that there are many, many people who would value you for yourself. As I do.'

He shook his head. 'There *is* nothing in me to inspire a woman's love. I did everything I could for Lucinda, and she still could not love me.'

'Let's leave Lucinda out of this, shall we?' said Helen tartly. 'She is not typical of womankind, let me tell you! You had a particularly unfortunate experience with her, but it was not your fault. Not your fault at all! *You* were not the one who failed in that marriage.'

'Miss Forrest,' he said, 'if you love me…if you truly love me…'

'I do!' she said, stroking his cheek very gently.

'Then do you think you might change your mind about marrying me?'

'Yes,' she said simply. 'So long as I know you love me, too.'

He wrapped his arms round her waist, burying his face in her lap. She felt his great shoulders heave as though with relief. Then he looked up into her face, searching her features intently.

'You say you love me? You really believe you love me?'

'Yes. Yes, I do!'

'And I, in spite of swearing I would never let another woman touch my heart, have fallen in love with you, too. I did not want to, mind,' he said ruefully. 'I did my utmost to evade the silken coils you were winding round my heart.'

'You make it sound as if I did it on purpose...' she objected.

He shook his head vehemently.

'No. I have had experience of a woman who truly tried to entrap me. What happened between us was something very different. We neither of us sought it. It was...a gift. Love came unbidden, unsought. And we are both richer for it.'

'Yes,' she said, her face lighting up. 'That is exactly how it happened! That is exactly what I feel!'

For a moment or two they just gazed at each other, as though neither of them could quite believe in their sudden reversal of fortune. And then Helen reached out and plucked the bunch of mistletoe from his buttonhole.

'I know this is not quite the done thing,' she said, plucking a berry and holding the sprig above their heads with a hopeful expression.

'You never do what anyone would expect, do you?' he said, his eyes lit with adoration.

Sometimes her impulsiveness had put him very much in mind of the way Lucinda had been. And it had made him wary of her. But it had not taken him long to see that the similarities were only on the surface. Lucinda had never thought of anyone but herself—never considered anything but her own pleasure.

Helen was all heart.

'Which is why I love you.'

And then he pushed himself up off the floor so that he could reach her lips and kissed her. With tears now streaming unchecked down her face, Helen flung her arms round his neck and kissed him back. And, just like the night before, the moment their lips met she felt as though she was entering a different world. A world of sensation, of need. She clung to him. He traced her shape, running his hands all over her body as though he could not quite believe she was real and he had to make sure.

And before long Helen felt restricted by the barrier of clothing that separated them. She was glad when he tore open the buttons of her coat, undid the hooks at the front of her gown, and freed her breasts from their confinement. For a while she was content to lie back and let him feast on her. But soon that was not enough. She had to get rid of some of his clothing, too. Pushing him half off her, so that she could reach his own buttons, she pushed aside his jacket, undid his waistcoat, yanked his shirt from his breeches, and sighed in satisfaction when her fingers finally met with skin.

He shuddered as she ran her hands up the satiny smooth muscles of his back, then tore away his neck-cloth and cast it to the floor, before lowering his mouth to her bared bosom once more.

Helen moaned as he began bunching up her skirts. At last she could move her legs apart, so that he could lie between them. This time when his hand slid over the tops of her stockings she arched up to meet his questing fingers.

'Miss Forrest, are you sure?'

She looked up at him in astonishment when he reared up and slowly began to remove his hand. He could not stop now! Not when he was finally touching her where she had been aching for his touch since they had been interrupted the night before.

'Helen—my name is Helen,' she managed to gasp, grabbing his hand and holding it still. 'You cannot address me in such a formal manner while you are doing that!'

'Sebastian,' he said, and, as though sealing a pact, he slid one finger inside her.

'Sebastian!' she breathed. 'Oh, Sebastian!'

He began to probe and withdraw. She reached for him then. He sucked in a sharp breath as she fumbled open the flap of his breeches.

'Helen, are you sure?' he asked again. And then groaned as she delved inside and tentatively caressed him. 'Oh, God,' he breathed. 'If you don't stop doing that I shall not be able to hold back…'

'Good,' she purred with female satisfaction. 'I don't want you to hold back.' She wanted to shatter his self-control. Make him break through his rigid self-restraint and just once behave completely outrageously!

So she stroked him again, exploring the length of him with inquisitive fingers, revelling in the way he jerked in her hand, his whole body quivering with the force of what he was feeling.

And then he snatched her hand away. Not to stop her,

but so that he could take charge. He grabbed her by the hips and tugged her down so that she lay flat on the sofa beneath him. Then pushed one of her legs down to the floor and hooked her other knee up so that she was fully opened to him.

For a moment as Helen glanced down at him she feared it was going to be impossible. She knew, of course, that people had been doing this for centuries. That it brought men and women great pleasure. But when he entered her, just as she had feared, there was such a fierce stab of pain that she thought the pleasure might be gone for good.

And then Sebastian stilled. He kissed her cheek softly, and stroked her hair back from her brow, and told her how much he loved her. The pain ebbed a little. And then he gave a groan and began to move again.

And just like that she forgot the pain as a fresh wave of sensation swamped her. Sensation which built and flooded her as he loved her with his hands and his mouth, his whole body.

But, most importantly, with his heart and soul.

And then she grew quite frantic with need, writhing and bucking under him, until it rose into a crescendo of ecstasy and every part of her throbbed with untold pleasure.

And Sebastian came with her, shuddering and throbbing deep within her.

Leaving her feeling complete. At peace.

And boneless.

He seemed to be feeling much the same as her, since he collapsed on top of her, his head buried in her neck.

'You are so generous,' he said at length, when he had got his breath back. 'I noticed that about you from the start,' he murmured into her ear, 'that you have a kind heart.'

'The start?' she said, lazily running her hands across the width of his shoulder.

'Was that while I was shouting at you to make yourself useful?'

He reared up and looked down into her face, a grin tugging at the corner of his mouth.

'That incident certainly served to make me take notice of you,' he said. 'After that I could not help watching out for you, to see what you might do next. Most girls of your age would do nothing but complain about their lot. But you never did. Not once. All you seemed to care about was your aunt's health.'

'Well, I love her.'

'You have a loving disposition,' he agreed, his eyes growing dark. 'I want that love for myself,' he said. 'I am greedy for it.'

'You have it.'

He kissed her then—not wildly, as he had done earlier, but with a tenderness that made her heart melt.

'So,' he said, after a short interval, 'now we have a wedding to plan.' His face abruptly fell. 'You know what this means?' he said.

'No,' said Helen, a shiver of foreboding slithering down her spine. Surely he had not had second thoughts?

'It means giving a grand ball. Half the county will have an excuse to come traipsing through Alvanley! And more than half of those currently staying up at the Hall will use it as an excuse to stay on for at least another month!'

He sat up and began to restore order to his clothing.

'You…you do not need to give a ball on my account,' said Helen. 'We can get married quietly. I only want a simple ceremony, with my aunt as witness. I do not care about anyone else…'

'Oh, no,' he said grimly. 'You deserve better than that. If I do not throw a ball and celebrate our union publicly people will think I am not proud of you. And I am,' he said gruffly. 'I want to show you off. You are going to be such an asset to me, and I mean to show everyone right from the start that this is no convenient marriage I am entering for dynastic reasons, but a love match that I enter into with my whole heart.'

'And so you will throw a ball…?'

He nodded, his face set.

'And invite your family to stay on while the banns are read?'

He squared his shoulders. 'I will.'

Helen giggled. 'Oh, Sebastian, you must love me very much to go through all that for my sake.'

He looked down at her where she lay, her white limbs still spread against the red velvet, her hair tumbled across the cushions, and his heart turned over.

'I do,' he said. And then, with a wry twist to his lips, 'Just think if that bank had not collapsed, and your aunt had not lost all her money, you would never have come here for Christmas and I would never have met you. I would still be cold and lonely and utterly without hope.'

She sat up, put her arms round his neck, and laid her head on his shoulder.

'And if you were not so determined to honour the season each year, in spite of wanting to have nothing more to do with the family that caused you so much unhappiness, I would never have found you.'

He turned and hugged her tight. 'When I was a very small child I had a nurse who told me that Christmas is a time for miracles. And somehow, deep down, I don't think I ever quite let go of the notion that it was the one time of year when hopes and dreams might come true. Every year when I came back here I wondered if this would be the year when things would change for me. And this year—thank God—at last it has. For this year you came. And brought love with you.'

'Thank God, then,' she agreed soberly. 'Thank God for Christmas.'

* * * * *

*Harlequin Presents® is thrilled
to introduce the first installment of
an epic tale of passion and drama by*
USA TODAY *Bestselling Author*
Penny Jordan!

**When buttoned-up Giselle first meets
the devastatingly handsome Saul Parenti,
the heat between them is explosive....**

"LET ME GET THIS STRAIGHT. Are you actually suggesting that I would stoop to that kind of game playing?"

Saul came out from behind his desk and walked toward her. Giselle could smell his hot male scent and it was making her dizzy, igniting a low, dull, pulsing ache that was taking over her whole body.

Giselle defended her suspicions. "You don't want me here."

"No," Saul agreed, "I don't."

And then he did what he had sworn he would not do, cursing himself beneath his breath as he reached for her, pulling her fiercely into his arms and kissing her with all the pent-up fury she had aroused in him from the moment he had first seen her.

Giselle certainly *wanted* to resist him. But the hand she raised to push him away developed a will of its own and was sliding along his bare arm beneath the sleeve of his shirt, and the body that should have been arching away from him was instead melting into him.

Beneath the pressure of his kiss he could feel and taste her gasp of undeniable response to him. He wanted to devour her, take her and drive them both until they were equally satiated—even whilst the anger within him that she should make him feel that way roared and burned its resentment of his need.

She was helpless, Giselle recognized, totally unable to withstand the storm lashing at her, able only to cling to the man who was the cause of it and pray that she would survive.

Somewhere else in the building a door banged. The sound exploded into the sensual tension that had enclosed them, driving them apart. Saul's chest was rising and falling as he fought for control; Giselle's whole body was trembling.

Without a word she turned and ran.

Find out what happens when Saul and Giselle succumb to their irresistible desire in

THE RELUCTANT SURRENDER

Available January 2011 from Harlequin Presents®

HARLEQUIN®

A Romance

FOR EVERY MOOD™

Spotlight on

Classic

Quintessential, modern love stories
that are romance at its finest.

See the next page
to enjoy a sneak peek from
the Harlequin Presents® series.

REQUEST YOUR
FREE BOOKS!

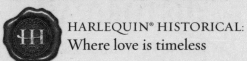

HARLEQUIN® HISTORICAL:
Where love is timeless

2 FREE NOVELS PLUS 2 **FREE GIFTS!**

YES! Please send me 2 FREE Harlequin® Historical novels and my 2 FREE gifts (gifts are worth about $10). After receiving them, if I don't wish to receive any more books, I can return the shipping statement marked "cancel." If I don't cancel, I will receive 6 brand-new novels every month and be billed just $4.94 per book in the U.S. or $5.49 per book in Canada. That's a saving of 20% off the cover price! It's quite a bargain! Shipping and handling is just 50¢ per book.* I understand that accepting the 2 free books and gifts places me under no obligation to buy anything. I can always return a shipment and cancel at any time. Even if I never buy another book from Harlequin, the two free books and gifts are mine to keep forever.

246/349 HDN E5L4

Name _____ (PLEASE PRINT) _____

Address _____ Apt. # _____

City _____ State/Prov. _____ Zip/Postal Code _____

Signature (if under 18, a parent or guardian must sign) _____

Mail to the **Harlequin Reader Service:**
IN U.S.A.: P.O. Box 1867, Buffalo, NY 14240-1867
IN CANADA: P.O. Box 609, Fort Erie, Ontario L2A 5X3
Not valid for current subscribers to Harlequin Historical books.

Want to try two free books from another line?
Call 1-800-873-8635 or visit www.morefreebooks.com.

* Terms and prices subject to change without notice. Prices do not include applicable taxes. N.Y. residents add applicable sales tax. Canadian residents will be charged applicable provincial taxes and GST. Offer not valid in Quebec. This offer is limited to one order per household. All orders subject to approval. Credit or debit balances in a customer's account(s) may be offset by any other outstanding balance owed by or to the customer. Please allow 4 to 6 weeks for delivery. Offer available while quantities last.

Your Privacy: Harlequin Books is committed to protecting your privacy. Our Privacy Policy is available online at www.eHarlequin.com or upon request from the Reader Service. From time to time we make our lists of customers available to reputable third parties who may have a product or service of interest to you. If you would prefer we not share your name and address, please check here. ☐

Help us get it right—We strive for accurate, respectful and relevant communications. To clarify or modify your communication preferences, visit us at www.ReaderService.com/consumerschoice.

HH10R

COMING NEXT MONTH FROM

HARLEQUIN®
HISTORICAL

Available December 28, 2010.

- **WHIRLWIND REUNION**
  by **Debra Cowan**
  (Western)

- **TAKEN BY THE WICKED RAKE**
  by **Christine Merrill**
  (Regency)
  Book 8 in the *Silk & Scandal* miniseries

- **THE ADMIRAL'S PENNILESS BRIDE**
  by **Carla Kelly**
  (Regency)

- **IN THE LAIRD'S BED**
  by **Joanne Rock**
  (Medieval)